Season of Retribution

Rock Hollow Series, Book 1

Shanna Nichols

Cover Art:

Publisher's Note:

This is a work of fiction. All names, characters, places, and events are the work of the author's imagination.

Any resemblance to real persons, places, or events is coincidental.

Solstice Publishing - www.solsticepublishing.com

Season of Retribution

Shanna Nichols

For Mike, J, and MaRita.... my rock, my guidance, and my test subjects. For Poppy, thank you for showing me life.

Chapter One

"Alright stop! There is nothing here for anybody to find," Lilly heard Drew saying on the other side of his office door.

"Look, I told you there's nothing here. They would have found it when they were crawling all over the place if there were. " Drew paused. "Fine. You're right, I know. I was stupid and careless once, only once. It won't happen again." There was another silence, then Drew erupted in laughter, "Yeah, she's having *memories*. Look, I've got it under control. Don't worry about her. She's never been anything. She doesn't know anything−" Lilly heard the wheels holding a drawer in the tracks of his desk roll, and the drawer clapped closed.

She barged into the office and threw the watch she was bringing from the repair shop onto his desk. The bright copper penny rattled in the center and Lilly thought of the quip he said so often, *"Penny for your thoughts."* How clever. The shrink offers a penny for your thoughts. Every time she heard him say the words it ignited a deep rage that would climb close to the top but never quite boil over. Lilly didn't understand why she hated hearing him say those words. She'd heard far worse from him every day that elicited no reaction.

The small woman who sat at the reception desk was the only person in the building to have even noticed her, aside from Drew. The snarky Mrs. Ehrin watched as Lilly exited the elevator. The condescending smile she gave

Lilly every time she saw her began to etch onto her lips. Lilly was having none of it.

"Have a wonderf—" she began.

"Oh, shut up," Lilly snapped, and slammed her palms into the exit door. The hag needed to let go years ago, she thought. Dr. Ehrin passed away just after Drew had taken over the operation of the clinic. The wife, on the other hand, would never give up the ghost.

Secure, huh? Lilly thought as she looked around her husband's office on the first floor of their home. She started going through everything she could think he would store information on. The only thing in the room was his computer, three banker's boxes full of patient files he had hidden from auditors during the Medicaid fraud investigation that was only a few months old, and a file cabinet. The file cabinet was only a piece of furniture. There was nothing in it except the green hanging files it came with. Paperwork had never been Drew's thing. Pride, condescension, humiliation, that was more Drew's thing. He was cocky, he was ruthless, and he was mean. A combination none of his colleagues or peers would ever see.

He looked the part of the good doctor with his deep brown eyes that, to some, may have been comforting; to Lilly they carried a silent warning. He kept his raven hair cut into a military high and tight that was refreshed on the fifth of every month, no exceptions. He displayed his tall, trim physique in five hundred dollar suits that Lilly had to ensure were laundered and pressed to perfection with creases he measured to the centimeter every week; then hung in the closet in order of darkest to lightest. The product of all that was the Drew everyone else saw. Lilly was certain he saved the real Drew, the hellion, just for her.

The computer was the only place he could hide something, and the only place she couldn't check. Drew had spent countless hours working on security to keep all eyes besides his own from viewing the contents. Cheap bastard wouldn't spend a penny hiring someone that knew what they were doing.

He caught her on his computer. That was why he hit her. She heard the door knob turn and the creak of the hinges as he came in. She knew, right that moment, she was his prey. Her fingers stopped pecking at the keys and she slid the chair back, but it was no use. He stood in the doorway glaring at her. Her cheeks were burning as his legs started toward her. The carpet crunched beneath his weight. Her heart pounded in her chest and rose to her throat as her hands began to tremble. Words were a distant memory as he closed the gap between them.

She closed her eyes and tried to find words or an excuse that would explain her being in this room, in this chair. When she opened her eyes he was looming over her, his shadow seeming to block all light. She struggled to breathe as her heart raced. His eyes bore into her, wild, like an animal about to pounce. When he opened his mouth, his voice came out even and measured, but she knew better. His tone was scarcely above a whisper, yet the words he spat at her held enough vituperation to have choked her.

"Listen young lady," he hissed in the slow measured tone that indicated he was about to make her feel as small and senseless as he thought her to be. She clenched her eyes shut and wrapped her fingers around the padded leather arms of the chair. He knew those three words summoned Lilly's ghosts. He knew saying them to her was the best way to spark a volatile reaction. He knew those were the words used by her high school algebra teacher when he was making her earn grades in ways that had more to do with the bible than math. Drew knew. Drew had never given a damn, and wasn't starting then either.

He wanted to provoke her, to command her, and to dominate her. The tiny vein that inched its way up his forehead bulged out as he said the words. It made him look like he had a small, blue crack forming and his head may burst at any moment. It didn't usually appear until well into the fight. For only the second time in nine years, Lilly was scared. Scared of Drew, scared of what he was about to do, scared that she may not have a tomorrow to get away from him.

He mocked her. He frowned like a baby and pretended to cry as though she were doing that in front of him. He stumbled for words in a mimicking voice.

"Stop it, Drew. You're gonna make me remember what a whore I've been since I was a kid," he said in a child-like playground taunt. "You know I'm just dressed up trash, Drew." Lilly's hands were shaking, and her legs felt like wet noodles as rage boiled bile up into her throat. She jumped from the oversized chair, sending it careening in his direction, and tried to scramble toward the door.

"Where the hell do you think you're going?" he roared, grabbing her by the arm. "Prying little bitches don't get to run away when they get caught." She turned toward him, her body shaking, and held to the desk behind her to steady herself.

"I am your *wife*," she screeched, "I shouldn't have to pry."

His eyes were wild, maniacal. His laugh sounded throaty and deep. She screamed the loudest high-pitched noise her small frame could muster, fearing he'd snap any second. The housekeeper had left hours before, and the closest neighbor was at least a half block away. No one was close enough to hear her. No one cared enough to help her. Drew stopped laughing and stared directly into Lilly's eyes, taking small, slow steps toward her from less than a foot away, keeping a thin smile painted on his face. He overshadowed her, being a foot taller and at least eighty pounds heavier. Lilly backed herself against the desk until it dug into her skin. She clenched her teeth and held firmly to the corner, trying to make the desk swallow her.

"You stupid little bitch," Drew said as his fist came hurtling toward her. The explosion in her mouth happened as tiny blasts in her head lit the insides of her eyelids like a firework show. Her head snapped backwards and collided with the computer monitor. Before she could piece together what was happening, his other fist landed in her jaw.

She spat blood at him and landed a kick as hard as her runner's legs could into his groin. He made a gurgling sound as he doubled himself and reached for the armchair. Lilly slid from between him and the computer desk and ran up the stairs, locking the doors behind her. She grabbed her worn duffle that had held every belonging she owned since she left home from the closet, and began to shove anything she could grab into it.

This time, she had to get away for good. *No chickening out now,* she thought as the metallic taste of blood in her mouth made her gag and her chest burn with hatred.

She worked as quickly as her heart raced, forcing clothes into the duffle. She heard Drew slamming doors on the floor below, and finally the front door rattled windows as he yanked it closed. She watched out the window until his car was a tiny speck, turned her pillow over and slid her hand into the case to retrieve the thin silver chain with the crimson vial, placing it around her neck. She took one last glance out the window to see Drew's car was still gone, hoisted the duffle over her shoulder, and walked out the front door.

She drove for hours with the radio on, but the only thing Lilly heard since leaving the driveway of her lavishly furnished, acutely manicured, perfect hell was her mother's voice telling her, "One day you'll wake up and see what an ass that husband of yours really is."

Of course, as always, Momma had been right, though she would never hear it from Lilly's lips. There was no way Momma could know just what Drew really was, nobody did. Nor would anyone have believed it if anyone told them. Momma, though, she saw right through him the day she met him.

"He's got a slick smile and drifter's eyes. Don't you turn your back on him, girl. He's a snake," Momma told Lilly after Drew off-handedly compared Rock Hollow to a Saturday night variety show. The muscles in his arm had tightened around Lilly's waist as the words tore through him. Momma never minced words, and she never held back. If she thought it, rest assured she would say it. That filter had broken years ago.

Drew could not get away fast enough. He shoved Lilly, nearly toppling her into the car, smirked back at Momma who was standing in the doorway, and held a peace symbol with his first two fingers. Not that he particularly cared about any sort of peace movement.

He stewed the entire drive and decided Lilly needed what he called 'limited contact,' aka zero contact, with her family. It was in her best interest, in his opinion. Everything about their lives was his opinion, his thought, his way. To be fair, his was a well-regarded opinion among the people who mattered—to him.

Maybe that bastard was right. Maybe she was just nuts. Hadn't he told her a thousand times? Or, maybe Drew took away everything that ever meant a damn thing, and she had nothing left to lose. Whichever the case, hell was in the rearview.

Her hair was blowing in all directions as she fumbled through the car for a pair of sunglasses. The asphalt looked like water as the heat drenched it. Drew would never have allowed her to keep the window down. "*You* may have been born trash, but you're not going to make me look like I went slumming," he said, more than once.

The familiar tune bellowed from the radio and Lilly caught herself twirling the crimson vial on her necklace between her fingers; *Leather and Lace,* by Stevie Nicks and Don Henley. Thoughts of Brad flooded her mind, as they often did. This was their song. She could see him clearly, in her mind's eye, as he was the night she'd met him.

***

"I wrecked my Harley," he said, taking the seat next to her at The Sunken Ship, a bar Bea Drake owned just outside of the county line.

"How's the bike?" she asked after looking him over and seeing no scrapes or cuts. He smiled at Lilly, a crooked devil-may-care grin, chipping away at some of the ice she'd encased her heart in. Something twinkled in his big gorgeous cerulean eyes. He looked at her with a blank stare that, to someone else, might have made him appear daft, but she could see the savvy, refined man that lurked beneath. He did not mask himself, yet he was not laying all of his cards on the table.

"Two beers please," he said to Bea with a confidence Lilly had only heard in movies. Real people could not possibly be as sure of themselves. Bea knew Lilly was not old enough to be there, much less drinking, but when no one else was in the bar, she could have cared less what Lilly did.

Bea looked from Brad to Lilly and finally shrugged and handed him two long-necks, uncapping them as they passed over the bare wood of the bar. Bea was suspicious of most customers that came in, especially the ones that were not 'regulars.' This new guy was no exception. She kept her beady, bronze eyes on him as he offered Lilly the bottle he'd bought her. "Dance with me?" he only half asked as he stood behind her offering his hand.

She looked at the dusty bar floor where only a single row of tables separated the long bar and the door, no dance space. There was an old jukebox in the corner Lilly assumed came with the ancient building, and was not sure it even worked.

"What? Here?" she asked. "You're nuts!"

After a quick assessment of the room, he sat his beer on the bar and began to pull tables together, the legs scraping against the wooden planked floor, creating a space big enough for them to dance. He moved with an air of class and refinement, a sort of sophistication she had never encountered. When he walked, there was an ever so slight twitch in his step Lilly thought emanated grace. Even the way he held his bottle, between his two first fingers and thumb, oozed finesse. Yet, he was in The Sunken Ship, moving old furniture that had seen its heyday come and go, just to share a dance with her.

He made his way to the old jukebox and inserted a couple of ones after he finished his rearrangement. Lilly watched him entranced. She couldn't hide her intrigue with him, or what music he might request. She knew nothing about him, aside from how captivated she was, yet there was a familiarity as if she'd known him for years. As he strode back over to her with a swagger that kept time with her heart, she heard the music begin.

Brad approached her and offered her his hand a second time, "Now?"

She laughed and shook her head.

"Don't tell me I did all of that and you're just gonna say no again," he smiled, and when he did his eyes danced to their own beat, the same one her heart was pounding out. She could see she posed a challenge to him, and he rose to meet it valiantly.

She took his hand cautiously, trying to display enough distrust to ward off any bad omens he may be carrying, and allowed him to lead her to the spot he had just cleared, where they swayed with the tune. His face at her ear, she heard him attempt to sing along, which stayed with the tune but the words came out as, "Aww Ooo" over and over. Everything about him made her heart speed up. Electric tingles raced through her chest as she let him put his arms around her waist. She laid her head on his shoulder and inhaled his windswept and mild woodsy cologne scent; it made her dizzy. Desire and curiosity inched her closer to him. He tightened his arms on her back, and she felt his heartbeat through his shirt.

He requested no other songs, and that one played three more times. They swayed back and forth with it each time.

"Thank you, my lady," he said, bowing to her after the song ended for the fourth time. She smiled at him, and stared into his eyes, trying to figure him out.

"You should do that more. You're stunning when you smile." He took one last long pull from his bottle and made a wide sweeping motion toward the door.

Once in the parking lot she saw the Harley he claimed earlier to have been wrecked. "Don't look wrecked to me," Lilly said, hooking her thumb toward the bike.

"I didn't say I totaled it. I laid it down a few weeks ago," he said, shrugging. "Got your attention didn't it?"

Laughter boiled from deep in her stomach and burst forth despite her best effort to staunch it. This man was something wild.

"Are you the one my momma always warned me about?" she asked him amused.

"Depends. What were the warnings?" he said as he lifted both shoulders, and watched one booted foot kick at gravel as the moon cast a long shadow beside them.

His energy and passion radiated as they walked together. It lit up the air around him and drew her to him like a magnet. His presence sent chills down her spine. As she laughed, his hands cupped both of her arms. When she looked up at him, his lips pressed hard against hers. She was shocked and started to pull away, but the tingle in her chest had grown stronger and spread like a warm blanket. The tiny voices in her head warned her this was a bad idea, this was the start of something she would never be free of again, but the smallest, most uninhabitable part of her heart made her kiss him back.

"That wasn't so bad, huh?" he said when he finally pulled away. He touched her lips lightly with his finger, gnarling the butterfly wings that flapped in her chest, and mounted his Harley. "I'll be here tomorrow night, can I see you then?" he asked.

"Maybe, if you play your cards right," Lilly answered playfully.

"Oh, I can play some cards," he winked as the old bike rumbled to life. She felt the vibration in her stomach and noticed that her knees were wobbling as she leaned against her car.

"What the hell just happened?" she asked aloud as she watched a cloud of dust rise from the gravel parking lot. She watched the red glow of his single tail light until it disappeared on the highway. She glanced through the window at Bea, who pretended to wipe the bar down with her eyes glued to the scene outside, and climbed into her beaten down 77 Nova her brother had warned her against driving.

***

Her heart fluttered, even now, all these years later, as she fumbled for her purse in the bucket seat of her Audi, and remembered the first time she'd laid eyes on him, the night she'd lost her heart.

"Crazy ass man," she laughed as she tucked the tiny vial that contained a bit of Brad's ashes into her shirt before she realized she no longer had to hide it. Pain jabbed at her busted lip and swollen cheek, sending her a not so subtle reminder of the urgency to put miles between her and the scripted, controlled, and now violent life she had lived.

Chapter Two

The text came from Lilly early in the morning, before he'd even had a coffee, which was a feat in itself. Ty wasn't sure why she would have even been out of bed at such an hour. The well-to-dos usually sleep until noon, he thought.

"I'll be home tonight. Meet me at the house," she had written. No explanation. The text jolted Ty through his usual morning routine, and he opted to take his coffee and head into the station rather than on the porch swing. As his old black Ford rattled to life in the driveway, he couldn't shake the knot that was tightening in his chest. Eight months earlier he'd received a call that had brought Lilly back into his life. She'd called in the middle of a double shift on a Sunday afternoon, asking him to drive three hours to meet her for lunch.

He heard the underlying panic in her voice, though it would have gone unnoticed by anyone else. Having a mother that doted over the novelty of her children, Ty had heard all of the stories and research of twin telepathy and could attest that it held at least some truth.

Two lanes of asphalt wound down the hillside as Ty replayed the entire lunch in his mind. He couldn't help but think of how much life had been lived in the years since Lilly left, and Ty missed his sister sorely. He never quite let go of the nagging thought that he had driven her away. Lilly and Momma were never able to get on solid footing after the Ricky Drake thing, and Ty stayed locked in his own hell, unable to quell the battles that raged between them.

Lilly, once a smart ass, foul-mouthed fireball that would just as soon tell you where on her body you could plant your lips as she was to look at you, sounded almost conservative on the phone. She didn't sound like the person he grew up with at all. She was distant, like she was hurrying to get off of the phone, but asking about everyone and everything at home. She sounded distracted, which he attributed to the bastard she'd married.

Ty, as the only York to have ever abided by the law, much less gone into a career enforcing it, had been working the only murder in Rock Hollow, Kentucky in over fifty years. It had happened three weeks to the day after he was elected sheriff. Two seventeen year old boys had gone to The Hollow, a cleared spot at the top of Rock Hollow Hill where the local kids go for their rite of passage, hanging out on weekends, loud music, and alcohol when they could get someone to buy it for them. The two boys never returned.

Every moment of his life since that early morning had been sacrificed to solving the murder. Even Tara, who had grown up in a house of police officers, had given up on him and left. Since Lilly's call, Ty had the distraction that he desperately needed. He could put his energies into piecing his family back together, whatever that looked like.

The winding hill gave way to the valley where tiny housetops poked above the fog. A tractor ran alongside the fence beside the highway as an old farm hand in his overhauls threw his hand up without ever glancing to see who he waved to. Ty rarely waved back, no one ever noticed.

One left turn and two miles later, Ty pulled into the parking spot reserved for him. Ben Hale, Ty's best friend since they attended the police academy together, was already in the office. His large frame, dark brutish features, and nearly eidetic memory intimidated some, but the guy had a heart of gold. Ty thought of him as the brother he never had.

"What's got the FBI in Rock Hollow before dawn?" Ty teased Ben as he walked between the rows of desks on his way to the coffee pot.

"Same thing that brings the sheriff in before dawn every day," Ben answered.

"You're looking into cold cases, too, are ya?"

"It's the FBI. We are always looking into cold cases."

Ty scooped the dark grounds into the filter and inhaled the bitter aroma, allowing its robust scent to jar his senses into action. He looked at the text from Lilly again as he waited for the brew to end.

"If you weren't so damn cheap you could have one of those single serve things in here. They're quicker," Ben announced without looking away from the computer.

"Mhm," Ty grunted.

"What's up?" Ben asked, finally looking at Ty.

"My sister."

"What about her?" Ben rose and dodged between empty desk chairs to look at Ty's phone. "So, she's on her way here?" he asked.

"Yeah. I wish I could figure out what's going on with her."

"Are you still talking about that lunch thing you two did a while back?" Ben mused.

The coffee pot gave an exasperated puff and Ty poured himself a cup. He would have to take it black; no one ever replaced the cream and sugar. Ty and Ben walked into Ty's office as steam rose from the Styrofoam cup, heating his palm.

"She was so different. I mean, sure everybody grows up and all, but it was more than that. She was almost hollow. She didn't even look like Lilly."

"Have you done any more follow up on the drug company?" Ben asked.

Ty shook his head. He hadn't thought about the drug company since the day of their lunch, when he'd followed Lilly without her knowledge. She went into a building to see what Ty presumed was a psychic, and he made his way to the clinic Drew operated. He collected the brochure for Sounds of Hope psychiatric clinic from the top drawer of his desk where he kept his 'follow up later' stuff. Ty winced at how full the drawer was getting.

He remembered the massive five-story building with its rolling green hill and glass façade. It looked like a country club instead of a medical facility.

He had hoped to find that everything was normal, though, in truth, he had no idea what 'abnormal' may look like at a psychiatric facility.

"I picked this up a couple of months ago when I dropped Momma off at the hospital," Ty said tossing the brochure across his desk in front of Ben, who had taken the seat opposite him.

"What is it?" Ben asked, turning the colorful glossy pamphlet in his hands. "Sounds of Hope? Psyche place?"

"Yeah. Lilly's husband runs it," Ty said, pecking at the keys of his ancient computer.

"Andrew Wilt is your brother in law?"

Ty nodded, sucking on his bottom lip. The screen in front of him was just beginning to illuminate.

"What was that drug company again?" Ben asked.

"Glick. The guy driving the box truck nearly branded it into my forehead, remember?"

Ben nodded. "They must be a big contributor to the clinic, this was printed by Glick," he said handing the brochure to Ty, thumb on the script at the bottom center. "What was weird about it again?"

"Besides me nearly becoming the new hood ornament for the truck? I'm not sure, really. Two guys, dressed like delivery men, got out and rang the bell by the back door. A tiny lady that I later found out was the receptionist opened the back door, and one guy pushed in a hand truck with several large red crates, the other one who had the name 'Ian' embroidered on his shirt waited for Drew and another lady. When they came out the conversation looked intense. The lady stood there with her hands on her hips and her mouth pinched tight and Drew was pointing this way and that way. I heard the guy, Ian, say that 'Loose has more.'"

"Loose? Is that the name of a person?"

"I don't know. I don't know what they, or it, or he, or whatever has more of either. The guy said that he was going back to Memphis. Not sure what's in Memphis either. I have looked and can't find an office or warehouse in Memphis for Glick."

"Maybe it's not Glick you're looking for. Did you look for any other pharma in the area?"

"No. I don't even know what I would be looking for," he said, glancing at Ben who was consumed in the pamphlet for the clinic. "I don't know, something just wasn't right about the way Lilly acted, ya know? Before she left the only thing she talked about was getting out of this hellhole town and never looking back. It wasn't *home*. But, that day, she referred to it that way several times. She'd stare off in the distance, then snap back, then do it again. I thought she was gonna cry once."

Ty was staring at his computer screen as he spoke. He had opened his email and saw that he had received a few reports from his deputy, Kari Spear.

"So why's she coming home?" Ben asked, breaking the silence that had grown thick.

"She didn't say, just said she was coming," Ty shrugged. "I keep thinking about Drew and that lady he was with at the back door. After the whole thing with the drug delivery, they walked out front, close to where I was parked. It looked like she was chewing him a new backside. I don't know, like she was his mom or something. But, she got into a car with Ohio official plates on it. Maybe she was an inspector or something."

"Doubt it. Inspectors don't really take part in deliveries of medications, and they do their backside ripping in a written report, not the parking lot," Ben said. "Did you say Ohio plates?"

Ty nodded.

"Hey boss, did you get my reports?" Kari Spear, Ty's second in command, poked her head in the door, auburn curls springing from her ponytail. Dark crescents under her eyes suggested she had worked all night.

"Sure did. I haven't read them yet, but they are in my email."

"Ok, I wanted to make sure. We've got an empty house."

Ben cocked his eyebrow at Ty.

"Everyone has been released, all cells are empty," Ty told him. Ben nodded.

"Sorry. I guess that sounded weird," Kari said, tucking her head, hiding the heat rising to her pale cheeks.

"It's ok. We're the same kind of weird, Spear. I'll go over the reports in a little bit."

Kari turned and walked to her desk without glancing back into the room. She was a smart, tough cop. At only five foot four, she could, and had, taken down everything from the 'good old boys' that got too rowdy, to the hardcore, violent offenders.

"So, the clinic is in Kentucky, yes?" Ben asked. Ty nodded. "Then that would not have been an inspector with Ohio plates."

"Probably not. I don't know, man, but something is off there."

"I do not know, my friend, but it's probably nothing," Ben said sliding the pamphlet across Ty's desk as he stood. "I've gotta get back to it. It's still cool if I crash at your house for a while right?"

"Oh, yeah. I meant to ask if you were still doing that."

"Ok, cool. I'll be a little late tonight, I still have to finalize a few things at my old office," Ben said standing in the doorway.

Ty could not get Lilly out of his head. She had looked so different. Even her hair, which was once a thick mane of honey blonde waves, was dyed platinum and straightened. Her perfectly circular golden eyes were barely visible under fake eyelashes and make-up she had never needed.

He thought of how easily Lilly lashed out when he told her about his ex-fiancé, as though time and distance had never separated them. Ty knew, somehow, Lilly had been trying to tell him something that day. Call it his 'twin-sense' or whatever, but the knot in his chest, now working toward his stomach, told him that Lilly needed him now more than ever.

Chapter Three

"*Welcome to Rock Hollow, Kentucky,*" the old wooden sign in need of fresh yellow and green paint announced. It had nestled between two smaller grassy hills since the early fifties, where the wives of town council members used to pride themselves on the attractiveness of their flowers. The hills were now grown into tall brush and untrimmed trees with no council members that cared about such things anymore. Wilderness seemed to be reclaiming the hillside.

"Welcome to Nowhereville, USA," Lilly scowled. As hard as she had fought to get out of this place, to find the 'something more' she had heard about, here she was, tail tucked between her legs, crawling back after yet another of the epic Lilly York disasters. The debacle that had been her marriage definitely topped the list of catastrophes.

The single stop light in town was perpetually red for the highway entrance. There was hardly any traffic that came in from the outside world until hunting season, so there was no need to stop the locals on their daily doings.

As she expected, Lilly was able to admire the newly refurbished courthouse that held its regal place in the center of the "square," that was actually round, in the middle of town since the town's inception sometime in the 1800s. The exact date was scripted on several of the buildings surrounding the courthouse if anyone were interested enough to look for it. The remodeling made the building taller, and gave it a fresh coat of paint. Otherwise it was the same building it had been for years.

There were two attorneys in town with offices on opposite sides of the square. One was the local divorce lawyer, the other handled real estate and wills. Aside from drug charges, a more recent problem, there were few other legal needs.

Rex's Drugs sign on the corner of the square was just beginning to light as it did every night. There was no traffic at this time of day. Papa always said that the town 'rolled up the sidewalks' at dusk. It took Lilly years to figure that phrase out.

She would have loved to bring Brad here. She had told him many stories of growing up in this small town. They planned it one night, the same way they planned everything that they did, as they lay basking in the quiet after sex.

***

"How many kids do you want?" she had asked him, breaking up the silence.

"None," he growled.

"Boys or girls?" she asked, ignoring his last response.

"Neither."

"Why not?" she whined. She knew that she would get her way with him. He made it too easy.

"Because I don't want to pass on this craziness to a kid. Why saddle them with that before they've even had a chance at the world?" he said, raising his pale, hairless body onto his right elbow, exposing the tattoo of a skeleton riding a motorcycle on his left bicep. "Lil, you may not have noticed, but I'm broken. I'm a walking catastrophe. Why do you want'em so bad?"

Lilly shrugged her shoulders, jutting her lip out.

"You don't really want to have to deal with snotty noses and shitty diapers, do you?" he laughed.

"There's more to it than that," she said rolling into him and folding her arms across his naked chest, her chin just above his heart that was beating a rhythmic hymn holding her in his trance. "Imagine, raising our own human being. We could teach them how to treat other people, how to love other people, and how to be a person that just doesn't suck. We could keep them safe from the nastiness that screwed both of us up so bad. Call it a favor to the stupid, hurtful worlds we grew up in."

He had laughed at her naivety, took her in his arms and kissed her wildly. Every time his lips played across hers, she knew the world slowed for them. Time was gone. Hurt was gone. All that mattered was that she was in his arms and, for a moment, he was hers. This wild, restless, crazy man was hers.

"And just how, my sweet Lilly, do you suppose we can protect this child? Should we hide from both of our families? Keep our baby a secret," he whispered with his forefinger across his carmine lips. "Tell no one? Or do we run away to some tropical beach, change our names and live like royalty?" His eyes danced wildly as he mused.

"Well, now you're just being ridiculous. You know we could keep a baby away from what has hurt us. We do it for each other now," Lilly said, rolling off of his chest and turning away from him.

"Tell ya what," Brad declared, his delight in getting Lilly worked up evident. "We'll take the Harley and ride straight through the middle of, what was it again? Rock Hollow. Let the judgmental jackasses gossip, I don't care. Hell, we'll burn the damn place down. You can show me that monster house you grew up in, show me the Hollow I've heard so many scathing stories about," he hissed, bringing his face inches from hers with his eyes wide and a playful grin curling his lip. He climbed to a stand, wearing only his boxers, in the center of the bed, and began jumping up and down, slapping the ceiling with both hands as he jumped. "We'll make a story from the Hollow that'll give the little town hens something to cluck about," he shouted.

As he toppled onto her, sending them both into hysterical laughter, the neighbor in the apartment upstairs stomped on the floor, shouting for them to shut up. Brad buried his face in her chest that was covered by white sheets, and they both laughed harder.

***

That was Brad. He didn't pull punches. He didn't like serious talk, he wanted to have fun. He wanted to laugh and be crazy and do crazy things; he wanted the people around him to enjoy life.

Lilly had not been a virgin when they met. But she had only been with guys her age, maybe a year or two older. Brad, at 16 years her senior, was experienced in ways that made Lilly's skin tingle when he touched her and her heart pound from her chest when his lips brushed hers. He was the definition of class to her. Just watching him walk next to her made her feel like the type of person she had always wanted to be. He had seen and done so many things. He told Lilly stories from almost every place on Earth as if there was nowhere that he had never been. Life had hardened him in ways that broke Lilly's heart to think of. She could see the crazy, the fun, the drunk, the high. Of course she could see it. But it seemed nobody save for Lilly could see the man that lived inside all of that. They didn't know the Brad that made her knees weak and caused her to break into a sweat with just a smile. They had never known the heart that held her captive.

She lifted the crimson vial that contained some of his ashes that she hadn't scattered over Vegas, their town, out of her shirt and kissed it as tears threatened at her eyes when the house began to come into view.

The old York Place, as the people in town knew it, was a capacious Queen Anne style house seated at the top of 'Shiner Hill,' so named for the family business. It was the largest structure in the countryside, built by Lilly's great-great grandfather in the late 1800s for his new bride, Molly. She was from Vermont, earning her the title of The

Yank York from the town's finest. They didn't like northerners invading their territory back then.

The covered porch that had welcomed Lilly since childhood wrapped around to the back where she remembered her mother sitting in the cast iron chair, sipping sweet tea. Kentucky summers could be brutal. The yellow painted boards were as bright as the sun, exactly as Papa had always kept them, and the stained glass windows on the second floor shone just as brightly as when they were new. The balcony overlooked the front lawn from the second floor, and jutted out above the tree line with ornate wrought iron posts that looked like they may have once been used as weapons. Lilly had named the gargoyles seated at each end Leo and Patrick as a child, at Papa's suggestion, because they frightened her and she refused to sleep for fear that they would come into her room in the middle of the night.

Angelica York, Lilly's mother, so named because Papa said she was angel-like when she was born, had been telling stories of York's past for as long as Lilly could remember. There were pictures of Amanda, Lilly's great-grandmother, and her two twin girls scattered all over the second floor of the house, where most of the family slept, and in the study on the first floor Papa had fashioned into his office years earlier. When it was especially hot he would do his timesheets and accounting for the paper mill from there.

As she looked at the house from the driveway, considering going inside and the inevitable questions that would bring from her mother, the landscape surrounding her changed, and the radio faded. Memories of a small, innocent girl padding through the yard with bare feet hanging onto Papa flooded in. His laughter filled the world, her world, as he'd toss her into the air.

"As high as the sky, Lilla girl," he'd say as he caught her and ran through the yard.

"Higher, Papa! Higher!" her tiny voice would shout as he threw her over his shoulder.

Guilt seeped into the pit of her stomach. She hadn't kept in touch with Papa; Momma or Ty either for that matter. She had walked away, lit a match and let the proverbial bridge burn in her wake.

"You make time and you find a way for the things you want," she could hear Momma say.

Her heart dropped and tears threatened as she touched her stomach absently. If only she *knew* the memories were real and not just 'what she wanted.'

She could hear Drew howl in her head. *"There is no kid, never was,"* he was saying over and over. *"Just your stupid daydreams. You're delusional, crazy!"* Her head throbbed, and she thought she was going to be sick. She clenched her stomach tighter.

"Stop it!" Lilly screamed to the empty car. "Go to hell, Drew!" She sobbed, only making his laughter grow louder and more defiant. "Just stop," she whispered, clutching the steering wheel, trying to drown out Drew's voice.

Three loud taps beside her head made her bump the horn and set off a honk. She looked out the window and saw Ty standing beside the car.

"Need some help?" he asked, his voice muffled beyond the closed door. Lilly swiped the moisture from her cheeks with her palms, placed the best fake smile she could muster across her mouth, wincing as little as she could, and shook her head. She had to pull it together. Neither Momma nor Papa could see her like this.

She took a deep breath and opened the door, keeping her head down so the first thing her brother saw would not be Drew's damage.

He cupped his thick fingers under her chin and lifted her face. She expected this was coming. Ty was a cop, a hero by nature, and he knew her better than she knew herself.

"What the—"

"Later, Ty. Please," Lilly pleaded, staring into his furious eyes.

Ty clenched his jaw, heaved a deep breath, and wrapped his large arms around her. He squeezed until she felt the broken pieces of her life begin to line up. She knew that there was nowhere else she was supposed to be at that moment, and followed him inside.

Chapter Four

Walking into the house she had grown up, cried and laughed in, been heartbroken for the first time in, all of the ghosts from lives of the past began to stir. Time had stood still inside these walls. Momma had not moved or changed even a single picture.

Momma herself, once the most beautiful woman in Berger County, was showing her age, but her class hadn't left her. Beautiful yellow-white hair rested where once she had a raging fire. Her eyes, the same as Ty's, looked like she had put in too many days' work. The smile, also identical to Ty's, lit up the house, though. That smile. Why could Lilly not have inherited that smile? Instead she had received Momma's wanderlust, her love of the written word, and her inherent ability to fuck up everything she touched.

"Come in here and let me see you!" Momma said with her arms open wide. Lilly tried to keep her wounds in shadows. Momma was bound to see her busted face, trying to hide it was useless. Lilly only wanted to keep Momma at bay until she felt strong enough to talk to her. Wrapped in her mother's arms, she looked at the family home, drank in all of the memories proudly displayed on the walls.

Rumors surrounded the York family. It was rumored, but never proven, that Shiner Hill had once been the site of the only still in the county, owned and operated by Jeff York, Lilly's great-grandfather. The family knew it was true. The police never found the still, or the brewery for that matter, on the massive six hundred acre patch of land that he had called home.

There were stories of midnight runs across 9 counties, bodies buried on the family's land of people who had crossed them and the law that tried to stop them, and the one time a real Chicago mob boss visited little Rock Hollow, Kentucky. The latter was actually documented. In Hershell's, the tiny diner in town, there was a picture hanging on the wall beside the third booth of a heavy man in a dark colored suit and fedora eating a plate of Marvin's fried chicken. The man was surrounded by five other men, all wearing suits, all stuffed into the booth, all eating fried chicken. The caption below the photo said, *"Even the mob can't resist Marvin!"*

Momma held her at arms-length, sizing her up. Lilly watched her mother grimace as her eyes scanned past the battle scars of Lilly's marriage.

"Well, this supper ain't gonna eat itself, and I'd wager that you could use some good home cooking. Sit down, let's eat. We can do all the catching up girly stuff later," Momma announced when her eyes had fully taken in the sight of her prodigal daughter.

"Where's Papa?" Lilly asked.

"He's in bed, honey. He goes down with the chickens these days," Momma said as she went about the business of getting plates and silverware for her children. Ty, as always, stood by to reach the dishes that were just beyond Momma's grasp.

Dinner was spent listening to Ty tell fascinating stories of his time on the narcotics unit. Lilly laughed at the ridiculous ways he said criminals try and avoid punishment until her stomach and sides were sore, all the while trying to avoid the grinding pain shooting from her lip. She saw Ty glancing at her lip and cheek and knew a storm was brewing inside him. His sapphire eyes held no secrets.

Meals with Drew used to be silent; only interrupted if Lilly took a larger serving than he thought she needed. She never dared make a sound until he was gone from the table. Then she and Gretta, the housekeeper, would mock his ego. Gretta loved to laugh at Drew, and, truthfully, so did Lilly.

"I'll get the dishes," Lilly announced after dinner, giving Ty a sideways glance to make sure he caught her meaning. Momma nodded and left the room. Lilly had wondered since she was a child if her mother knew how close the twins were, or if she just wanted to give them time to talk.

Just breathe, she thought as her hands dipped into the warm, soapy water. Ty was standing behind her, left hand propped on the back of a chair, shifting his weight from one foot to the other, waiting to hear what she had to say. Lilly could feel his eyes boring into the back of her head, and imagined his expression of impatience waiting for her voice to fill the silence.

Finally, words began pouring from her. She dared not turn around for fear she would no longer be able to talk. Telling her brother everything she could about the past nine years flowed freely, as long as her back was toward him. Eye contact seemed like a monumental feat Lilly was not prepared for. She watched his facial expressions through his reflection in the window as she spoke.

She told him about the cruelty that Drew was capable of, how he belittled her in public, especially at the massive power summits, her name for the political parties they attended, where she would be the butt of the jokes between him and his colleagues, and how he would dump her off onto whomever he could when they went anywhere. He couldn't be expected to take care of his 'hick' wife who lacked any sort of social grace, he had appearances to keep. He had said those words more than once.

She told Ty about the brutal way he spoke to her when they were at home; how he tried to convince her that she had mental health issues. Drew had, on many occasions, threatened to lock her in the clinic. That intensified when she began asking about the memories. She tried asking in different ways, asking about certain details rather than telling him the memory as a whole. Anything she said to Drew was sure to be thrown back in her face in the most humiliating, dehumanizing way he could find. Sadly, Drew was intellectually superior to her. She knew that, he had proven his salt in that category repeatedly.

She wanted to tell Ty about the terror she had seen glint in Drew's eyes the first time she told him about the memories. She was watching the birds fly freely above her on the patio, wishing she could taste their freedom, feel the warm air wrap her body as she floated above the cares that weighed her to the ground. The memory only lasted seconds, but left her with sweat beading her forehead, and her stomach churning. What she glimpsed in that moment ignited the war that rumbled inside her. She trembled even now, even after having seen it hundreds of times over, when her mind unlocked for small interludes.

Making Ty understand why the memories affected her so deeply was risky. In order for him to fully comprehend, she would have to tell him about things she wasn't ready to acknowledge aloud, especially not to him. The way he would look at her if he knew the full truth would break her, and she needed his strength.

She would have to tell him about Brad, at least who he was to her. She had never been able to tell anyone about him. The very thought of his name still made pain in her chest burst as it had the day that he had died. No, Brad was hers and hers alone. The things they had done together, she was certain, had nothing to do with the memories.

"What did he do to your face? Was it his fists?" Ty asked startling her into a conversation she hoped would wait until later.

"Yes. Last night. It was the first time he ever hit me," Lilly admitted. "That's only a part of why I left, why I came home."

"A part?" Ty questioned. "A pretty big part I would hope. What else is going on, Lil? I've got to tell you, I've tried to keep calm with Momma in here and all, but I will not let any man put his hands on my sister like that and walk away."

"I've started...well..." Lilly stammered, searching for the words that would make him understand and not believe her to be nuts. "I've been having memories. Not like something from when we were kids, but from a time I don't remember, like from an alternate reality or something. I don't see everything, only pieces. I don't know where I was or...anything really...." Her voice trailed off, her body shaking. She found a chair and slid onto it before her legs gave way.

Ty seemed to sense the pain Lilly was holding onto. She saw the lines around his dark sapphire eyes deepen. He knelt in front of her, putting his hands on each of her arms, and drew her close to him. She put her head on his large chest and stayed there until the air seemed to leave the room before plunging forward.

"I see a place with white walls. I hear people screaming like they are being tortured. In the memory I am in pain. Labor pain, Ty."

Saying the words aloud sounded surreal and made her feel as if she was on display. Like the rest of the room had been darkened and light only shone on her, making every word that came from her mouth become more proof that she was unstable, unbelievable, just like Drew said.

"*Stupid little hick. Have you gone so far that you can't even tell a daydream from reality?*" she heard Drew's voice echo in her head, the words he'd say when she brought up the memories. The first time she had seen it she was jarred enough to actually talk to him about it. Each detail she saw seemed to have a deeper meaning, a meaning that resonated to her bones. She knew better than to ask Drew for help. She tried to appeal to the medical Drew, the 'good doctor' that everyone else knew, the one she had yet to meet.

She gave Ty her most precious bit of information, her notebook recounting every time she had seen the memory and each new detail that it offered.

The silence was thick as Ty read the notebook. Lilly crossed her legs then crossed them the other way, hooked her foot around the leg of the chair, and propped the other leg in the chair across from her. She never knew what to do with her body during awkward situations. Page after page he submerged himself into what Lilly had been living. He covered his mouth and closed his eyes as he finished the last page.

"I'm so sorry, sis," he said, shaking his head.

When his eyes opened again he laid the book on the table and stared at Lilly. Her stomach was wrapped up in needlepoint. She had grown so accustomed to the memories, to feeling less than human, when he looked at her as his equal it was foreign to her. She could see the pain that haunted her shining out of his eyes and trickling down his cheek. He kept his mouth covered as though he feared speaking would only damage the both of them more.

"Ty, I... I don't know what you want me to say." She averted her eyes from his, as tears were waiting at the surface to begin falling.

"Why didn't you tell me this? When we were at lunch that day, why?" he gasped, holding his emotion in. Lilly shrugged. "You have a child, sis."

"I know," she nodded, releasing the dam she had been holding back. She sobbed into her palms, her body jerking, allowing the sadness that overwhelmed her to flow out of her with each gush. Ty stood and put his arms around her shoulders as he had since they were small and let her weep.

As the tears fell, Lilly pictured a small child, a boy she thought, large blonde curls swirling across his frightened face. Aside from a teddy bear that had spent many nights comforting an abandoned baby, he was alone in the dark. Guilt, cloaked in bile, crept up her esophagus. She saw the child wipe his eyes as he cried out for her to no avail.

"*Just imagination*," she heard Drew's voice howl through her thoughts. "*You want a kid so you dreamed one up. God, you are a loser.*"

She wanted to shout that Drew was wrong. She may have wanted a child, but not with him. She had never given thought to bearing his heir. Certainly not after his having told her just after they were married that he couldn't medically spawn a child. For any child's sake, Lilly always thought, that was a gift from above.

"I don't know anything more than what I have written in there. I came here for your help," she said as she pulled away from Ty, wiping her eyes with the back of her hands. "I wanted to tell you. That day at lunch, I mean. I wanted to tell you what I remembered. Drew...he's....you don't know what he's like. He made me think I was losing it. I wasn't sure what I was seeing, I questioned everything. I still do sometimes, but I know how seeing it makes me feel. I can't explain it, Ty. I just know it's real."

"And then?"

"What do you mean, *and then*?"

"*If* we find your child, find out what's going on with your memories, what then?" Ty said, staring directly into Lilly's eyes. She felt a shiver course through her chest.

"Well, then, *after* we find my child, we will stay here. In Rock Hollow. I'll raise him right here."

"Him?" Ty asked. Lilly shrugged. She could not explain that everything inside told her she had a son.

Ty stared into her eyes for what felt an eternity. She felt a chill settle in the deepest pit of her stomach. Her leaving must have been hard on him; there was no way for it not to be. He did not know all of the times she dialed his number but hung up before it rang, or all of the times she tried to talk to him through the 'soul connection' Momma always spouted about. He had no idea what she had seen and done while they were apart, but she was panicked that he was somehow reading it in her eyes.

Ty stood abruptly, taking her notebook and the stolen drive in his hands and walked out the door. Lilly wasn't sure what to do or think. He was never one to just walk away. Did he not want her in Rock Hollow? No, that's ridiculous.

Lilly took her phone from her purse as she watched his taillights fade, and saw she had missed twelve calls, and had as many voicemails. They were all from Drew. Never, in the nine years they were married, had he called her twelve times. She had never taken anything important to him either. She dialed the voicemail number and held her breath as she heard Drew's voice with the ever-present threat just beneath the surface. The threat only she heard.

"Where the hell are you? What did you think you could do with my computer? What the hell is going on? You need to call me back. Now. Don't do this Lilly. Don't make me chase you," Drew said to the voicemail. It shocked her he would leave a message at all. He normally assumed his number being on the missed call list would prompt a return.

"Okay, I get it. You're pissed off about something. Answer the damn phone, Lilly," was his next message, his voice growing more agitated with each call.

"Dammit! What the hell are you doing? I need to hear from you! Now! I will come for my computer and you know that. You just get off on pushing my buttons, don't you? Damn you!"

"Shit! I made it clear. Even you should have been able to understand this. Call me!"

"I'm coming, and you better have your shit together."

*"Lilly! Damn! I'm leaving and I want my computer.
I can only guess that you want out of our marriage, and
that's not going to happen. I will be in Rock Hollow
tonight, and you will be coming home with me."*

She punched the number 4 to get the time of the
call, which was made two hours earlier. That meant she
should have about four hours, depending on his driving,
before he was near.

She called Ty, and it went to his voicemail. She left
a message telling him about the calls from Drew, and sat at
the table, waiting. She had kept the volume turned down on
the phone while she drove, so the inevitable call from Drew
did not deter her plans. She turned it up three notches so
that she could hear it, but not so loud it would wake her
mother. And, on cue, Drew called again. Lilly answered it
quickly to avoid her mother hearing and interrogating her
for the rest of the night. So far Momma had said nothing
about her battered face, but it was coming.

Lilly took the phone and retreated to the front
porch. This conversation was bound to be ugly.

"What the hell do you think you're doing?" Drew
said in that measured, calm voice that started her skin
prickling. She could almost feel his breath on her face
through the phone. Lilly could hear the anger hiding
beneath the stillness in his voice. She had heard it too many
times. She could imagine him, that little vein in his
forehead popping out, making it look like there was a tiny
blue crack in his face. He continued talking, but she
stopped listening. From necessity, she had learned to block
out words when he was like this.

She could see him, eyes lighting up like a wolf's,
face contorting into that of a mad man, and fists swinging
wildly through the air. Nobody knew that Drew, nor would
they believe that he existed. As far as anyone outside of
their marriage knew, he was the kindly doctor, bent on
saving every patient.

"I don't have it," was all that she could manage to force from her lips. She wanted to yell at him, plant her fists into his chest, anything. She longed to be able to vindicate herself with every ounce of hatred she harbored for him, but the words were gone.

"What do you mean you don't have it? You took it out of my computer, you idiot. Did you throw it off a bridge? Hell, no you didn't, you're probably sitting there reading through my papers, you and your Podunk brother. I'll be there tonight, soon, and I want it."

The line went dead. Drew was coming. Of course Drew was coming. His prisoner had escaped and she had taken something he valued. What value it held was still a mystery and she was bent on solving it.

Standing in the sticky night air she eyed the old liquor cabinet just past the kitchen door, still fully stocked. A large green and gold bottle of chardonnay with grapes and silver embossed script scrawled across the label called to her. She could taste it in her mouth; feel the relief wash through her as it slid down.

"*It's only sanctuary,*" she reasoned with herself as she pulled a glass from the cabinet. She traced the rounded top with her finger and thought of all the nights she and Brad had opened a bottle together.

Her hands trembled as the cork came out effortlessly. She watched the amber liquid cover the bottom of the glass. "*After all this time, stupid, stupid girl!*" she thought. Her lips rested on the edge, her hands shaking. She closed her eyes and lifted the chalice. It was smoother than she remembered as fruity notes lingered on her tongue. Licking the last drops from her lips, she remembered where Papa kept his revolver hidden in the study. Drew would soon be there, and she was not ready to die.

She found the weapon in the empty book in Papa's desk and spun the cylinder. There was one bullet, all she needed. She eased it into the back of her jeans and glanced out the door to double check that he wasn't there. She hadn't touched a gun in years, and hoped she could remember how to use it. *"Bastard wants a fight, he'll get one,"* she thought.

She slid onto the porch swing, still carrying the wine glass, now empty, closed her eyes and saw Brad the morning he died. His head lying on the pillow beside her circled by dried blood, pale blue eyes staring directly through her, though they were already glassy when she awoke. His beautiful blond hair disheveled as always after a night of raucous sex. Dried blood, mixed with clumps of white powder, the remnants of the rest of the cocaine he had purchased, were on his nose and upper lip. He was not breathing, just staring at her. She touched his cheek, as she always did when she awoke beside him. His cold, clammy skin felt reptilian to her hand. He didn't move and his expression didn't change. She had no illusions, he was dead. The world faded from her as life drained out. She could not produce a sound, though her mouth was open wide. Tears scalded a path down her misshapen face.

Everything in her world was wrong. Everything in the room was wrong. Curtains blocked out the daylight and she wanted them to block out the cruelty of the world. Sobs thumped in her chest as her mind begged for reprieve. Brad could not be dead. He was not supposed to leave, he'd promised.

She grabbed the receiver and pushed 911 into the keypad. She knew that he was gone, but what if? As the operator answered the phone, she remembered Brad begging her not to seek help.

"If I die tonight, take the money from my wallet and leave. It won't matter where you go, just go. Don't be here with my body, please. Promise me, you have to promise," he would say every time he used drugs.

She slammed the receiver onto the phone and held her head in her hands. Brad had shown her many times, just in case, how to remove traces of herself and exit the hotel. He didn't want her to have to answer uncomfortable questions or face his crazy family.

"I don't know what to do, Brad!" she sobbed. "I need you. Please, don't go."

Hot bile bubbled up in her throat. Her heart was racing, and the room was fading in and out of view. The only man she had and would ever love was gone. She shook him, slapped at his face, screamed his name over and over, and begged him to wake up. She cried on the edge of the bed until she ran to the bathroom, vomiting until her stomach was raw. Her insides had lurched into the small toilet for what felt like hours.

She laid her body onto the cold, tiled floor and closed her eyes. The coolness calmed her stomach and kept the dizziness at bay. Brad's body lay feet from her in the bed they'd made love in less than twelve hours ago. His face, angelic as it always was, held the same expression like a wax figure.

She had lain on the bathroom floor, her face on the cold ceramic tile, her tears collecting into a puddle that, in her mind and memory, formed two halves of a heart, now broken.

When she finally dressed and retrieved his wallet for the money to get home, she lay beside him one last time and stared into his eyes. The allure that held her soul captive so many nights was fogging over. The laughter that played in the translucent blue irises was gone. What was left in the bed was a shell.

Brad was not addicted to drugs, and Lilly would level anyone that claimed otherwise. At least, he was not addicted to the one he put up his nose. He could go for months at a time without even a mention of getting high. He was a functioning alcoholic. Period. Sure, he did enjoy cocaine, and would go far out of his way to get it, but a lack of having it was not going to ruin his night. The same could not be said of alcohol. He rarely went more than ten or so hours without it, and never for an entire day. For four blissful years before Brad died, before she met Drew and gave her soul to the devil, Lilly never saw Brad completely sober, and never questioned it. She was never sober herself.

Knowing that Drew was coming, knowing that he was angrier than he had been when he caught her on his computer and struck her caused her heart to sink low into her stomach. She knew he was capable of doing anything, and given his mind set, she panicked. She contemplated running as far and as fast as she could get before Drew got there. The thought was tempting. She had his car. She had some of his money, which is probably what he wanted more than the damn computer anyway. She remembered counting it just before she'd left, and there should be enough to get to Vegas, or farther if she chose. She could get out of his grasp for a while, she thought.

The small boy in the dark returned to the forefront of her mind, his small face distorted with tears. He must be crying out for her. A child should want their parent, right? This must be what Tonya, or Madame LaCura as she is called these days, had seen. The promise of the other part of Tonya's vision, finding out what happened to her baby, Brad's baby, kept her seated on the swing. Waiting.

Chapter Five

The front porch swing may have been the greatest invention ever. Rocking slowly back and forth, trying to collect thoughts, calming the mad, crazy voices that screamed in her head. The thought of him harming Momma, or God forbid, sweet Papa, plagued her mind. For the first time she could remember she wished she had let Brad buy her a gun when he'd offered.

"You gotta be able to defend yourself, Lil," he had said. "People aren't all good, and you could hurt yourself if you don't know what to do with it."

Brad was never without his. He carried it in the saddlebags of the bike or in the glove box of the car wherever he went. She never thought she would need one.

Her phone began playing the orchestral ringtone version of one of Beethoven's works that she found the least obnoxious of the presets. A pop song would never blare from her purse as she had heard in many of the malls. She turned the phone over to see her brother's name displayed.

"Where have you been? I called you hours ago! Drew—"

"I know. I'm on my way. Don't say anything or do anything if he shows up before I get there, and for God's sake don't tell Mom what's going on. She won't let—" His voice broke into static. Cell phone reception had always been horrible in this part of the county, but right now it was taunting her. What if Drew was already in town? How long had she been on the swing? What would he do to her before

Ty got there? What could she not say or do? How would it even matter now?

She looked at the time on her phone and calculated the hours. Drew should be close. She pulled the small revolver out of the back of her jeans, her hands trembling, and stared through the sights at the tree leaves rustling in the breeze. Finally she laid it on the swing beside her. She held the wine glass to her nose and inhaled. The mild aroma eased the knots from her shoulders as she laid her head back and stared at the sky.

Every noise in the calm, still night reverberated from the trees. She heard the leaves rustling with the breeze, she heard crickets and frogs singing to the skies, she heard the low rumbling of a motorbike of some sort. With the hills and thick woods a lot of the teen boys were given four-wheeled ATVs for hunting. Instead of hunting four-legged prey, the boys would take their date for a ride, usually ending in some remote spot, expecting sex to reward their showmanship. But this didn't sound like an ATV, nor did it sound like it was in the woods. She strained to hear where the sound was coming from, resisting her desire to look up. She was certain that whatever powers controlled the universe, they were tormenting her. Brad was dead. His Harley sold. Their relationship may have been wrong, but was being unable to find their child not enough punishment for it?

She heard the gravel popping before she saw the headlights. She knew he was coming; she had been psyching her mind up for it. Hearing his arrival, she was still stricken like a deer in the headlights, paralyzed. He was out of the SUV and on his way toward her before she could even get off the swing. Her heart was pounding loud in her head, drowning out the sounds of the night. Desperate to keep him away from the house, away from her family, she leapt toward him, revolver in hand. The porch swing made a loud creaking sound and lurched from under her, sending her into the bannister of the steps. Undeterred, and scared to death, she took another long stride down the steps, landing in the gravel in front of him. She raised the weapon and stared at a spot between his eyes through the sight. Her hands shook as Drew inched closer, his eyes wild.

She pulled the hammer back and squeezed the trigger, only to be met with a dull, 'click.' *Shit, I turned the cylinder,* she thought. Her thumb yanked the hammer again as she squeezed a second time. Again, only click. Drew chuckled, sending rage from the pit of her stomach straight to her hands. Without a thought, she slammed the hammer back, squeezed the trigger, and was nearly blinded. The loud boom rang in her ears and she dropped the revolver in the gravel.

"Jesus! You fucking shot me you crazy bitch!" Drew howled. She could barely hear him, and certainly couldn't see him. Lilly stepped back toward the porch, willing her eyes to focus.

Drew grabbed her neck with his spiny fingers and held her still. There was no pretending that she wasn't panicked, he could feel her heart pounding. She tried to back away from him, and he squeezed tighter, dragging her through the gravel and throwing her against the monstrosity that he drove. His mouth formed into a heinous grin, and his eyes lit like tiny bulbs. He made her think of horror movies with the antagonist being possessed by demons. *He's snapped,* Lilly thought. She saw blood on the sleeve of his arm that was dangling free, and her heart dropped.

"Listen, bumpkin," Drew began in that calm voice that trickled out through clenched teeth. The voice he'd had on the phone. "I don't know what kind of game you think you're playing, or who you think you're playing with." His hand tightened more around her neck. "But you *will* give me my hard drive. I'm not asking."

Lilly tried to swallow. She tried to force words out, allowing air to escape. Drew wedged her body between him and his vehicle, he towered over her. She was reaching and slapping the car searching for anything to stop, or at least hinder him. As his grip on her neck got tighter he leaned harder against her. She gasped for a tiny breath as the pressure dug her ribs into her lungs. She was certain he would crush her.

The motorcycle roared into the driveway sending gravel in all directions. In one quick motion, the driver dismounted and threw himself at Drew, falling with him to the ground. The headlight was left on, creating a shadow play on the front of the house. Lilly saw her shadow melding into the vehicle as she heaved air into her newly freed lungs. The shadows of the man on the motorcycle and Drew were picking themselves up, growing to enormous heights on the yellow painted boards. The man on the motorcycle was about Drew's height but built much larger with wide shoulders that made his shadow on the house loom over Drew's like Goliath.

Motorcycle Man pushed Drew back down to the ground as he steadied himself on the rocks. He scanned Lilly with steely grey eyes then turned back to Drew.

"Who the hell are you?" Drew spat, drooling blood from his lip.

"Ben Hale, detective. FBI," Motorcycle man said, reaching toward his back.

Drew put his hands in the air signaling surrender. Lilly's eyes darted to where the motorcycle man was reaching and saw the holster.

Drew's face went as pale as it had when he saw Lilly at his computer desk. He looked like he would either pass out or vomit, or both. He kept his eyes locked on Ben Hale as he gently raised himself from the ground.

"FBI?" Drew finally managed.

Ben nodded.

"What the... Why...?" Drew said, searching the ground for whatever words he needed. "I just want my computer back." He sounded much more like the good doctor.

Drew looked from Lilly to Ben, back to Lilly. He recovered quickly from the identity of the motorcycle man. The hatred that oozed from his eyes may have, at that moment, rivaled hers. His loathing covered her like a thick coat in the middle of July. Drew's lip curled as if he smelled something putrid, his nostrils flaring with each labored breath. His lips began to part and the evil that Lilly had seen for years, the evil that made her feel like the small trapped rabbit when the hunger crazed wolf licked it's drooling fangs, crossed his face. As he rose from the ground Lilly could see that she had only grazed his arm with her shot.

"I didn't drive six hours to go home empty handed," Drew said, again in the calmest tone she'd heard him use in nine years.

Ty's old black Ford roared to a halt. He parked on the side of the street and got out, carrying papers and the hard drive. He handed one of the papers to Drew and a stack of them to Ben.

"Emergency Protective Order?" Drew said after looking at the paper. "She leaves me, takes *my* property without *my* permission with her, and I have to stay, what was that—" he searched the paper for the exact distance. "50 feet away from her at all times?"

"Look at her face, you piece of shit! You did that! Do you feel like a big man now?" Ty shouted, a rare occurrence. "Yes, you have to stay 50 feet away from her. Today. Tomorrow. Forever. As far as your property goes, she's your wife, it's half hers."

"Give me my computer, and I'll stay 600 miles away from her forever," Drew shouted, blue crack in his forehead growing. Ty threw the hard drive at his feet, little circuits and wires getting lost in the gravel. Drew scrambled to grab the parts splaying in the driveway, shooting his darts at Lilly through his blood shot eyes. Ty may as well have punched her in the gut. She sacrificed everything to get it, holding to the hope that it would lead her to her child, and he just threw it at Drew. It was useless now, having fallen apart in the driveway, but that did not lessen the risks she took.

Drew lunged at Lilly with the weight of his entire body, sending her careening into the car she'd taken from him, his body crushing her again. She could feel the heat of his breath in her eyes, making her close them and turn her face away so she could hear only his hideous voice. "You have no idea what you've started," he whispered.

Ty and Ben Hale pulled him off of her, throwing him into the side of his behemoth of a vehicle. Lilly heard him hit the metal, the sound like a bludgeon.

"No, you son of a bitch. *You* have no idea what you've started," she said, her voice and body void of any emotion that he could once use against her. She turned away from them and walked into the house, collapsing onto the Cherub bench that had consoled her years before. The roller coaster of this day left her spent and hollow. She wanted to have something to use against Drew. She thought of nothing else since last night, seeing his reaction to the sight of her on his computer. *There had to be something on there*, she thought. Unless he was just so controlling that the thought of her having bested him ate away at him. And she knew he was a controlling thug.

She glanced back out the door at the scene still unfolding in the driveway and saw Drew in handcuffs, Ben Hale from the F.B.I. on his left, and Ty on his right. Lilly knew Drew would be out soon, if Ty even managed to book him before the dog and pony show arrived. She watched the two men as they put Drew into Ty's truck, and saw the

F.B.I. man's wide shoulders turn toward the door. His thin, brutish face scanned the front of the house.

"What now?" she whispered. She could only imagine what Drew was filling their heads with; what secrets he was knocking the dust from. She would have to tell Ty about her past before Drew had the chance, but how would he react? Would he still accept her as his sister, or would he renegade her? Would he look at her the same? Her gaze fell onto the wine glass that had rolled under the swing. She closed her eyes and put her head on her knees. How had life come to this?

Lilly was exhausted, her neck sore, her lip and cheek ached, and she wanted a drink more than she had in years. This was not the homecoming she had dreamt of.

As she leaned her head against the hard backing of the bench she closed her eyes, and visions of Brad played in her mind. She had gone to The Sunken Ship the night after they met and sheepishly waited to see if he'd show. After the last patron—an angry drunk guy that wanted to go fist to cuff with anyone that looked bigger than he—left, Bea gave Lilly *that* look. Lilly shrugged. It was better Brad hadn't come. She held up her forefinger, and Bea poured Jack straight over ice, Lilly's favorite poison.

The slow burn as it inched down her neck with each sip took with it all thoughts of hurt. It cleared the fog that set itself up in her head. She sipped slowly until the corners of her mouth were curling upward—her body's signal that the alcohol was there, pain could not permeate its defense.

"Hello, gorgeous," she heard his deep voice growl in her ear. Lilly jumped and nearly fell from the bar stool, spilling a bit of her whiskey on her lower lip. She turned her head slightly with her hand wiping at the amber liquid creeping down her chin, and was staring into his translucent eyes.

"I'd ask if you come here often, but that's a horrible pick up line, and we've both been here two nights in a row.

Nice touch with the whiskey, by the way," he said, wiping a droplet from her chin.

"You scared the hell out of me! I didn't even hear the door!" she screeched.

"You and your buddy Jack there were deep in conversation when I walked in. Darts?" he asked.

"What?" Lilly demanded.

"A game of darts?" The amusement in Brad's eyes was infuriating.

"Oh, I don't play. I don't think I want to either, so no moving furniture again."

"Fair enough, cards then." He produced a deck from his pocket. "You did say if I play my cards right, so, let's see if I do."

"It was figurative."

Brad's smile lit his eyes, and Lilly could not look away. She was fighting her face to keep a scowl firmly planted. He did, after all, come late enough to make her worry he wouldn't show up at all, and he did cause her to spill whiskey down her chin like a toddler. She was losing the battle. His daft stare was chipping at her ice-encased heart further. Without looking away he dealt them both five cards each.

"What are we playing?" she asked.

"Poker, silly goose. What do you have for ante?"

Lilly assumed he wanted her to offer up her clothing, and no way was that happening. She fought the alcohol mudding her brain, and remembered that she had two peppermint candies in her pocket. She slapped them onto the bar and straightened her back as she smiled triumphantly at him.

Brad chuckled and began rummaging in his pockets. Finally, after minutes of digging, he took out a slim, yellow pack of chewing gum.

"I'll see your mints, and raise you a pack of gum." He produced a second pack of gum and laid it on the growing pile.

Lilly looked at her hand, and her heart skipped when she saw two kings smiling gracefully back at her. She took a one dollar bill from her back pocket and stacked it on top of the candy.

"That should do, I call you." Confidence oozed from her royal pair.

"Ace high garbage," he chuckled as he laid his cards face up on the bar. Lilly turned her hand over and showed her pair. Brad shook his head.

"Are you hungry?" he asked.

"A little."

"Ever ride on a motorcycle?"

Lilly shook her head. Her hands began to tremble at the thought. She was fascinated with bikes, had been forever, but still carried a healthy fear of her head meeting pavement.

"Come on, let's go strap on a feed sack," he said, taking her hand. His touch calmed her pounding heart, and stilled the tremors that were working down her legs. He laid the money for their drinks on the bar and led Lilly out the door.

***

The screen door slammed, shaking the bench Lilly was perched on, and dragging her back to the present. Back away from Brad, again. She opened her eyes and saw Ty standing over her, glaring down at her.

"He's in jail, you're safe. Go upstairs and get some rest." He reached for her arm.

"I can walk, Ty," she shot at him.

Chapter Six

As she opened her eyes, the sun was beaming in the narrow crack between the pale green curtains hanging in the bedroom she'd grown up in. Posters she'd hung years earlier still decorated the walls. Time had been unable to change this room or the feeling that lying in this bed gave her. For a while, she could lay here and be seventeen again. She could forget the lies, manipulations, and pain and just be imperfect, insecure Lilly.

As she lay awake staring at the ceiling, the image of Ben Hale coming out of nowhere and taking Drew down played in front of her. He did not seem to notice that she was there, clinging to the car. It seemed completely natural for him, like he was born to do exactly that. She heard three knocks coming from the floor and smiled. Momma would use the broom handle and knock on the ceiling to signal her to get out of bed and come to breakfast. Lilly wiped the sleep from her eyes and descended the stairs. She could hear Momma and Ty in the kitchen bantering whether the heat would soon break.

"I need to go to Rex's and pick up your grandfather's meds, and I want to ride in that fancy thing you drive," Momma said as Lilly walked into the room.

"Momma, I really don't—"

"Hush! I have to go into town and I haven't been able to be with my baby girl in years. It's settled, we'll go after breakfast. Now eat up. Coffee's fresh."

Ty turned his head and chuckled silently once Momma's back was turned. Lilly scrunched her nose and narrowed her eyes at him. Pain rushed through her cheek, but she would not let her brother best her, and fought the wince back.

This was what she dreaded, going into public and showing the town that had made no secret of their collective disdain regarding her, the latest of her epic fails with a nice battered face. She could already feel the sneers and hear the whispers as she strode down the sidewalk. Momma was unbothered by the looks and hushed tones that always accompanied the Yorks in public, but Lilly was not as hardened.

As they walked to the car Lilly glanced back at the enormous old yellow board Queen Anne with the beautiful wrap around porch, and rounded tower that made Lilly think she were a princess growing up in a castle as a child, and saw Papa peering out the window. Momma climbed into the car and sat stoic. Not even a glance in Papa's direction. As far as Momma knew, Lilly was unaware of the latest feud between father and daughter, but Ty had told her all about it at lunch.

"Look at poor Papa," Lilly cooed staring at the window.

Momma sat motionless, as if she hadn't heard her.

"Momma? Are—"

"I heard you, Lillian. I am not going to look at that man. Poor Papa my eye. You don't know the half of it."

"What happened this time?" Lilly asked, making an effort to avoid the inevitable eye roll. Momma was known to be contrary, and Papa could be stubborn as a bull. Fighting and, at times, all-out war, were not uncommon in this house.

Momma gave her a stern look letting her know that it was not her business, and not going to be resolved any time soon. They drove in silence. No stories of York lore to pass the time. In less than 24 hours Lilly had come to a harsh realization. You really can't go home again.

Their first stop in town was the Rex's Drugs. The seats and counter were still there, but there was no one to dip ice cream, no coolers to house the sweet treat, not even the wall-sized mirror was still behind the counter.

She saw a familiar face lurking in the pet care aisle. Mr. Holloway, a mail carrier for all of the years that Lilly could remember, was debating with himself which flea collar would be best for the dog. Judging from the boxes he held, it was a large dog, over 50 pounds at least.

"Hi, Mr. Holloway," she said.

He looked up, annoyed by her greeting, and grunted. Lilly didn't remember him ever being particularly chatty, but he always at least greeted her when they would meet. She remembered that he had a child, a boy. The boy should have been grown up by now, and usually that meant they were off to State.

"How's your son?" She was trying to keep smiling. The humiliation would come sooner if she held her head in shame, or acted like a beaten puppy. Her mother was coming toward her quickly with her arms outstretched and eyes as wide as Lilly had ever seen. Mr. Holloway dropped his packages and was twisting his lips unnaturally.

"No no no no no!" her mother said, taking her by the arm and leading her out of the store. Mr. Holloway was still in the same spot he'd been in, staring after them, his face distorting and twisting, reminding Lilly of Drew.

Once they were on the sidewalk, Lilly yanked her arm out of her mother's grasp and put both hands on her hips.

"Let's go to the park," her mother said somberly.

Momma picked a bench close to the playground so the children's laughter would drown out their voices. She was kicking at the dirt, looking to the cloudless sky, and sighing.

"Momma?"

"There was a murder. A few years ago. At the Holler," Momma began.

"I know. Ty told me about it."

"He didn't tell you it was Oral Holloway's boy?"

Lilly shook her head.

"Or that the other boy was Bess Spear's boy?"

Again, Lilly could only shake her head. She had known these people since she was small.

"Well, they were."

The women sat silent on the bench for a long while. Lilly watched as people busied themselves with their daily routines. Things weren't at all how they used to be. So few people looked familiar, so few places held their original charm. Mr. Holloway had not come out of the drug store and Lilly thought that was odd. If he never bought the flea collar, it could do no good for the animal.

"He lost his mind, you know. Mr. Holloway," she jutted her chin in the direction of the pharmacy, apparently picking up on what Lilly was thinking. "Went stark raving mad after it happened, and Tyler had no suspects. He killed the only dog they had the night after Jake died. He goes to the pharmacy and just holds flea collars now for hours, then goes home." Her mother was shaking her head. "Blames Tyler for not finding the killer."

The tank top Lilly had found in her dresser drawer she had left behind was at least a size too big now, but sweat was sticking it to her skin. It was one of the hottest days she could recall, and the sun was bearing down on her. She knew her pasty skin would be blaze red by the evening, even if she got out of the sun now. Her skin had two color settings, white as a ghost or bursting into flames. There was no in between.

Lilly heard a familiar high-pitched, obnoxious voice behind her. She only knew one person that could sound like that and slowly glanced behind her to see.

"Oh, God," she whispered.

"What?" Momma asked, alarm rising in her voice.

"Trenia Willis," Lilly said flatly.

"Oh, good Lord, I thought you saw your husband back there. It's Trenia Drake now. She's been coming and doing Papa's home health care for a while."

Despite the years that had passed, Lilly still felt the punch in her gut when Momma told her that Trenia had married Ricky Drake.

"Momma, I really don't want to see her. Can we go somewhere else?"

Momma acted as if she hadn't heard her, and Lilly couldn't take her eyes off Trenia. She was wiping dust from the playground off of a little boy's cheek that had just fallen from a swing. From across the park Lilly could see that he had small, strawberry curls covering his head. He looked about the age she thought her own child would be. Her heart froze as the small boy, freshly clean faced, ran to the see-saw and waited on the seat for someone to join him. He seemed content to just wait. Lilly's heart ached to watch her son play on a swing, or slide, or teeter-totter.

Trenia sat on a bench facing the playground, and Lilly turned around and watched the people on the sidewalk across the street, mindlessly doing their normal routine. There were spectators snapping pictures of anything and everything, town people going from building to building, always managing to wave at each other, regardless of whether they actually knew one another.

Momma, while driving, would wave to the oncoming car and smile so properly. Once the car passed, the smile morphed into a scowl, and she would let loose whatever gossip she knew about them. Ty—usually in the front seat with Momma— and Lilly would eye one another and laugh silently at their mother's rant.

Momma kicked at the dirt beneath the bench. Her eyes were glassy and she seemed like her mind was in another world. Lilly watched her click her fingernails together and stare at nothing in particular.

"What is it, Momma?" she asked.

Her mother barely acknowledged the question and kept clicking.

"Mom?"

Her mother sighed and turned to face her. The muscles in Lilly's neck tightened, bracing for what was coming. Her mother had a dramatic streak, but when she meant business, there was no room for doubt.

"Let's go up to Hershell's, Lilly. We can talk there."

The walk to the other end of the square to Hershell's was silent. Momma scoffed as they passed Patsy's Hair Emporium, signaling that she and her former trusted friend were still on the outs. Lilly couldn't hide the amusement she found in the spat. Everyone that crossed paths with Momma had been on the outs with her at one point or another. It was commonly known that if you don't want to hear the harsh truth, don't let Angelica York know your business.

Once they were seated in the booth, Lilly turned her attention to the picture hanging just above them of the mob. A new picture had been placed above the next booth over; this one of the Berger County Bulls football team from Lilly and Ty's senior year. Ty was in the front row. He used to be a star in high school. The last half of his senior year he was recovering from an injury, though.

Lilly was at the Hollow with Ricky Drake when Ty, the hero, came to get her. Lilly hadn't asked for a hero, she hadn't needed one. Ty just shows up in his save-the-day way and thinks he is just going to swoop in and rescue the poor damsel. Lilly had gotten angry and started walking back down the hill. Ty came after her in his truck. When he caught up to her she refused to get in. Ty got out of the truck, and forgot to set the brake. The hill was too steep and the truck started rolling. He pushed her out of the way, but the truck caught his ankle underneath the front tire, shattering the bones and the full scholarship he was to receive. Neither Momma nor Ty ever said anything, but she could feel the blame every time his football greatness was brought up. She kept the guilt tucked safely away in her ever growing train of emotional baggage.

"Lillian, you have no idea how perfect your timing is. You couldn't have picked a better time to come back," Momma said, yanking Lilly out of her trudge down memory lane.

"Why, Mom? What's going on?" Lilly knew there was no way that her mother knew all of the reasons she was there.

"Honey, I need to tell you something." She paused as the waitress set their water in front of them. Lilly could feel her eyes growing larger, trying to urge her mother on.

"I went to see Dr. Farley a couple of months ago. I was having dizzy spells a lot, and I thought all the problems I've had with my ears were coming back." She took a sip from her water glass. "He ran some tests." Momma cupped Lilly's hands in her own. "Honey, I have leukemia."

The news landed on Lilly's head like a boulder. She watched Momma's lips moving, tried to comprehend what she was saying, but the world around her was in a tailspin. Anger began to sprout deep in the pit of her stomach. How dare Momma put this on her right now! How dare she be sick! After everything else in Lilly's life, why couldn't she just be Momma?

"Ty knows?" Lilly nearly spat the words. She cleared her throat trying to mask her animosity.

"No," Momma said, her voice coarse. "Nobody knows except you now. Honey, I am sorry. I had to tell somebody."

Remorse coursed through Lilly's chest. Her mother's jade eyes had gotten watery, and she was blinking profusely to hold back the tears.

"Are you... I mean, of course... well... what about...." Lilly couldn't bring herself to the question of treatment.

"I have had three chemo treatments," her mother told her, sparing Lilly from playing with more words that she could not force out of her mouth. "Tyler thinks I've been volunteering at the hospital. That's all that he needs to know."

Resolve oozed from her. She was set. Ty would not know until Momma was ready to tell him, if such a time ever came.

Lilly found herself staring at her mother's resplendent hair. She could not imagine her without it. Even as a small child she found comfort in the mass of deep crimson curls that spewed from her mother's head.

"It's a wig. I shaved it off before I started chemo," her mother said, once again reading Lilly's thoughts. "I didn't want wads of it falling out in my hands. Couldn't bear it."

"My God, Momma. Ty has to know."

"No. It would break his heart. You know as well as I do he's a momma's boy. Always has been. The last thing I need is for that boy to fuss over me."

As true a statement as it was, no one within the family ever spoke the words. Lilly had believed she was the inconvenient child for as long as she could remember; like she was being blamed for having taken a cluster of cells from Ty in the uterus. She was sure Momma had never intentionally tried to make her feel that way. She and Ty had a closer bond than that of Momma and Lilly.

The drive home was mostly silent, only broken on the occasion that Momma found another button or gadget that she had never seen before. She could have the damned car; Lilly had not ever wanted it. Drew would not allow his wife who, like it or not represented his family, being seen in anything that wasn't the latest and greatest. As they turned into the driveway, Lilly saw Ty's truck and Ben Hale's motorcycle parked in the yard, and the two men on the porch, waiting for them.

Chapter Seven

"Lose your key?" Momma teased Ty.

"Nah, waiting on you lovely ladies to get back. Wanted to see my big sister."

"Well, there's nothing big about your sister," Momma chided.

Lilly wanted nothing more than to hold her brother. He had no idea what Momma was going through or what he would be faced with eventually. She was following Momma into the house, but Ty slammed the screen door after their mother was inside. Anger mixed with the heat of Kentucky June, snapped in her chest, and Lilly spun on her heels to glare at him. As she turned, Ben Hale's scent, a mild woodsy cologne, wafted to her nostrils and sent sharp longing through her chest. It reminded her of Brad so much that she stopped and glared at him. It was cruel.

"Ben's found some stuff. He's, well I mean we, were hoping you could answer some questions," Ty said.

"Like?" she shot at Ben. She could feel his eyes on her. She knew how these things ended; there was no reason to allow it to start. She wanted to find her child, nothing else. Never again would she be caught up in some dizzy daydream about happily ever after. That wasn't real, and that was that.

"Well, to start, Ty copied the information that was on the hard drive onto this." He laid a flash drive on the railing of the porch. As he moved his arm Lilly saw the ink of a tattoo peek out from the sleeve of his black t-shirt. Ben's bronze skin nearly masked it. She was sure it was letters. She tore her eyes from Ben's brawny arm, feeling heat flushing through her cheeks, and glanced at the drive.

A renewed hope leapt into her chest as she stared at it. Light was starting to break the surface of the tunnel again.

"You really aren't as dumb as you look, baby brother." Lilly picked up the tiny piece of hope and turned it over in her hand.

"Ha-Ha. Ten thousand comedians out of work, and my big sister is *dying* to be funny," Ty said, flashing a wink in Lilly's direction. Ben cracked the slightest smile but did not take his stormy grey eyes off Lilly. His smile winded its crooked way up the left side of his face, etching lines around the edge of his eyes the way Brad's used to. Rage boiled at the edges of Lilly's chest. Fate, she thought, was the cruelest hag.

"Did Drew talk about the clinic with you?" Ben asked, leaning against the porch rail, arms folded across his hefty chest, bringing the heaviness back into the moment. Lilly shook her head. "Nothing?" Again, Lilly shook her head. "He never mentioned a fraud investigation?"

"The only time he said anything to me was the day he unloaded the boxes of files into his home office. He said no paper trail, never happened. That was it. He didn't tell me about the investigation, I had to hear about that from Anne. She called to discuss my plan to help him," Lilly said, making air quotes with each hand as she said 'help him.'

"Anne?" Ty asked.

"Anne Hodge," Lilly answered, thinking of how Anne was going to react to her separation from Drew.

"The senator?" Ben asked. Lilly nodded, not looking at either of them. "Damn, you've got some big time friends."

"They're Drew's friends," Lilly said, still staring at the edges of the tattoo.

"Still, I'd love to have friends with that kind of clout," Ben complained. "Did you think to ask her for help?"

Lilly shook her head. "Like I said, they are *his* friends."

Ben shuffled the stack of papers that he was holding until he found what looked like a letter that someone had typed.

"Have you ever heard the name Lüx Pharmaceuticals?" Ben inquired.

Lilly shook her head.

"What was the name of the pharmaceutical company?" Ty asked.

"Lüx. It's German." Ben told him.

"When I checked out the clinic that day, the guy driving the truck for Glick told Drew that 'Loose has more'. He meant the pharmaceutical company, not loose like a bolt that needs tightening. That makes more sense." Ty scrolled through his phone until he found the picture he had taken, and turned the screen for Ben to see.

"Yeah, I was gonna tell you I found it earlier but hadn't had a chance."

Lilly narrowed her eyes as she looked at Ty. "When did you check out the clinic?"

"That day we had lunch. I drove up and had a look at the place," Ty said, crinkling his forehead, forming lines that stretched the width of his face. "Which reminds me, what in the hell were you going to see Madame LaCura for?"

"Dear Lord, Tyler James! You followed me?" Lilly snapped.

"Yup. Answer the question, please."

"My God, Ty, it's none of your business."

"Lüx has more what?" Ben asked, probably trying not to let the conversation veer too far off course. Ty lifted one shoulder and continued tapping on his phone. Ben made a note on the letter and looked back to Lilly.

"Drew never mentioned it?"

Again, she shook her head.

"What about a man named Haim?" Ben handed her the letter. It had a date from June ten years earlier and was addressed to Drew.

Dearest Mr. Wilt,

Congratulations! You have worked extraordinarily hard to obtain your fellowship with

The Sound of Hope Psychiatric Facility. I have found your research and subsequent essay on the multiple layers of dissociative disorders and the variations thereof, and how they differ from schizophrenia captivating. I have passed the paper up to my superiors, and have been met with overwhelming enthusiasm to induct you and your research into our scholastic endeavors. I do look forward to meeting with you as well as reading further research that you may be considering. If ever I can be of any type of assistance, please feel free to contact me.

Respectfully yours,

Haim Koehler, President
Helping Hands Research/Fellowship Grants

"I've never heard of any of this," Lilly said, handing the letter back to Ben. "Drew didn't tell me anything besides how stupid I am. I thought you said Lüx was a pharmaceutical company. This guy was interested in research projects."

"They are. They supply a lot of medication to Mexico and China for next to no money. They were banned in the US a little over 10 years ago."

"Banned? Why?" Lilly asked confused about what any of this had to do with her or her child.

"They put a diet pill on the market, called it *'herbal'*. FDA doesn't really regulate the herbal supplements. It was herbal, alright. One of the herbs was

Dinitrophenol. Works great, gets rid of the fat as is advertised. Unfortunately, the drug also causes hypothermia, makes your heart beat too fast, causes you to sweat at unheard of levels, and makes you take fast shallow breaths, and twenty-five people died as a direct result of taking it. At least, that's what the lawyers that took the case to trial claimed."

"And Drew was doing research for this company?" Lilly asked, knowing the question sounded stupid. She had just read the letter herself. It blatantly stated he had given them research. She assumed he had done more over the years. *You're sounding like a school girl*, she told herself.

"I don't know if he has done anything further than the one paper for them. I don't even know that he did the paper specifically for them. Sometimes companies offer top tier graduate students a fellowship for excellent projects. It gets pretty competitive."

"I have no idea. The only thing I ever knew was what my credit limit was on the cards, and how to dress to look like his wife. I can't imagine him doing anything to help people get medication cheaper. He was constantly complaining about people getting everything for nothing on the back of his hard earned dollar."

"There are a lot of grants going to Sounds of Hope Rehab Clinic, to the tune of over six million dollars. Do you know who would want to direct this much money to the clinic?" Ty asked.

Lilly shook her head again. "Don't you still have him in jail? Can't you ask him this stuff?" she asked.

"We did," Ty answered

"I can't open a separate investigation without more to go on. I'm gonna leave this as part of the Medicaid fraud. I looked at the file this morning. The auditors closed the case. They did mention that there were a few files unavailable, but the records clerk had just been let go so they were working to recover them," Ben said.

"Why would they close it with files missing? That seems counter-productive," Ty said. Ben shook his head as he buried himself into another document in the stack of papers he had.

"Guess his friends in high places gave him a hand."

"I doubt that Anne would. She's not like that," Lilly said. Anne had befriended her at one of the 'first power summits', how Lilly liked to call these political galas.

"Just sayin'. It doesn't hurt to have friends that high up in the food chain," Ty said.

Lilly shrugged. Drew had never allowed her even a glimpse into the affairs of the clinic. She picked up the drive and went to Papa's office where the computer was set up in a corner. Momma and Papa fought over the space for years. Momma called it hers, Papa complained the only thing she ever did on the computer was play games or browse social media; one of the many things capable of starting a York war.

She opened the drive and started looking through the files. How Ty and Ben understood any of this was beyond her comprehension. There were a few letters written by the Haim guy. They all looked identical to the one she had just read. The research projects that were typed on the letter were different on each one, but the basic form letter was the same. She saw all of the grants they had asked her about. The only thing out of place about any of them was the one that he had gotten for indigent care. Drew was not a believer in pro bono work.

She clicked through year after year of records. Nothing. She thought that her memories were probably from the time just after they married because she could clearly remember the last nine years. She clicked on the file labeled for that year only to find the same grants, receipts, and letters as every other year. The last file was labeled with the year just before they married. She clicked on it. There were only two document files inside. The first was from the office of the Helping Hands congratulating Drew for his fine work in med school, graduating first in his class, taking the lead in the research field of psychiatry, and offering the chance to qualify for the charity's annual endowment. He apparently qualified because in every other year the grant money was being put towards everything in the clinic.

The second file was of a patient at the clinic. She was 22 years old, and according to the file, suffering from bi-polar disorder. She was admitted to The Sounds of Hope three days after the letter from Helping Hands had been written. The woman's entire medical chart was on the screen in front of Lilly. Ben and Ty gathered close behind her to read it as well.

The file said Drew had tried a number of anti-depressants, two anti-hallucinogenic drugs, and one antipsychotic. The woman had been in the clinic under his care for eleven months. There was no change noted by any of the nurses during the entirety of her stay. At the end of the file there was a discharge disposition form with the word, 'Deceased' typed at the top. There was no disposition offered as the form's title implied, just that the patient was dead.

Lilly turned to the two men and stared. They appeared confused as she was. It was not normal practice to have a patient file on the personal computer of the doctor. There were plenty of HIPAA laws to ensure that sort of thing doesn't happen. Not to mention all of the lawsuits against doctors for doing unspeakable things to patients while they were incapacitated.

"Probably his dummy file," Ben said, finally breaking the silence. The dumbfounded look on Ty's face conveyed that he had no more idea than Lilly what Ben was talking about. "I've heard of med school students keeping a dummy file for practice, exams, that sort of stuff. He was into research, so this is probably his dummy file."

Maybe, but Lilly did not buy it. Drew thought himself a god. He didn't need anything as inane as a 'dummy file.'

Chapter Eight

Drew was only being held on assault charges, and Ty didn't know how long he was going to be able to keep him in jail. He had already had a visit from a lawyer. Not that they were getting anything from him before, but since the visit he just sat there staring straight ahead. Ty spoke with Jay Marsh, the Commonwealth Attorney prosecuting the case, and gave him everything he could on Drew, including the Medicaid fraud. Ty needed the jackass exactly where he was.

"I'll do what I can, but I can't hold him any longer than the judge says. It's just assault," Jay said.

"I know, but he's threatened to kill her. He attacked her twice in front of Ben and me last night. I know he'll go after her again," Ty told him.

"She's got the EPO. And she's got a brother that just happens to be the sheriff. That's how the judge will see it, Ty. I can't change it. I have asked for a continuation to buy a couple of days. "

Dammit, Ty thought. He only had a couple of days, but he needed weeks. He looked over to the interrogation room and saw Drew, with the same expression he'd had since the lawyer left, staring straight ahead. It looked like he was staring directly at Ty, but Ty knew he couldn't see him. The mirrored glass wouldn't allow that.

Ben came bouncing in. He had been on the phone since this morning with the office that investigated the Medicaid case. He knew the law as well as most people know the alphabet. He also knew how to close loop-holes, something Ty thought they would need once Drew's team started hammering on the case.

"It's re-opened. Got a search warrant," Ben said, grinning as though he caught the prize bass in a contest. "I need Lilly to tell me where those banker's boxes are that she told you about. I've got people on their way to the house now. I'm gonna go meet them in Lexington and pick up the boxes there."

Ty nodded, not taking his eyes off of Drew. Ben looked from Ty to Drew. "Is that helping?"

"What?"

"Staring at him like that."

Ty shrugged. "He's been like that since the lawyer left. Won't speak. Won't look at you when you talk to him. Just sits there."

"Let me have a crack at it," Ben laughed. "I think I just may have something that's gonna make him want to open up and share his feelings with us." In the academy, Ben had excelled in interrogation techniques, Ty had excelled in physical training. The instructor, Sgt. Dave Lannum, told them both that they'd make one hell of a cop if he could splice them into one person.

Ben walked into the room, slammed the door, and spun the chair on its back legs so that he could straddle it, and sat across from Drew. Drew never so much as winced or acknowledged Ben's presence. Ty watched Ben slap the paper on the table he assumed to be the search warrant. Ty saw Drew flinch, and for the first time since the lawyer had left, he turned his head to look at Ben. Ty could not sit still, whatever came out of Drew's mouth right now, Ty wanted to hear firsthand. He flipped the switch activating the mike in the interrogation room.

"The boxes of files? You remember, you told Lilly, 'No paperwork, never happened?'" Ben said, making air quotes with the forefinger of each hand. Drew, who had moments before been the most collected, together individual, was unraveling. His eyes were wild, staring knives into Ben.

"You believe that stupid bitch? There's nothing in my house. Talk to my lawyer," Drew said.

"I'm talking to you. It would make things much easier if you just told me what we'll find. I can help you if there's a discrepancy in the records. If that's what you are afraid of. You just need to talk to me," Ben said.

"Go talk to Lilly. I want my lawyer." Drew said.

"I will talk to Lilly. I'll call your lawyer, but I gotta tell you, I'm thinking that I'm going to find something pretty big at your house," Ben taunted. It was a bluff, neither of them had any idea what they may find. "I'm thinking something that will make this Medicaid stuff look like playing in the sandbox, am I right?"

Drew stared straight ahead, hands folded on the table in front of him. The loosened tongue was restrained again. Ty could stand it no more.

"What about the child?" Ty shouted into the microphone, his voice like a deafening boom in the steely silence. Drew turned his icy glare to the mirrored wall, and the smirk they had seen the previous night was etching its way onto his cold lips.

"There's no child. There never was. Lilly made it up," Drew spat as though the words themselves were too imbecilic for him to be sitting here wasting his precious time saying.

"She remembers," Ty shouted.

"She remembers what?" Drew called over Ty's voice. "There was never a kid. Jesus! She's your sister, your twin. Did she ever call you to tell you that you were going to be an uncle? No? That's right. She didn't. Because she was never pregnant." Drew shook his head, and for the first time Ty saw a fragment of concern in his eyes. "I've tried to help her. Offered her medication that would do her a world of good. She refuses it. All of it. And now she's having *memories.*" He held up his hands in surrender, and gave Ty the look of a man beaten at his own sport. "It's not real, Ty. She made all of it up."

"Why would she do that?" Ty asked.

"People do things that even those of us in the field don't understand. Maybe she's not happy with our life. Maybe she wants something that I can't give her. Maybe she truly believes that it is real. I don't have an answer, and she blocks all of my attempts at helping her." Drew planted his head into the palms of his hands and let out a frustrated sigh.

Ty turned the microphone off. He had to admit, if only to himself, he was having problems with the 'memories' she had told him about. It did sound fantastical. Lilly had been known to exaggerate the truth occasionally, but it did seem unlikely she would make up such a far out story. The thought of Drew telling him the truth about something sent a pang of rage through his chest, but, he was right. If she had been pregnant she would have let him know.

"The truth will out," he could hear his mother's voice say. She had said those words to both Lilly and Ty throughout their teenage years, usually when Ty was covering for his sister's late night shenanigans.

Drew was not to be trusted. That was a fact. He was into something, and Ty had to figure out what. How Lilly played a part was the biggest uncertainty. The cop in Ty said there was the possibility she was into this with him, got mad after getting cut out of the deal or whatever and decided to roll on him. That didn't sound like the Lilly that he knew, but he hadn't known her for years. She had led a life that nobody knew anything about, except possibly Drew. The thought tied knots in his stomach as anger began to rise up.

He had been the one who had stayed and taken care of the family after Lilly took off for greener pastures. He'd held everything together. He heard their mother cry herself to sleep when she had no idea where her daughter was. It was him. Not Lilly. He hadn't realized the resentment he was finding himself unable to quell ran so deep. He couldn't protect her if she was into whatever this was, and, truth to tell he didn't want to. If she had knowingly gotten herself in over her head with Drew, then ran to him for help, only God could help her. He had to talk to her. Something about her story nagged at him. If she knew anything and withheld it, no matter how little a thing, he had to know, and the sooner the better.

Ty was becoming keenly aware he was pacing, pounding his fist into his palm. He stopped and turned to see Ben emerging from the room, shaking his head.

"Text from the guys. They went to the house to get the boxes, and the housekeeper wanted to talk to *him* first," he said, nodding his head in the direction of the interrogation room. "There were only two boxes when the guys got there."

"Two? Lilly said three."

"Yeah, I know. They are heading to Lexington with them now. You need to sit your sister down. I don't know what he's doing or has done, but it doesn't look good. I'll be back tonight, man."

"Yup." Ty felt his nostrils flaring.

"Look," Ben started, putting his hand on Ty's shoulder, "I don't think she knows what he's into, and you don't either. I know you. Don't let your judgment be clouded by that piece of shit."

Chapter Nine

Lilly walked quietly so as to not wake Papa if he was sleeping. As a young girl, she and Papa would walk the property, looking every inch over to make sure nothing was out of place. The York family was prone to visits from the local law, Papa told her. He shared stories of his own childhood, watching his father and uncles make 'the shine' as he called it. Papa hated the stuff.

On one of the walks of the land Lilly saw a small wooden building, no bigger than the outside toilets scattered among all of the older homes. It was in disrepair and Papa had told her to never go near it. She listened, for the most part. She was 14 before she opened the doors of the building and found the demon that changed the course of her life.

"My Lilla girl," she heard Papa's feeble voice say through the open slit in the door of the study. She pushed the door open and saw him sitting in a wing chair, a dank blanket draped over his legs. His hair, which had been white for years, was reduced to a few scattered hairs across a freckled head. His glasses clung to the tip of his narrow nose, showing the sunken eyes of the kindest, smartest man she had ever known. He was a pillar and a hero to her. He used to have the strength of an ox, physically and emotionally. He'd pulled the York name out of the trash all alone. He was now a mere shadow of his former self, but he managed a bright smile that made Lilly run to him and throw her arms around his neck.

"What did you do? You're too skinny, girl," Papa said.

"I'm fine, Papa," Lilly said, still holding him.

"Your mother was like that, too. She wanted to be so thin that I could read the paper through her. I think you've got her beat," he said with a wink.

Lilly doubted that poor Papa's sight was what it used to be. She heard a movement in the corner and looked over to see a young man, no older than 25, she thought, holding a tray of what appeared to be Papa's lunch. The man was tall, probably 6'4 she guessed, wearing light blue scrubs. His appearance was dark, from the stubble on his head to the scowl on his face. Something about him sparked a memory in Lilly. Not a flesh and bone memory, just a déjà vu feeling. She knew she had looked into his face before. His name badge said Phillip, but she wasn't sure that was right.

"Lunch," Phillip proclaimed solidly, and sat the tray on Papa's folding table, pulling the table over so he could reach it.

"Haven't we met somewhere?" Lilly asked him, her eyes narrowing as she searched her memory. Phillip shook his head without looking at her. "Where do I know you from?"

"We haven't met," Phillip said, dismissing her and leaving the room.

"Not the friendliest fella, but he's good so far. That girl they were sending out here was driving me crazy. She wouldn't shut up all day. Lilly this and Lilly that," Papa said, waving his hand as if to shoo her away and cutting his already quartered sandwich into smaller pieces. "I asked them to get me somebody else, just took them a while to find somebody. Not a lot of folks around here want to come take care of an old York man." He put a bite into his mouth and Lilly saw a sparkle glint across the room from the small gold band still sitting on his dry finger. She thought of the kind of love that lasted long after death, the love Papa had with her grandmother.

Lilly and Brad had never used the word love. It was something they had agreed on early in the relationship.

"What would you call us?" Lilly had asked late in the evening as they held each other on the floor in front of the sofa.

"Brad and Lilly. Why?" Brad stroked her spine.

"I don't know. Just curious, I guess," Lilly answered lazily. "Are we a couple? Are we headed anywhere?"

"Anywhere like where?"

"I don't know. I mean I guess I just want to know what we are."

"I'm not going to tell you that I'm in love with you, if that's what you're looking for," he declared flatly.

"No, that's not…well….why not?"

"Because I don't believe in it."

"Me neither. Love is something that you feel, you almost see. It's tangible, if it's real, that is," Lilly said.

"Yup, words are just words," Brad said, pulling her in close for a long, deep kiss that left clothes on the floor. She did not need the hollow expression; she knew what was in his heart. She could see it every day, from his insistence in being ready for work before her so he could microwave breakfast sandwiches for both of them, to his eyes lighting up whenever she walked in. She did not need to hear it.

"Go get the pictures, Lilla girl," Papa said after he finished eating, bringing her back to the present. She checked the time and saw she had four hours before the meeting started, so she grabbed the case and curled up next to Papa on the chair, ready for the trip down his memory lane, wondering the entire day what he might have thought of Brad.

She made up a number of scenarios that she thought would have played out if such a meeting between the giants in her life were to have happened. She could see her precious Papa scowl, as he did at every suitor, and laugh heartily as Brad was known to make everyone do. She knew Papa and Brad would have gotten along wonderfully. Papa never gave Drew the time of day during the one visit they made to her home. His dislike of Drew was not spoken, but then again, it didn't need to be.

Chapter Ten

The Honorable Judge Gerald Scheckel signed the order of release at 3:43 p.m. Drew didn't even spend 24 hours in jail. His lawyer showed up with a city boy grin, and demanded his client be given his personal effects and sent on his merry way. Ty was furious. Marsh didn't even have the cojones to tell Ty himself. He gets to walk. Again.

Drew, who had been stone faced in the interrogation room for hours, sprung to life like he was at a frat party when his attorney walked in. Ty watched them shake hands, talk for a few minutes, and fist bump until he was nauseous. He could see why Lilly feared him. He'd witnessed this man ferociously attack her. He'd finally seen the beast that lived in Drew. The one she said existed, that nobody would believe was there. Now he knew exactly what she meant.

Reid, one of Ty's trusted deputies that had been with the previous two sheriffs, handed him the paperwork to sign, and left to retrieve the few personal items Drew had come in with. Ty poured his fifth Styrofoam cup of coffee, and looked over the pages on his desk. They were properly signed by the judge barely a half hour ago, releasing him to his attorney's recognizance. He'd serve community service in Yuppyville, Ty was sure of that. A slap on the wrist and Lilly gets to stay in fear of him. Sometimes the law just don't work, Ty thought.

The lawyer and Drew came out of the room talking and laughing loudly. Reid handed him the release for his belongings, and the envelope. Ty watched as he pilfered through his own effects with cartoonish gestures, as if something might just be missing. The heat in Ty's cheeks grew to a boil. He texted Lilly with a fury that should have cracked the screen on the phone. She had to know he was loose again.

Drew flashed a smile at Ty and tipped his invisible hat before he walked out the door. Ty stored the release papers in the folder, and turned on his computer. He googled Lüx Pharmaceuticals as soon as the stooges were out of the parking lot. The video the website required before you entered was fast and flashy. It was in Swedish, but had subtitles he could read. The 2 minutes intro video explained that Lüx, which was founded in 1948, was on the cutting edge of medicine. With researchers working worldwide in every facet of medicine, development of crucial drugs was becoming more and more possible. The company, based in Gothenburg, was a privately held company, whose president and CEO, a man the website called John Smith—Ty didn't believe for a minute that was his real name—with salt and pepper hair and vibrant blue eyes, was still actively researching in the lab. It ended with a map of Sweden that transformed into a street view shot of the building.

Ty clicked on the tab that said, "Our Staff" and scrolled until he found Dr. Haim Koehler. The bio the site gave said Dr. Koehler was the lead researcher in the Gothenburg facility, overseeing more than 600 projects worldwide. Dr. Koehler was a 1985 graduate of Columbia University School of medicine and had joined Lüx the same year.

Not a single American physician, researcher, or facility was listed. They were in every other country and province. Ben said that they were banned so Ty expected to see no American companies or names. He scrolled through the list looking for Drew's name anyway. Cover all bases, look at every angle. That's what Sgt. Dupree had drilled into Ty's and Ben's brains in the academy.

Twenty-five minutes later, he was pulling into his mother's driveway. Lilly's car was gone, and Momma was on the porch, swinging. She waved as he pulled into the driveway.

"Where is she?" he asked, stepping onto the gravel.

"I don't know," she said shrugging. "She was in there with your grandfather, then changed and left again. She was on the phone the whole time. Couldn't very well demand that she stop talking and tell me where she was going, Tyler. She's grown."

Yeah, he thought, she's grown all right. "Shit!" he said slapping the truck and kicking the gravel.

His mother started at his reaction. "What? That's it, Ty, what are you and that sister of yours not telling me?" She demanded, pointing to the empty spot next to her on the swing.

Ty sat next to his mother and told her everything he knew about Lilly's life. He only left out the questioning part about whether or not Lilly was involved in whatever Drew was doing.

"He was here? In my driveway last night? And beating on Lilly again?" Momma asked when he finished. Ty nodded. "You couldn't wake me up and tell me?"

"And what would you have done? Come out like Annie Oakley? There was no reason," Ty said. Momma crossed her arms over her chest and pursed her lips looking into the wooded thickets rather than at him.

"He got out this afternoon." He let the words sit still in the soupy air.

"Is he coming here?" Momma asked after several minutes.

"Not if he has any sense, and I'd bet that he does. I have to find her, Momma."

She nodded, but otherwise remained quiet, swaying back and forth, staring into the trees. She had never been an easy person to read. Nor had either of her children, which made the mood stale quickly. Ty walked to his truck and grabbed the file out of the seat after Momma gave up and went inside. He was opening the file when she was back at the door like a shot, glaring at him.

"You mean to tell me, I have a grand baby somewhere and Lillian hasn't mentioned it? Do the two of you think I'm…I'm…How could you keep something like *that* from me?" Momma waved her hands in the air, becoming more animated as her indignation rose.

Ty was fuming. He hadn't wanted to tell his mother. This was Lilly's story to tell. Once again, she pushed her responsibility onto him. She had no idea what she was in for when she got home.

Chapter Eleven

Lilly had a text from Ty, and two voicemails when she checked her phone while she was putting Papa's pictures back into his room. Ty's text told her that Drew was out of jail. She knew he would be. He had lawyers on retention at all times. He always said that any doctor worth his beans should keep one on the payroll. He wasn't the type to be caught with his hand in the cookie jar very often. But the helpless look on his face last night was worth the bruises on hers today. Seeing him unable to find words, unable to defend himself, unable to manipulate her; it wasn't quite the karma she wanted, but she was willing to accept it for now.

The two voicemails were from Anne. She was planning a new fundraiser, next year there would be a new election after all, and wanted Lilly to help. In the second message she didn't just want Lilly to help, she wanted her to host it at Drew's house. Lilly pictured Anne's reaction to her news of leaving Drew. She hoped Anne would at least be saddened she was gone. She didn't care what any of the others from the soiree clique thought. Anne wasn't like them, though. She was more person than power hungry weasel.

Of all the dinner parties and fundraisers that they would go to, and often times host, she admired the political couples most. There was no denying many of those marriages were held together only by their shared lust for wealth and power. If you didn't know beforehand, you'd have no idea who was married to whom. They were as cold as dead bodies toward each other, usually barely within reaching distance, and rarely did they speak. To each other that is. The wives were socialites, the men politicians, or vice versa, as in the case of Senator Anne Hodge.

She was a stately looking woman, about Lilly's height, graying hair that had once been deep chocolate, and a smile that said, "Give me your best shot." She looked tough. She seemed as though she would have been equally at ease in a thrift store as she was at these fundraisers. Anne was the first woman Lilly had ever known that kept her maiden name after she was married. Anne's father was some sort of big time lawyer at a major firm with a reputation for being hard as nails. Anne wanted it known that she was his daughter. She was the most personable woman of power, if not the only woman of power, Lilly had ever known.

Being raised in Rock Hollow, Kentucky, with only a single prom to teach her formal social etiquette, she was unprepared for the expectations of her new role as the wife of Dr. Andrew Wilt. Lilly was a quick learner – as most Kentucky girls are – and she was rapidly picking up on dos and do nots of her new life. She and Anne clicked instantly. Kindred spirits, Anne called it, and stayed by Lilly's side most of the evening. She taught Lilly the art of working the crowds. It became so commonplace to see the two of them together at an event that Drew would dump her off onto Anne as soon as they arrived and disappear into the mixture, only resurfacing when he was ready to leave.

These soirees were pomp and circumstance. Lilly hated them. Drew loved them. Anne was what made them tolerable. She had the ability to walk into any conversation and turn it to something she chose to discuss. Lilly would interject the occasional thought, normally controversial to whatever direction the group seemed to be leaning despite what her true feelings may have been, turning it into more debate than discussion. Anne reveled in it.

"My little hell-raising buddy!" Anne would say. She introduced Lilly that way.

Lilly could not imagine Anne Hodge putting up with the life she led for years. But she also could not imagine William Henry Foster, Anne's husband, having the gumption to do any of the things Drew did. Anne wasn't necessarily controlling, but when your wife is a U.S. Senator, you tend to do what she asks. And, as she often said, she doesn't ask twice.

Lilly went to the back porch to return Anne's call. She answered on the first ring. "Hey, little lady!" she said.

Lilly listened as she explained how the other venues fell through, leaving them with nowhere to have the event on the weekend she wanted. She went into detail about how good people, the right people, were getting harder to find. She even thanked Lilly for being so gracious as to allow her to use the gardens.

"You remember at the Hall's Social last month I told you about the drug company that was thinking of increasing prices, right?" Anne asked guardedly.

"I think so," Lilly replied, though in truth she couldn't remember a word from any social, anytime, anywhere.

"Well, I really hoped I could use your gardens because they're so private. I need to get support. They just raised the seizure medication that a lot of people, mostly kids, use by 450%! It pisses me off to think these greedy bastards are causing working families to go without milk so some damned CEO can buy a bigger summer home!" Anne was getting louder the longer she spoke. Lilly was holding the phone half a foot from her ear and still the near shouting hurt. "I have the senate hearings in a few weeks and I want to know who I have. They *will* tell me where they think they can get off gouging like that."

"You'll have to discuss it with Drew," Lilly finally managed to say as Anne was taking a breath.

"Oh, of course. Ideally, you would discuss this with your husband, but if you prefer that I do, that's fine."

"I'm not there, Anne. I've left him. It's a long story, but there are so many things that you don't know. Drew is into something up to his eyes. He even hit me the night before last, attacked me last night and spent the night in jail. I'm sorry, I can't help you with this one," Lilly told her.

"Oh, I had no idea," Anne paused. Lilly could imagine her beady eyes searching the desk in her office for the proper words to say. "Forgive me, but it is hard to picture Drew doing anything like that. He's a healer, after all. And he's always so genteel."

"Yeah. He did do something like that," Lilly told her, frustration rising. She knew once she left him there weren't many people who would believe her, but the walls were getting tighter just the same.

"Is there nothing you can do? Have you tried counseling or anything?"

"He's a psychiatrist, Anne. I doubt that any amount of counseling would help. The therapist would likely be too awed by my husband to be effective," Lilly explained.

"I'm so sorry, Lilly. Is there any way that I can help? I really don't want to lose my little hell raiser at those things." Anne sounded near pleading. Lilly's pride swelled a bit.

"I don't think so. There's so much you can't possibly know. This will be a good thing for me. For him. For both of us."

"I do hate to hear that, little lady. I do understand, I'll try someone else then. You take care," Anne said.

Lilly knew that the so called friends that she had made while playing Mrs. Andrew Wilt would be long gone after she left. This wasn't a shock. But shock or no she couldn't help but feel the stab of knowing that she alone had never been good enough for these people. It had taken Drew's prominence for her to see that life.

Chapter Twelve

Ty was still in the swing on the porch, reading for the eighth time the order signed by a judge releasing Andrew Wilt when Ben pulled into the driveway. The sun was just starting to set, sending its orange and red over the hills, and he was worried about Lilly, and furious at her. He tried calling her several times, but it went to voicemail every time. If she had gone back with Drew after he and Ben started working on the information that she'd given them, there was nothing he could do for her. If she was involved in one of Drew's schemes, he didn't want to be able to do anything for her.

Ben dropped the tattered boxes in front of Ty's feet and put his hands on either hip like he'd just conquered a lion. The boxes looked like Ben dragged them behind the Crown Vic rather than inside it. They were charred and torn.

"What did you do to them?" Ty asked, looking up from his release order.

"I didn't. So, picture this, it's the middle of June right?" Ben paused, waiting for Ty to answer. Ty nodded. "Roughly, what ninety, maybe ninety-one out?" Ty nodded again. "Then it would be natural to build a fire in the fireplace wouldn't it?"

"Um…I don't think so. Why?"

"Well, that's exactly where these were. Apparently there was a chill in the house so Gretta, the housekeeper, had started a fire. She told Cam that she didn't have any firewood so she used these old boxes," Ben chuckled. "Cam said that the old woman told him that Ms. Lilly would want it warm in there when she got back."

"Yeah, when she gets back," Ty spat, his rage rising again.

"The place was clean. Nothing anywhere. Probably not much in these either," Ben said, pointing to the boxes.

"Dead ends. It's all dead ends," Ty said. "I'm not even sure what to believe. I mean you saw Drew at the station. When he talked about Lilly he seemed like a man that was just beaten."

"She's your sister, man. You know her better than anybody else. What do you think?

Ty shrugged and handed Ben Lilly's notebook describing the memory. Ben read it through, then flipped the pages over and read it again. He looked up at Ty blankly.

"I don't know. She says she's having this…memory thing. It's not a dream, it happens at all times of the day. She remembers a little more every time," Ty paused, listening to the doubt in his own voice. "I'm not sure about any of it, Ben. Hell, she's not even sure about it. But that's what I was trying to get out of Drew today."

"Seemed like he knew what you were talking about," Ben finally said. "If this is real, if she really went through this, we need to get her to a doctor. I know a lady in Louisville that we can get her in to see. She's an OB/GYN and she has done a lot of forensics, works with us a lot. I would ask, though…"

"I know. Did she have a brain injury? If so…." Ty sighed. He knew that any information that she gave him would be questionable at best if she suffered from head trauma.

"So, where the hell is she?" Ben asked.

"No idea. She disappeared right after Drew left jail," Ty answered, his fury evident. Ben was typing on his phone and acted as though he didn't notice.

Ty pulled on the lid of the first box and it crumbled in his fingers. The files were charred, but not burnt. They were patient files dating back ten years. No names were listed on the file, just patient numbers starting at patient two.

He opened Patient Two's file and began reading. The patient had presented complaining of heroin addiction. She was a 19 year-old female who had started sneaking the drug from her mother at 12 and had overdosed, landing her in the ER. Dr. Andrew Wilt was assigned the case. In his notes, which were nearly illegible, Drew had administered a drug and began therapy immediately. The drug name had been replaced by ####. Nurse notes in the file claimed the patient was prone to seizures and found wandering the halls telling staff that *he* was after her, though she never elaborated about who *he* was. Staff never found anyone aside from the patient. The patient had stayed in the clinic for six months, gotten a GED and a job, and was discharged to her grandparents.

Ty put the file back and withdrew Patient Three's file. This one was a 20 year-old female who started using many drugs at 16. She was addicted to cocaine. Like Patient Two, Patient Three had been assigned to Dr. Wilt, and also like Patient Two, she was immediately administered a drug. Drew's notes about this patient were much more in depth. She had developed an eating disorder early in high school. When her mother insisted that she stay in a hospital to recover from bulimia, she met someone that introduced her to cocaine. She began using regularly, was wearing a size zero within weeks, and couldn't imagine herself not having it. She only stayed in the clinic for four months and was released to her mother. As in the previous file, the name of the drug that Drew had administered had been replaced with ####.

Patient four was a 22 year-old female who had started drinking at 14 and using cocaine recreationally at 18. She, too, was assigned to Dr. Wilt. Drew's notes on this patient were sporadic. She had been in the hospital for six days before his first note, which said she was difficult. She had suffered severe seizures and hallucinations before coming to the clinic as a result of trying to stop drinking without help, and was belligerent about the effectiveness of any treatment. After six weeks of therapy and drug ####, she was beginning to emerge from her room and had befriended another patient. She was discharged after seven months to the care of her husband.

All of the files were the same. All of the patients were assigned to Dr. Wilt, all administered a drug, all of the drug names were replaced with ####. And all of the patients were women.

Ben was looking in the second box which contained more patient files. He shook his head, pulling out a file, then replacing it and reaching for the next.

"Any drug names other than the ones they are addicted to?" Ben asked Ty.

"Nope," Ty answered, reaching the last file in the box. It was turned the opposite direction of the rest of the files, labeled 'Patient One,' and was thicker than the other patients' files. On the inside was the same page they had seen on the computer the night before. The disposition said "Deceased" and nothing more.

The patient was 23 years old and, according to the file, suffered from bi-polar disorder since childhood. She received treatment from several psychiatrists and facilities and had been prescribed a host of medication, all to no avail. Her symptoms were sporadic, usually rendering her unable to function.

Drew noted that he began treating her with what he called 'Trio.' Ben tried searching for it but what came up were only porn sites, nothing in the medication field.

The patient grew gradually more aggressive, at times prone to violent outbursts. She had been restrained after attacking another patient, calling her Satan's spawn, injuring her. 'Trio' was then recalculated with some noteworthy success. She befriended Patient Four, whom she had previously attacked.

The notes left out the three months leading up to death. As if they didn't happen or were misplaced.

"Still think it's a dummy file?" Ty asked Ben. Ben shook his head and stared at the papers.

Chapter Thirteen

It was nearly 10 p.m. as Lilly pulled into the driveway and noticed a light on at a window upstairs. It was the forbidden room; Amanda's room. Knowing Papa had been in bed since the sun went down, and Momma likely not far behind, Lilly figured someone forgot to turn it off. Papa was always a stickler about turning off lights, even when she was afraid of the dark as a child.

She climbed the old wooden steps leading to the door trying to make as little noise as possible. She didn't want to alarm anyone, especially at this hour.

She ran her fingers above the doorjamb where they always kept the key and found it, then shook her head. That would be the first place a thief would look. She touched the knob and the door slid open slightly, sending a pang of fear through her stomach.

She slid through the door, pushing it nearly closed as it was when she arrived, and started toward Papa's room. She opened his door and heard his slow breathing to indicate he was fast asleep when she heard footsteps directly above her that sounded like someone upstairs was trying to be as quiet as she was downstairs. Easing the door closed again and reaching for her phone to text Ty she heard the footsteps heading in the direction of the stairs. Her heart was pounding so loud she feared whoever was in the house would hear it thumping long before they heard her making any noise.

The phone locked itself, and her fingers were fumbling, trying to unlock it. The footsteps on the stairs were getting lower, and she was panicked. She couldn't find Ty's name in her contacts, and the light the phone was emitting was surely going to capture the attention of the person in the house, so she ducked into the kitchen, pushing her body as close to the wall as possible.

Finally, Ty's name appeared on the list and she pressed it too hard, the phone locked again. Stupid thing. She had dropped it the night Drew hit her, and it had not been the same since.

The footsteps were on the first floor now, coming down the hall toward Papa's room. Lilly looked around the kitchen for a knife or anything she could strike the person with and found a large butcher's knife. *Cliché*, she thought. *It was the granddaughter, in the kitchen, with a butcher's knife*, she was saying in her mind, remembering her childhood playing the game Clue with Ty.

The steps stopped just across from the kitchen. She put the phone against her leg to keep the intruder from seeing the light, but she could not make her heart quiet, or her hands stop their wild trembling. A good cop she was certainly not. Whoever was in the house was standing quietly just out of the door.

Her phone vibrated against her leg causing her to jump and hit the counter with her elbow. Tears immediately sprang into her eyes as she was silencing her desire to yelp from the pain flashing through her elbow. The phone vibrated again, and she turned it over to see Ty's name displayed across the front. She pushed the answer button.

"I'm at home, get here now, somebody is in the house!" she said then put the phone on the counter so Ty could hear anything happening at the house.

As soon as she spoke, the footsteps, no longer trying to be silent, were heading toward the front door, ripping it open and dashing across the yard toward the woods. Lilly, armed with the butcher's knife from the kitchen, ran after the person, stopping once she saw them dash into the woods. She was not able to see much of the person, couldn't even tell if they were male or female, tall or short. Everything was hazy, and she was panicked.

Ty's truck roared into the driveway just as the intruder headed into the woods. Lilly pointed the blade in the direction the intruder was running, and Ty and Ben took off on foot. Ben paused to take a second glance at the weapon in her right hand. Both had their guns drawn as they ran.

Lilly watched them until she heard Papa stirring in the house. As she opened the door again, Papa was coming out of the kitchen, his walker clanging against the floor.

"What's going on in here tonight?" Papa's sleepy voice asked.

"I dunno Papa. There was a light on upstairs and I wanted to turn it off," Lilly answered.

"Did ya get it?"

"Not yet."

Lilly told him about the intruder being in the house and how they had ran into the woods and now Ty and Ben were chasing them. Papa stood looking at her, his precious face expressionless as she told him. *How much those eyes have seen*, Lilly thought. He went to his chair in the study, claiming he would wait there for all of the 'excitement to die down.'

Ben and Ty came clamoring in the door after a twenty minute search through the woods. Whoever had been in the house had managed to get back out and run away from them unscathed.

"Have you checked the house? Made sure nobody else is here, or see what they took?" Ty asked Lilly. She shook her head and the three of them went up the stairs.

The room in which Lilly saw the light on had been forbidden to them since they were small. She had no idea what they may see inside, but the prospects were exciting, given the excitement the night already produced. As Ty opened the door, she caught herself peeking around him trying to get a first glimpse.

Lilly's eyes were wide as Ty pushed the door open. She stood on tiptoes trying to see the room in its fullness. She was not sure what she expected, but she was disappointed. With the lore of the family's history she thought there would be something more than an old secretary's desk and file cabinets. The walls were lined with old furniture. Pictures of different York men adorned the walls. Most she did not know and would never meet. Their pictures were in Papa's case.

Nothing looked out of place in the room. File drawers were all closed, scribe desk intact. The pictures had not been moved as far as they could tell. Ben and Ty did a sweep of the other rooms upstairs and Ty texted Kari, his deputy, to get the crime team out and dust for prints. Everything inside the room looked like it was as it should be.

They went back downstairs and assured Papa everything was fine. Lilly scolded him lightly for continuing to keep the key above the doorjamb, but then tucked him into bed with a light kiss on his forehead.

Ty and Ben walked the perimeter of the house, and Lilly checked on Momma who was dead to the world and snoring loudly, so she went outside to see what the guys found. Ty had given Lilly some unsettling looks since he'd gotten there but barely spoken a word to her. Now, in the driveway, he spun on his heel and stared daggers through her. "Where the hell have you been tonight?" he demanded.

Ty's words were like a punch in Lilly's gut. Even with shattered bones in his ankle while they waited for paramedics years ago at the Hollow, he had not spoken to her like this.

"I'm pretty sure that I'm an adult, Ty!" she retorted. His actions were stinging her. After him not believing what she had told him, he hadn't said that but she could see it every time he looked at her, scaring her with the hard drive, and now looking at her like he was, talking to her like he was. Her heart ached. She had wanted nothing more than to come home to the security of her small town, and here she was, meeting with her own twin's suspicions and anger.

"With Drew out of jail and us investigating his clinic, it's probably best if we know where you are at all times. Ty's just worried about you." It was Ben who talked. The sound of his voice stirred something deep in Lilly's belly, something long dormant. She tightened her lips, and struggled not to look at him.

"Well, I'm a big girl, Tyler. I've been taking care of myself for a long time now," Lilly said, trying to mask the shame she wore. Where she went was between her and her past. Ty did not need to know about it. Not now. Hopefully, not ever.

Ty stormed back into the house, slamming the screen door behind him. Lilly watched him, his fury evident in his stormy eyes and clenched fists, until he was out of sight. The light in the kitchen flashed on and she knew he was in for the night.

"He's just worried about you," Ben repeated softly.

Lilly stared, for the first time, directly into his eyes where it appeared a deep storm was brewing. Momma would have described them as 'old eyes'.

"He doesn't have to worry about me. I'm not a child; I'm not going to do something stupid," she said, trying to loosen herself from his gaze. He took her hand in his and led her to the porch swing. His touch was a foreign comfort and that frightened her. Warmth that once electrified her was tingling through her chest. She did not know how starved she was for human touch until she tasted his presence.

She stared out at the tiny stars dotting the night sky. The first time she had ridden the bike with Brad was a night much like this, muggy and serene.

"Beautiful night," Ben said, breaking the silence. She nodded, though she would have preferred the quiet.

"I've known Ty for many years. We have seen some of the worst shit you can imagine. He knows how people like Drew think; he knows what could happen to you. He's worried and, from what I've seen, he should be."

"Why?" Lilly asked the question more sharply than she intended. Frustration was evident, and she knew that. "I mean," she began, her voice softer, "I'm sorry, I've just been through a lot and I don't mean to...."

"I get it." Ben looked sideways at her. "Ty was a good friend, the only friend, to me at a time I don't think I would have survived without him. He's a good man. Trust him."

"I do trust him. More than anyone." Lilly turned to Ben, narrowing her eyes. "How did you and my brother meet?"

"We met in the academy and worked on the force in Nashville together for a while. I was gonna be his best man, but, Tara left and all."

Lilly nodded. She wanted to hear more of the story, be closer to this man who, no matter how hard she tried, she could not stop thinking about. But her head was pounding, and she was exhausted.

"I think I'm going to go rest now. Thank you. For everything."

She left Ben seated on the porch. As she ascended the stairs she heard Ty and Ben's voices behind her. She knew they were talking about her. She also knew she had to tell Ty the rest of the story; she had to tell him about her past. Fear of what he would say, what he would think of her, nearly paralyzed her on the steps. A large lump lodged itself in her chest, and the only way to remove it was eating away at her. She could not stand the thought of losing her brother again.

Chapter Fourteen

Ty was awake for most of the night, pacing the floor. He was trying to figure out what he was missing. Whatever Drew was doing, it was right in front of them, he knew it. He could feel it. His gut told him this thing with Drew was bigger than he had given it credit. He'd only scratched the surface with the Medicaid stuff, and he wanted deeper, much deeper.

As a sheriff in a small Kentucky county his hands were tied. He had absolutely no jurisdiction over any of it. Drew was knee deep in something, and Ty was not about to drop it.

Papa had never had issues with intruders. Not at home anyway. Once upon a time nobody in their right mind would have the sack to sneak into the York house. Not if they wanted to live to tell the tale. Papa had nearly done away with all of the theatrics of earlier generations. He spent his entire life trying to make the name something to be proud of. Even still, not many people had it in them to come all the way into the house.

Enter Andrew Wilt into the picture and everything is turned upside down. Ty hated that man since he met him. Lilly, as ambitious as she was, would have been so much better off if Drew had just left her alone; if Drew would have just kept walking instead of stopping to talk to the hot college girl. It made Ty furious to think of how many times he'd made men leave her alone, and she fell for the worst of them all. Or had she fallen at all? Had the thought of marrying Drew's money been more than she could walk away from?

Lack of answers. He couldn't sleep because of lack of answers. It was going to haunt him until he could find them. Just like the boys at the Hollow haunted him most nights. Lack of answers. Nothing is adding up, nothing is making sense. What was Lilly remembering? What were the drugs that were being given to the patients in the files? What does any of this have to do with his niece or nephew? Where was the child? Where had Lilly been in her memories? What had his sister endured?

The sun was beginning to poke its way into the windows as Ty started measuring the grounds for his third pot of coffee. His cell phone rang from his pocket nearly causing him to drop the glass carafe. He flipped it over to see the name of Jay Marsh, Commonwealth's Attorney.

"Yeah, Jay, what's up?"

"Ty, where are you?" Jay asked with an edge to his voice that Ty didn't like.

"Good morning to you, too, Mr. Prosecutor. I'm at home, why?" Ty answered.

"I need to talk to you. Stay put. I'll be there shortly."

Ty, already jumpy from the caffeine, was more curious than ever. He'd investigated some serious cases in Nashville with Ben just after they graduated from the academy. They had worked on the Nashville PD together until Ben got the call he was waiting for from the FBI. They had seen sadistic. They had seen evil. They had been through the boiler with a masochist that took months to bring in. All of those cases, every one of those perps made sense in their own sick ways. Nothing about Drew made sense, no matter how Ty tried to twist it.

Jay Marsh's car pulled into the driveway while another vehicle stayed on the road. Dangerous in these curves, but if it wasn't Ty's car, it wasn't Ty's problem. Jay started toward the house, and Ty met him in the driveway.

"You're making house calls early, Jay. What's up?" Ty asked as he approached Jay and a man he had never seen who got out of the other car.

"Ty, this is Agent Rod Jeffry, Internal Affairs, DOJ," Jay said.

"Tyler James York, a complaint of police brutality and false arrest has been filed against you by Dr. Andrew J. Wilt. You are being put on administrative leave until an investigation has been conducted. Do you have any questions about these actions?" Jeffry said with the best poker face Ty had ever seen. Jay stood at his side staring at the gravel. Ty had loads of questions, but shook his head, and the man handed him a paper with the written form of what he had said typed across the front. Attached to the back was the statement given by Dr. Andrew J. Wilt. The statement said:

'I, Dr. Andrew J. Wilt, am giving this statement of my own free will and am under no duress. It is my claim that on Wednesday, June 26th, Tyler James York, Sherriff of Berger County, Kentucky, physically restrained me after I informed him of my asthma. Sheriff York punched me in my stomach and laughed about it. He then shoved me into the gravel driveway of his home, busting my lip and causing $2,500 worth of dental repair. After he falsely arrested me for assaulting my wife, he hit my head against the bars of three different jail cells trying to find the most uncomfortable one for me. I have a concussion from this.

'I swear that this statement is true to the best of my knowledge and ability and in no circumstances should this man be allowed to remain in a position of authority in any jurisdiction.'

Ty read the statement through three more times to make sure he had not misread anything. The earth spun around him and he felt like he had stepped into an alternate universe as Jeffry began to speak again.

"I need you to come down and answer some questions. I also need your badge and weapon, Mr. York."

Ty felt his jaw tighten and his nostrils flare as he walked to his truck. He held his badge wallet and Glock and thought of the long hard battle he'd fought against his last name to earn them. It was just not right that this pig could claim 'police brutality' and strip them away.

Ty put the badge and weapon at his side, set his jaw, and took them over to Jeffry. He was not going to fight them, but he was not going to disappear either. He was the elected sheriff. He'd earned that. The people of this county had voted for him. He would win this, too. His mind was set; Drew would not take anything more from him or Lilly.

The men left after Ty handed them what they came for. Ty went into the house feeling empty. He planned a meeting for his deputies that afternoon, but that was not going to happen now. His chances for re-election were in the toilet with the murder still hanging over his head. This accusation successfully flushed the toilet.

Ben was at the table stirring his coffee as Ty walked in. He laid the paperwork on the table in front of him and began pouring his own cup. The words played in his mind over and again. *'Falsely arrested me for assaulting my wife.'* Lilly said thousands of times the man thought he was a god.

"Guess you can go with us to Louisville today," Ben said.

Ben had been trying for years to get Ty to come work with him at the FBI. Ty was convinced his place was protecting the town he grew up in rather than a huge region. It didn't hurt that the York family had such a bad reputation historically, and Ty got to revel in the irony of being the sheriff every day he went to work. Maybe now he would take Ben up on it.

"Not today, gotta go down and answer his questions. Does she know?" Ty asked pointing up at the ceiling. The room Lilly was sleeping in was just on the other side. Ben shrugged. "Probably should tell her, and, my brother, I'll leave that to you."

Ty took the papers and left. He would not admit to Ben how knotted his stomach was becoming. Sure, he'd been a little rough with Drew, but hell, he deserved it. He hadn't falsely arrested him; he hadn't beaten him. The scene played in his mind until he pulled into the Berger County Sherriff's Department parking lot. The spot reserved for him was taken by a dark SUV with Kentucky Official plates.

Jay and Jeffry were in Ty's office huddled at the computer when he walked in. Jeffry was typing something and Jay was digging through a file with TJY on the side. Both men looked up as he sauntered in.

"Tyler, please sit," Jeffry said pointing him to a chair on the opposite side of his desk.

"We don't need to go into the interrogation room?" Ty asked, not really needing to hear the answer.

"Do we?" Jeffry asked looking over his wire-framed glasses at Ty. "Maybe in a while."

Jeffry turned the computer monitor to face Ty. Drew's face and arrest record were displayed, though it was not the shot taken of him the night Ty brought him in. In the picture on the screen Drew could barely open one of his eyes, his cheek was swollen and displayed a nasty cut that looked like it needed a stitch or two, and his mouth was unrecognizable. His lips were puffed out with dried blood trickling down one corner.

"When was that one taken?" Ty asked.

"Really? You don't know when this was taken?" Jeffry retorted. Ty shook his head. "This is his mug shot from his arrest. It was taken right over there." Jeffry pointed toward Kari's desk where the camera was set up.

"No. No that's not his shot from here," Ty said, aware of the crack in his voice.

"This was in the system. It was uploaded from that computer right over there," Jeffry snarled.

"No it wasn't! I don't know what the hell kind of game you two are playing, but that is not from my arrest!" Ty shouted. His deputies gawked from their own desks out in the open space office.

"Mr. York, I'm not concerned with the theatrics, I just need to get your statement. This is the picture that is in the system from the arrest, your arrest. Contesting the photo is not going to do anybody involved any good. I need you to write out the events to the best of your recollection, in as much detail as possible. Dr. Wilt has already given us his, it was attached to your notice."

"Yeah, I read it. Thanks," Ty said. His throat ached for something cold, and constricted with every throbbing breath he took. He wrote exactly what happened the night Drew was arrested and signed the paper. Jay Marsh put the paper into the file he had created for Ty.

"We will also need statements from Lilly Wilt and Ben Hale," Jeffry said, trying to conceal his satisfaction. Ty nodded. "Did you have a statement on the night of the arrest from the wife?"

"Of course, it's in the file. That was uploaded from right over there. I had Kari do it when I got Drew here," Ty spat, his chest boiling.

"There is no statement in the file from anyone," Jeffry said. What Ty would give to be able to wipe the smug smile from this asshole's face.

"There has to be. There were statements from Lilly, Ben and me about what happened that night. I saw Kari scan them and upload them. Where is the paper file?" Ty was trying to keep anger out of his voice. It would not help him at all if these idiots thought he was out of his head. Jay handed him a file with nothing but the arrest record, the picture, and the statement he had just written inside.

"Where are they?" he demanded. Both men stared blankly at him. "They were put in this file and scanned into the database. Who has been in here? Who brought these to you?"

"Kari Spear," Jeffry answered, condescension flowing freely with every syllable he uttered. "She is the acting sheriff."

Ty searched through the glass between his office and the rest of the station for a glimpse of his once deputy who, at the moment, was nowhere to be found. The rest of the staff was milling through old files, pretending to have a conversation about something other than what was going on in their boss's office.

Rage boiled in Ty's chest. He could feel his face contorting and twisting, but was incapable of quelling the raw hate he harbored for Drew and for whomever he'd managed to convince to help him in his abashed attempt at getting Ty out of his business. Drew had no idea how up in his business Ty was about to get.

Jeffry explained the procedures and what would happen next in the investigation. Everything sounded like bureaucratic bull that Ty had no choice but to accept. Accept or resign, and no way in hell would he resign and let Drew have an inch more than he had already taken.

Ty had not drank in the middle of the afternoon since before the academy, but a cold beer or twelve sounded like what was on tap for the day. He bought his dozen bottles and waited on the porch swing to hear from Ben and Lilly about the doctor visit.

Chapter Fifteen

"Get up!" Lilly heard a male voice shout. She only vaguely recognized Ben's deep growl. She bolted upright in her bed and tried, unsuccessfully, to shake off disorientation. Light streaming in through the windows was blinding her as she felt her way to the door with her eyes only half open.

Never having been much of a morning person anyway, she was livid at being awakened this way. Maybe she had just gotten too spoiled.

Ben was in the kitchen when she got to the bottom of the stairs. Momma had left for the day an hour ago and, to nobody's surprise, drove Lilly's car. Lilly knew she was gone for another chemo treatment, but Ty thought she was volunteering. Lilly smelled the coffee as her eyes were starting to accept shapes and forms. She poured herself a cup before attempting to speak to him. Holding the mug to her mouth, she allowed the aroma to fill her nostrils, jostling her to life.

"Why are you so damn perky in the morning?" she questioned him, not really needing or wanting an answer.

"I got you an appointment with the doctor I told you about last night. We have to leave in about twenty minutes to get there," Ben said.

"Are you kidding me? Twenty minutes? I have to get a shower and get ready and everything! Twenty minutes? God you are unbelievable, worse than Ty!" she said, storming out of the room and up the stairs.

She cursed him throughout the shower. This appointment was one she was desperate for. She should get the approximate age of her child, and maybe, more importantly, confirmation of her pregnancy proving she was not nuts, as soon as today. To have a baseline age to shoot for was the launching pad she needed to start searching. She already developed a list of adoption agencies. It did not seem likely Drew would have done anything aside from adopting the child out.

Nervousness tingled in her spine and jetted her through the steps of getting ready to go somewhere. Being away from Drew was still a process she was enjoying. Like a long walk on a beach she did not have to return from.

She reached the bottom of the steps with four of the twenty minutes to spare. She flashed Ben a smile that was building since the memories started. This day was second on the list of days she was looking forward to; finding out how old her baby was. The top of the list was actually meeting her child.

The weight keeping her from moving forward with her search was gone. She was giddy and could not contain it. She had not felt this light in years, if ever. She began wondering if the child looked more like her or Brad, a luxury she had avoided until today. She would bow at the doctor's feet, if necessary.

"Aww. I'd hoped we would take your bike to Louisville," Lilly teased Ben.

"I don't ride the bike on duty, but I'll take you for a ride on it later if you want," he said, blushing.

"So, you weren't on duty the other night?" she asked. His answer made no difference; her head was filled with images of her baby. Some were from the memories, others she knew she conjured.

"What's that goofy grin all about over there?" Ben's voice broke into her thoughts. She did not realize she was smiling, something that, while she was still getting accustomed to, was beginning to feel involuntary.

"Just thinking." She felt heat rush to her cheeks when she glanced at his intense eyes and turned to look out of the window, keenly aware she was clicking her nails just as Momma did when she was nervous. She scooted to the edge of her seat, waiting for the doctor's office to come into view.

As the silhouettes of the Louisville skyline shed their shadowy appearance and became a beautiful collage of buildings, her heart raced. Her mind was whirling with thoughts of Brad and the child. Thoughts of Drew were far removed. None of his howling laughter of how stupid or crazy or whatever adjective he chose for her could be heard.

The office of Dr. Marsha Kinman was in a deep red brick three story on a cul-de-sac. The neighborhood was rather cookie cutter and very clean, almost sterile looking. The bushes were all trimmed exactly the same, grass the same height, even the shutters were identical. Sunlight even seemed to reflect from the windows in an identical pattern.

Pushing open the forest green door, butterflies began to flap in her stomach. Her hands were trembling and she couldn't contain her schoolgirl giggling. The waiting room had only one other person in a comfortable plush chair. An older lady with short curly silver hair was reading a magazine, pausing to look at them as they walked to the receptionist's desk.

Ben told the receptionist they had an appointment with Dr. Kinman and she handed Lilly some forms to fill out, as per usual when visiting a new doctor. The questions were the same as with any other physician, and she answered them to the best of her knowledge. She thought it odd to answer some of them given that she was only there to be examined and learn the timeframe of her pregnancy. The butterflies were raging and she was getting nauseous. She put her hand to her mouth, trying to keep anything from lurching forth.

"Your first baby?" the older lady asked Lilly, laying her magazine on the table between their seats.

"Oh! I'm n–"

"Yes. Yes, it's our first," Ben interrupted her, laying his hand on hers, sending electricity up her arm, and grinning like and ecstatic new father to be. Lilly smiled at the lady who was beaming as if she knew something Lilly did not.

"I remember my first. She's in there now, 'bout to have her first."

Lilly nodded and returned her attention to the forms. She was thankful at least, Ben spoke up. Explaining the truth behind their visit to this person that they would likely never see again would have been time consuming and, frankly, it was none of her business.

Ben returned the forms to the receptionist and Lilly grabbed a magazine from the small round table next to her. Her attention would not focus on any of the words, so she settled on the pictures.

"Lilly Wilt," the medical assistant announced as she was still opening the door. Lilly followed her to an exam room and Ben remained in the waiting room. She was instructed to undress and put on the oversized robe, which she did with trepidation. She could hear the doctor in the room next to her talking kindly to her patient, and wished she could have had this type of treatment for her own pregnancy. She dreamed of listening to the baby's heartbeat for the first time, seeing the images of an ultrasound, creating baby books, feeling the baby move, and baby showers.

She and Drew did not host things like that. He would only ever attend a soiree that may further him socially, and baby or bridal showers did neither. Lilly made few female friends, and there was not a chance any of them would need one.

None of that matters if I can find you, Lilly thought and longed to say to her child. She wondered what he might look like, what he might like to do, or to eat.

Lilly was deep in thought and the knock on the door startled her. As Dr. Kinman walked through the door, Lilly knew she liked her. The gentle smile that she displayed put Lilly at ease. The flapping wings in her chest and stomach calmed.

"Wilt?" Dr. Kinman asked looking over the form Lilly filled out. Lilly nodded. "Drew is your husband?"

The world came crashing down on Lilly. Her heart lurched into her mouth, and she choked on her own breath. Her eyes narrowed as the doctor spoke.

"I was in undergrad with a Drew Wilt at Cincinnati, did your husband go there?" Dr. Kinman asked, staring out the window. Lilly nodded, anxious to talk about anything else. "Wow, small world."

"Yeah, we are separated so—"

"Oh! I'm so sorry. I wasn't trying to pry," Dr. Kinman stated, pulling a pair of purple gloves from the box on the wall. Lilly watched the doctors cheeks begin to flush as she struggled to get her fingers into their correct spots. Beads of sweat sprang onto the back of Lilly's neck. The once light, jubilant air had stiffened making Lilly keenly aware of the large knot forming in her chest.

"It's fine," Lilly said, watching the shadow of her feet swinging from the side of the exam table in the reflection of fluorescent light, wishing she could think of anything to talk about besides Drew.

"So, I'm doing an exam to determine the approximate timing of your pregnancy, is that correct?"

Lilly nodded.

"Ok. If I may be so bold, can I ask why this was scheduled through the FBI? You don't have to answer, but pregnancy is a pretty big deal. Most people don't need an exam to determine these sorts of things. Am I looking for something specific?"

"Just the timing of my pregnancy. Ben Hale is a friend of my brothers who is helping us and I have something going on with my memory." Lilly heard the sharpness in her own voice. "I'm sorry, I'm really nervous."

"Nothing to be nervous about. I'll be as gentle as I can."

The doctor proceeded through the exam with very little else to say. She was mashing on Lilly's stomach when Lilly looked up and saw her brow furrowed.

"What's wrong?" Lilly asked.

The doctor shook her head and gave Lilly a reassuring smile. The smile missed its mark, and Lilly was terrified. She could see Drew smirking in her mind, laughing at her trying to find a kid. One she didn't even remember.

"I'm going to get some blood work and do an ultrasound, nothing to worry about. Just relax, my phlebotomist will be in shortly," Dr. Kinman told her as she was leaving the room.

Relax? This woman had no idea what an impossible chore she so nonchalantly lay on Lilly's shoulders. It had been well over 9 years since she had been able to accomplish anything resembling relaxation.

"Brad, help me," Lilly whispered as soon as she was alone in the room. She whispered to him daily since he'd died, and more since the memories started.

Susan, according to her name badge, came in carrying a tray with different colored vials, a rubber tourniquet, and small packages containing differently sized needles. She opened her mouth into a full smile showing off her perfectly straight teeth. She didn't speak beyond telling Lilly what tests she was going to be doing, which may as well have been speaking her own made up language. She drew three vials with different colored tops on each, and was gone.

Dr. Kinman came back several minutes later, pushing an ultrasound machine. Lilly's name had already been typed in and was showing on the monitor. On the screen was an upside down cone shape of darkness with lines and notches.

"This won't take long, Lilly. I just want to see what I'm working with," Dr. Kinman said as she typed into the machine and shook the gel bottle. Lilly nodded as she watched what the doctor was doing.

The images the wand was capturing made no sense to Lilly, but the doctor was entranced. She swiped the wand just below Lilly's navel and pushed. She typed into the machine, captured the image and progressed to the next area she wanted to see. Every time she found what she was looking for she took several images and moved on further across Lilly's body.

After she had seen everything she wanted, she wiped Lilly's belly with a warm towel, pushed the ultrasound machine to the corner of the room and told Lilly she could get dressed. Just before she got to the door, she turned and asked Lilly if she would like Ben to come in and hear her findings. Lilly nodded. The lump that had been building since watching the doctor furrow her brow was too large to allow her to speak.

Ben knocked after Lilly had dressed and cracked the door open a bit to signal that it was ok to enter. He leaned against the counter across from her and stared at the floor over his crossed arms. They could hear Dr. Kinman in the next room talking to a nervous expectant mother, her voice so calming.

Lilly held the robe she had been dressed in, rolled around her crossed arms. Her mind was racing with the possibility of what was to come. The excitement that kept her moving earlier was buried beneath dread of what she saw on the doctor's face.

"Okay," Dr. Kinman announced as she walked back in. "As you know, I've done a comprehensive exam on Lilly today. During the exam, I noticed some abnormality of her ovaries, which is why I ordered the blood work and ultrasound."

The doctor put her hand on Lilly's arm and her stomach filled with tiny pins, all of which stabbed at her to let them out.

"Unfortunately, both tests confirmed what I thought." She paused as to give Lilly time to absorb what was being said. When she spoke again it came out slow and deliberate. "Your fallopian tubes are severed, Lilly. I don't see any scar tissue that would indicate it was surgical, and without a complete medical history it's hard to say whether or not it was a congenital anomaly. Your ovaries appear to have some damage as well." Dr. Kinman picked up a plastic model of a reproductive system from the counter and used it to show Lilly the flaws in her own body. "In a healthy reproductive system, we see the ovaries are shaped like these. Yours are shaped more like a cone. The process of maturing the eggs for fertilization is flawed. At your age, most women should have around 20 to 25% of their total eggs left. As a guess, without further testing, I would say that you have roughly 4% left. I'm sorry, Lilly. The chances of you having conceived are low, maybe one in a thousand."

The doctor's words trailed off. Lilly could not, would not, accept what she was saying. Drew was in her head again, laughing hysterically. *I told you there never was a kid.* She could feel the hot tears rolling down her face. The lump was exploding, and she was unable to comprehend anything. Her heart, what was left of it, was surely scattered on the floor so whatever was being touted as humanity could stomp out any hope of letting it beat in her chest. It was a liar anyway. Not once had anything it told her panned out. Drew danced around merrily in her head, stopping long enough to let out a howl of laughter and mock her cries for the child the liar in her chest ached for.

Vodka. This was a vodka blow. Vodka would be the only thing that would make the memory of today vanish. She could taste it already, burning the lump out of her throat and soothing the aches her stomach formed longing for it. It was definitely a vodka night.

Chapter Sixteen

Fear. Fear like he had never known before ran down Drew's spine. He had been so careful. He had kept her in line for years. He had done everything he thought would keep her from doing exactly what she was doing now.

He knew he would die if she wasn't stopped. She had no idea what kind of shit storm was on the way. She just wanted to find the truth. The damned truth. She just wanted to find her baby. He was powerless. Nothing he could say to her now was going to make a difference.

"Those damn memories," he raged, squeezing his glass of scotch tighter. Why hadn't it worked with her? So many others were fine. Why could Lilly just start remembering? If she hadn't taken off, he could have handled it. He could have convinced her she was just day dreaming. He could have put her in her place again, and she would have submitted. Hadn't he offered her the life she sought? The life Sissy made him give her?

Sissy was working on the collateral damage. She would see to it that Lilly York didn't cause irreparable turmoil. What she would do to Drew remained to be seen. She was a true bitch, but when in a jam he couldn't think of anybody else to call.

The police brutality case was all Sissy. She thought that Ty was the head of the snake that needed cutting off. She didn't know all of the facets of Lilly's family. If they knew enough, which not one of them did, they could be in contact with some potent people that neither Drew nor Sissy wanted to have against them. Sissy had tossed Lilly into Drew's life and, just like that, wiped her hands clean. Drew was the smart one. He'd done the research on the family. He'd found the corpses in the closet. Sissy would not hear it, though. She only wanted to deal with here and now.

Then there was the FBI guy. What the hell were they going to do about him? He already had his hounds snooping at the clinic, threatening to shut it down. He had people there night and day. Just when Drew was so close to perfecting his work, Lilly has to pull this. The boxes he protected at home were gone. What would he do if they figured out what any of it meant? *What about the other box?* he heard a voice in his head say. It was his mother. It was always his mother, rest her soul.

"They won't know what any of it means," he said aloud. She cackled, as she always did. She had never trusted him. Never allowed him to treat her the way she needed to be treated. He had gone to med school, had gotten the degrees. He had graduated first in his class and gotten the prestigious fellowship and internship. That was him; it had nothing to do with Sissy or anyone else. Certainly no favor from his father. Not this time.

Then there was Lilly. She was the wild card. She was the unpredictable, irrational piece to this puzzle. She was a threat, and he had never done well with threats.

"Dammit!" he shouted, throwing the remnants of his Scotch into the fireplace, the glass shattering over the freshly burned dregs. He had worked so hard for this, and she was just going to drag it all away. After all of these years of research, after all of the successes he had documented, he was so close, to close, to allow her to upend it.

If he could have taken away having ever met her, he would. If he could have told Sissy no when she put Lilly York in his care.… It wouldn't do. It just wouldn't do. He had to keep her from destroying it all. He had to stop her somehow.

Sissy would have a conniption fit. She could have it. Drew had to do what he had to do. Self-preservation was the only way to go. This breach had to be stopped. It had to be quelled.

He'd never wanted to marry Lilly. Yes, it was his idea, but not his desire. The only woman he would have willingly married wanted nothing to do with him.

"And what happened to her?" his mother's voice in his head chortled. "And your half-brother? Huh, where is *he*?"

"Shut up!" he shouted. "That idiot never deserved his last name! He sure as hell didn't deserve the time father wasted doting over the golden one." *If father had had the decency to live a few more years,* Drew thought, *he would know who the better son was.*

He heard the door close behind him and jumped, turning to see Gretta as she walked to the kitchen. Had she been watching him? Had she known what was going on? Was she spying on him for Lilly? That was it! The old lady had gotten close to Lilly. He had seen them talking in hushed voice time and again. She was helping Lilly, feeding her information. He had to stop her. Lilly may have gotten out and started poking into things beyond her comprehension, but he wasn't going to sit back and watch Gretta help her destroy him.

"Jesus, Drew! Rena's crazy ass genes are thick in your veins!" Sissy said when he had called her on the worst night of his life. Sissy knew the truth. She knew that their father had driven Drew's mother into madness. Reminding Drew how disturbed Rena was helped Sissy feel validated in the things father had done to her. She would raise nine kinds of hell again after he got rid of Gretta, but he had to.

Lilly's hillbilly brother was not going to stop just because his badge had been stripped, Drew knew that. Sissy was convinced that he would, but Drew knew better. He should text Sissy before he took care of Gretta. She would be incensed if he acted without her approval. But he knew the situation better than she did.

"You better get yourself in check," he heard his mother say. "They'll have you locked away just like they did to me."

"Shut up!" he shouted. He heard Gretta in the kitchen, pots and pans clanking together. It was now or never. Lilly had more information than she needed as it was. He would not allow Gretta to give her more.

He opened the hall closet and pulled out the straight jacket that he had gotten from the old doctor; he had used it several times before. Gretta, as sweet as she was, would put it on without asking questions. She was never a problem, until now. She had gotten too close to Lilly.

Gretta kept her back to him as he walked into the room. She acted as if she hadn't seen a thing. *Probably already texted Lilly. Told her that you're cracking up*, the voice in his head told him. He glanced at the old woman's phone lying on the counter beside the sink.

He walked to her and pulled the jacket over her head. It hadn't been unfastened since the last time. She was startled and turned to him. He saw the fear swelling in her eyes. *She deserves it,* his mother's voice told him. *She deserves this and more, helping that little skank.*

"It's just an experiment, Gretta," he lied, sliding her arms into their correct spot. "I've got a bunch of these and need to see if they still work," he said.

"No! I put it on myself!" Gretta protested, her eyes scanning the counters around Drew.

"It's okay, Gretta. I just need to make sure they haven't sat in storage for too long. It will only take a minute."

Drew yanked the jacket over her head, pinning her between the counter and his body. She wouldn't stop squirming, making this so much harder than it needed to be. When the jacket was on her, he gave one last yank at the bottom, forcing her to the floor. As she slid down the cabinets, she stared directly into his eyes. God that made him hard. If Lilly were here he'd do something with her he hadn't done since they were first married, when he still found her attractive and not a leech.

As he placed his hands around the woman's thick neck her eyes grew wide, and she struggled to speak. His fingers closed around the woman's windpipes quickly, he didn't want to hear her curse him. He knew it was wrong. He knew he'd spend eternity in hell for it. Hadn't he heard the nuns tell him that enough in his life?

Gretta thrashed under the weight of Drew's body straddling her, tugging and clawing at his wrists, but she didn't have the strength to put up much of a fight. *She doesn't even want to live. She wants away from the guilt of helping Lilly,* the old voice in his head quacked.

He squeezed until her eyes fixed on the ceiling, and she stopped trying to throw him off of her. His heart pounded in his head as her neck constricted. He watched as the life fled from her, just as it had from Tracey years ago. She gave one last tug at his wrist, her gaze went glassy, her pupils became tiny pinholes, and she was gone.

Drew slid his body between Gretta and the counter and laid his head in his palm, the other hand resting on his cock that was now as hard as bronze. Sissy would find a way to fix the mess he'd made. She would send someone to clean up, as she always did. She'd only refused him once, and now they were in *this* over their heads. She wouldn't dare turn her back on him again.

Now, that sniffling little momma's boy better do his part. Sissy thought that Ty was the head of the snake, but Drew knew the truth. She wouldn't have liked him sending the kid, but she will see; they all would. Drew could handle this. He could control the empire. He could be the son their father would have been proud of, even if he wasn't the heir that had been intended. The little prick, the boy that dad wanted, had disavowed everything. Now father and his precious little *chosen boy* were gone, and Drew would not apologize to anyone, including Sissy, for having bettered the world by ridding it of his half-brother.

Chapter Seventeen

Ty considered his next move. He would not get his badge back by sitting around here drinking beer. Maybe he should pay a visit to his dearest brother in law, but how would that help? He would not drop this bullshit case. He took a long pull on his bottle and grabbed the boxes of files.

There had to be something in them that he was missing.

The files, placed on the floor around him, looked exactly the same. Nothing was out of the ordinary about anything. Ty wasn't a physician, but he thought that the treatments Drew rendered were probably what should have been given.

"What do all of you have to do with Glick or Lüx Pharmaceuticals?" he asked aloud, as if the files would deliver up their secrets, paving the path to what Drew was doing. There were stickers on the pages of notes for Glick with serial numbers on them. Ty googled the serial numbers finding anti-hallucinogen medications, anti-seizure medications, and other psychological drugs. All of them seemed like they were perfectly in place. He scrawled the name of the medication each serial number stood for in the file so he would have it within reach when he looked at the files later.

"What is the drug he doesn't want me to know?" he asked aloud, looking at the #### on the notes. There were no serial numbers associated with them, no easy path.

He opened another beer and sat in the middle of the files. He heard Papa and his home health care provider in the next room arguing over medications. Papa never wanted any pill for any reason, and fought all of the people that came and tried to help him. Ty decided to go help the poor CNA that was there today.

The tall lanky guy in the study with Papa looked hopeless. He was holding a small cup with five tiny pills of varying color and size in it. The aide eyed Ty suspiciously as he walked into the room.

"Papa, you know you have to take your meds. The doctor told you that you do," Ty started.

"I don't have to take the stuff that no doctor told me to. He's trying to give me drugs!" Papa huffed.

Ty looked at the cup the nurse was holding. Nothing looked at all unfamiliar. He asked the guy, Phillip as his name badge identified him, what each medication was for, suddenly feeling like an expert at drugs after reading so many descriptions online trying to figure out this thing with the clinic.

Phillip pointed to each pill and told Ty the name and purpose of each. They all sounded like what Ty had heard the doctor tell Papa.

"He's just being stubborn today. Doesn't want to eat either," Phillip said. Ty noticed the guy had at least two days growth of beard on his face, and his hair was unkempt. Ty was no medical professional, but thought they usually looked more sanitary than this. This guy was a home health aide, so maybe the sanitization rules didn't apply to him so much.

"That little round white one isn't what I usually take," Papa said.

Ty looked at the pills in the cup and looked up at Phillip.

"It's his blood pressure medication," Phillip said shrugging his shoulders, "the distributor changed, so the size and shape changed."

"Papa, it's what you have always taken. Just take your medicines and eat your lunch," Ty urged.

"Tyler, did you look at the pills? Do you know what I take?" Papa asked. Ty, feeling a weight of responsibility that, even as the head of law enforcement, he wasn't accustomed to, nodded his head. He knew nothing about Papa's medication, and prayed what he was taking was the right stuff.

"Papa, what happened to your arm?" Ty asked, noticing a large bruise on his forearm.

"Nothing. It was there when I got up this morning," Papa said weakly.

"That's a mighty big bruise to have been caused by nothing."

"I noted it in his file and phoned his doctor just a little while ago," Phillip chimed in.

Ty went back to the library where he had the files strewn all over the floor. His phone alerted him that there was breaking news, and he clicked the article. The headline read, "*Berger County Sheriff, Tyler James York, Placed on Administrative Leave After Police Brutality Charges.*" He could feel blood rush to his cheeks as he read the account of how he had beaten Drew when he was arrested, falsely.

Drew's entire statement was in the article; every lie Ty read earlier in the day. Not a single statement from the York family. Crickets. To their credit, the reporter did not say they tried to reach out for comments.

At the end of the article, more was promised as soon as it was available. Ty needed to get out of the house for a while. He got in his truck and started driving. He had no place in mind, he was just going. His head was thick, and he needed to clear it out.

Chapter Eighteen

Lilly lay across her bed after the seemingly eternal ride home, falling into a dark abyss. Drew's maniacal voice tore at her, ripping every part of faith, memory, even hope she had ever known into confetti he was now spraying throughout her mind. The memory of being on the floor, feeling the pain in her groin, the pain in her head, giving in to the darkness taking over her sight was so vibrant. She was living it again. The darkness was surrounding her, threatening to lock her away for eternity.

Nothing was right. Nothing was okay. *"It will always be the same. I'm a winner. I'll always win. You, you're just a dumbass bitch, you'll always lose. Always,"* Drew was saying in her mind. Screaming it.

A familiar sound from beneath her called out to her senses, prickling her skin, causing her to stand and walk toward the kitchen. Ben was sipping beer from a bottle in the kitchen as she walked in. There were still several left in the fridge. She turned to the cabinet where the bottle of wine sat untouched since she'd opened it the night she left Drew. She slid a chalice from the rack and twisted the cork on the bottle until it popped. The sound of the liquid rushing into the glass made her dizzy as the fruity bouquet danced in her nostrils. She put the glass to her lips and inhaled the fragrance. She turned it up and emptied it of the wine in one long swill. She felt Ben's eyes watching her. She winked at him and poured herself another. As the wine rushed into the glass, she watched as Ben cocked one eyebrow and shook his head.

"What?" Lilly questioned.

"I've just never seen a girl do that," he laughed.

The fruity notes and mild burn were answered prayer as they slid down her throat. Her body began to relax from the first gulp. The second glass found her senses more deadened, but dulled senses and emotions were what she craved. She finished her third glass and glanced at Ben who was staring in amazement holding his first beer, still half full.

By mid-way through the fourth glass her teeth were markedly numb, her cheeks were sagging, and her movements had to be calculated. God, she had missed this feeling.

"The doctor is wrong, you know," she said, trying to force the words to come out right. Judging from the amusement in his face, she was unsuccessful. Back in the day that would have been no problem. She had convincingly gone to class almost daily after tossing back three or four.

"Why is she wrong? You must have thought exactly what she said at least once or twice. Is it possible that you were never pregnant?"

"No!" Lilly shouted. She couldn't think that. "I was sitting on the lounge at Drew's watching birds when the first memory happened. It really did just happen. I looked down at my pregnant stomach, about to give birth. Then I fell to the floor and lights were flashing, I heard people talking, I saw someone staring in through a window in a door, and then it was over." She felt her heart pounding in her neck. It was urgent that Ben understood her.

"Ty gave me the notebook, I read about your memories. Where do you think you were?" he asked, taking a long pull from his bottle.

"I don't know. Obviously a hospital somewhere, but I don't know where. I doubt that it was even in Kentucky."

She noticed that she was twirling Brad around her finger and tucked him into her shirt. She wasn't ready to share him and didn't want to have to explain him to Ben just yet. She walked to the porch and sat on the swing feeling the breeze in her hair. The swing dipped under Ben's weight. She traced his features with her eyes. His chiseled cheekbones and deep-set eyes gave way to his rounded nose and a couple days growth of stubble. His skin was tanned and clashed harshly against his black hair and grey eyes.

"If not in Kentucky, where is the hospital?" he asked without turning to look at her.

"No idea," she said, pulling her knees up and resting her chin on them. Ben dropped his head and turned to her with a grin that eased up the left side of his face, deepening the lines around his eyes that were dancing.

"We aren't getting anywhere with all the 'I don't knows'. You know that right?"

"Mhm," she sighed.

"You're drunk," he laughed and put his hand on the small of her back, rubbing her spine. Her body ached for more of his touch, like someone who'd been in the desert ached for water.

"I went to see a psychic," Lilly laughed. "She was going to *unlock* my mind for me." She used her fingers to make air quotes. "I know Tonya, I have known her since she worked for Drew several years ago. She was one of the few, no wait, the only person from the clinic I could stand to talk to. Most of them are horrible. You'd hate −" She stopped herself just as she realized she wasn't talking to Brad. Ben stared at her as though he understood exactly what she was feeling.

"Madam La...La...something. The one Ty saw you go to?" he asked. His eyes put her at ease. His voice was so gentle, yet surprisingly deep, just like Brad's. Ben was a taller, stockier man than Brad had been, and the booming voice seemed less out of place. The shape of Ben's head, the boyish wonder in his eyes, all reminded her of Brad.

Lilly nodded. "The first time I went she held both of my hands like this." She put the wine glass between her thighs and took each of his hands in hers. "She looked into my eyes and told me I had seen so much pain. Duh, right? I know, who hasn't, just a general thing to say to people. But then she said you have a little boy, but he isn't with you. I was blown away. Then she said you see your past, but you don't see all of your past. At this point I'm thinking, hey, there might be something to this. Ty wouldn't get it. He'd tell me it was nonsense."

Ben held her hands and watched in amusement as Lilly played out the visits to the psychic. For the first time she saw his perfect white teeth when he smiled.

"Madame LaCura told me that she could see something blocking my memory, and she thought she could help me get it out of the way. That's why I was still going to her. That day that Ty followed me, when I got there she told me that she saw my twin in my eyes." Ben frowned and looked sideways at her as if he didn't believe her. "I know, that one was weird, but I wanted to know what happened so, I kept going."

"When did you go to her last?" Ben asked.

"A couple of days before I left Drew," Lilly shrugged. She was trying to remember exactly when she had seen her. The fuzz that had taken over her mind was making it difficult. Then it hit her, she recalled the visit exactly. "She told me that I was going to go through the most difficult period, but I wouldn't be alone and that I would be with my baby again."

Ben looked at her differently when Ty wasn't there, or maybe the alcohol was making her see things in a different way. She thought she saw something flicker in his eyes she hadn't seen in a long while. Desire. She was certain that she had seen it. Then she recalled the car ride and how cold he'd been. She didn't want to take time for games. If she misread him, he would let her know.

She put her hand on his thigh and brushed it gently. He did not move away, and she didn't retreat. She leaned closer to Ben, and allowed her breast to linger on his bulging bicep. He turned his head toward her and she plowed her lips into his, wrapping her arms around him and holding on as they kissed deeply. Their tongues met, stroking each other, his passion growing. His grip on her tightened, and he grew more demanding.

She could feel her chest swell as her heart raced. Ben's hands were on her back, his fingers gliding along her protruding spine, stopping at the waist of her jeans.

His heart was beating against her chest. It seemed so natural to wrap her leg across his lap and ease herself onto him, knees on either side of him. She heard his breathing intensify and tried to control her own arousal. His lips danced across hers. Each breath gained momentum and she squeezed him closer to her. She wanted this man more than she could admit, even to herself.

She opened her eyes for a moment, and didn't see Ben. It was Brad looking through her as he always had done. His head cocked slightly to the right, his eyes open only in slits, but she could see the shine in them.

Ben clutched Lilly's waist, picking her up, and placed her on the swing. His eyes were deep, burning into her as he stood over her. She reached for him but missed as he stepped backward shaking his head.

"No. Not like this," he said, turning and walking into the house.

She was crushed. And humiliated. The world was caught up in a dizzy fog. She ran through the house and up the stairs, throwing herself onto her bed. She heard Drew begin to howl inside her head. *Loser!* He was proclaiming through his laughter. The entire world was against her. Drew owned it all, as he told her over and over.

Her body shook the bed as she sobbed. She heard the doctor's words, *"You were never pregnant."* Drew would scream his delight every time. Her stomach was doing the dance of death, and she barely made it to the bathroom before everything inside her came bursting forth. She held onto the toilet for her life. Hours must have passed as she knelt there, broken, crying, and rejected.

"I'm so sorry Brad," she moaned as she clutched his vial.

Lilly's hair was getting wet from her tears. It was making her crazy. Every time she opened her eyes she saw this white-blond mess all around her. It was Drew's mess. He wanted her to keep her hair long. He wanted it to be this light. It was all him. Everything about her seemed to be him.

She was going to be caught in his grip her entire life. At least, for his entire life. Even leaving him made no difference. She was six hours away from him, and she may as well have been in the next room. His control, his reach was astronomical. She could have gone to China and he would still be looming over her.

She had to get rid of him. Exorcize herself of him. Cut him out of the world. He was never going to let her go, he made that clear.

She hated the weak, sad, beaten person staring back at her in the mirror. Loathing was all she could muster for this poor helpless girl that couldn't stand up for herself. This fool who thought she would ever be good enough to rub elbows with the rich and powerful. She was just a scant little idiot. Brad would never have wanted her like this. He wouldn't have given her a second look. Why should he? Why should anybody?

She took the scissors from the bathroom drawer, lifted her hair into a ponytail on top of her head and began chopping until she had the length of her hair in her hand, and the image staring back at her looked formidable. She kept chopping and cutting until her hair was less than an inch long everywhere except her bangs on top.

She rubbed her head and liked the feeling of the short hairs poking her hand. Running her fingers through her bangs and tossing them around made her feel right. This was better. This was stronger. This was the woman that was not taking shit from anyone. Not anymore.

She grabbed her purse from the bed and headed toward the door. She heard Momma and Ty as she scurried past them.

"What did you do to your pretty hair?" Momma yelped, her face distorted, horror-stricken.

"Where the hell are you going?" Ty asked. The unabashed anger in her brother's voice caused her to flinch. Had Ben told him about the fool she had made of herself already? Had he been told about what the doctor said?

"I need to go out for a while. I can't breathe here, Momma," Lilly said, trying to avoid eye contact with her brother. Her mother tossed the bangs as Lilly did moments earlier. Momma's eyes met Lilly's. There was a knowing, almost accepting look in them.

She shook it off, got in the car, and drove away. The vodka was calling her, and it would take more strength than she had on her own not to answer.

Chapter Nineteen

"Not this time sister dearest," Ty said as he and Ben were getting in the Crown Vic. They followed Lilly's car, keeping distance between them. She was not paying attention to them.

"Taking these curves like a champ," Ben said from the driver's seat. "She best be glad there are no beat cops around here. I don't know where she's going, but she's in one hell of a hurry to get there."

Ty glanced at the speedometer. It was at eighty and climbing.

They followed her for forty-five miles and watched her pull into a church parking lot with only a few other cars. They pulled onto the shoulder of the road and watched her park and walk in through the basement entrance door. Ty was having trouble recognizing her with the short hair.

They waited until she had been inside for ten minutes, then pulled in and parked across from her car. Ty fought the urge to go in and grab his sister, shake her, and demand to know what she was doing. She had never been religious, far from it. At least, she wasn't when he knew her. There were so many things that were different about her he wasn't sure what he knew.

As they got to the door, Ty was overcome with dread. He had only been to church once in his life that he could remember, and that time hadn't gone so well. When Ben opened the door leading to the church basement it let out a loud screech, alerting anyone inside. The hallway inside the door was dimly lit. The place smelled like a mixture of damp rug, old lady perfume, and coffee.

"To accept the things I cannot change," they heard chanted by combined voices behind one of the closed doors in the hallway. It struck a familiar chord, but Ty could not remember what it was or where he'd heard it. Ty tried the first door and, no surprise, it was locked. There was no light coming through under the door. The second door, across the hall, opened with no problems, and to his surprise, no screeching.

The large, dull tiled room was set up with rows of chairs facing the wall opposite the door. A man stood at a podium talking to the group that was seated in the chairs. The man did not stop speaking, or even acknowledge their entering the room.

Ty found Lilly in the back row, watching intently. She had not noticed them coming into the room, and from the appearance of it, no one else had either. Ty took the seat to Lilly's left and Ben took the one to the right. Lilly looked up as they sat down with the wide eyes of a child caught with snacks before dinner.

"What are you doing?" she asked Ty.

"About to ask you the same thing. What is this? You into some sort of cult now?"

Lilly shook her head. The man finished speaking, and everyone clapped, then another man got up and headed to the speaking position.

"Hi, I'm Aaron, and I'm an alcoholic," the man said.

"Hi Aaron," the entire room replied.

Ty looked at his sister whose frame seemed to shrink as she stared at the back of the chair in front of her. She had not come for religion; she came to an AA meeting.

They listened to Aaron and several others tell the story of their hitting the bottom and reaching out for help. Most went to a rehab facility, a few had not. Those who went to a facility credited the places with their life, their survival. Of those who had not was a young woman by the name of Robin. Ty was struck with her story from start to finish. She was such an attractive woman he could not have envisioned her drunk.

"Hi, I'm Robin and I'm an alcoholic."

"Hi Robin," the group chorused.

"My story started out like many of yours. I was just a kid, experimenting with alcohol, getting drunk and laughing with my friends. I put the booze away once I got married. Grew up, ya know? Alcohol was just funny stories from being young and stupid." She paused as the group chuckled. "I started wanting to drink again after my kids were born. Just to relax a little. I knew that my husband was cheating on me. Hell, most of the town knew he was. He didn't try to hide it, just flaunting his little tramp all over the place. It started as just a glass after the kids were asleep. Then it was two glasses. I always told myself that I would stop doing it when the stress stopped. Then I lost count of how many glasses. I thought the only way that I could deal with all of the hurt was with the bravado a bottle of wine would provide." She paused as she took a sip from her water bottle.

"I've never been the sexiest or the cutest woman in the room so I didn't think I could compete with my husband's girlfriend. She was a blonde with long legs and a tiny waist. She was gorgeous. Of course, I'm just me. A bottle of wine though, whoo, those boys could care less what you look like, how plain you are, so, I turned to the bottle. My kids didn't understand. At first they laughed at Mommy when she was drunk. I can still hear them saying Mommy fell down again, or Mommy is sleeping at the table again. Over time I saw the laughing fade, and they just didn't know what to say to me. They didn't know who I was anymore. My heart was breaking for them, but I was trapped. I wanted the madness to stop. I didn't want to be *that* person in their lives. I didn't want my kids to hate me the way that I hated their father. I was desperate to not push them further away." Robin paused as she wiped away a few stray tears that wondered onto her cheek.

"We eventually divorced, and he sought custody because I was drunk most of the time. He and his leggy whore. Sorry, that was uncalled for. But there was no way in hell I was going to sit by and allow her to raise my kids and sleep with my husband, so I threw all of the bottles of any type of alcohol out. I even threw out mouthwash and cough syrup," she chuckled. "I had no idea what I was in for. The first night was okay, I just really wanted to drink. Sure I was biting off the heads of anyone that spoke to me, but hey, big deal, right? Not so much when your kids are the ones getting their heads bitten off; especially when those kids are what you are fighting for. The second night was worse. I could feel tiny bugs crawling all over my body. I couldn't brush them off. I was swatting at my arms and my legs but I kept feeling it. I saw them coming out of my body. It was awful. I ran a hot bath and just lay in it trying to make it stop." She paused again for a drink.

"The kids were at their father's, I knew that, but I kept seeing them run into the bathroom, shout things at me, and run back out. They taunted me, told me how useless I was, which I knew, I had been drunk for all the years they remembered. They kicked me in my face as they laughed at me. I questioned everything. I mean, I knew they were at their Dad's house, but I saw them as real as though they were there. They yelled and screamed at me and told me they loved Mindy, their Dad's girlfriend, and wanted to live with them. I know now that it was my fear playing with me, making me its bitch. I kind of knew that then. I lay there and listened anyway. I cried, I hurt. I survived. After about a week of no alcohol I'm thinking I'm doing okay. The urge to drink was still there, still strong, but I was learning to deal with it. The hallucinations were going away, I hadn't had the feeling of bugs all over me for a while, I was better. I was ready to take on the world. Yeah, not so much.

I had the first seizure while I was in the shower. I was singing along to the song Beautiful by Christina Aguilera, and all of a sudden I'm in the bottom of the tub thrashing around, my head banging against the enamel. I have a cast iron tub so it was painful. I banged my head so hard I lost consciousness for a moment. When I woke up there was blood trickling down my forehead. I was helpless. The only people in the house were the kids, and they were watching some kids show and playing. I thought, *Oh my God, if this is what I have to live with I'm better off drunk*, but the kids deserved better than that. I deserved better than that. I deserved sobriety, dammit. I went to the hospital. I told them that I had a seizure and banged my head on the tub. That's mostly true, right? They stitched me up and did x-rays and CAT scans, and during my five day stay, my ex got a judge to give him custody of the kids." She paused to take another sip from her water bottle.

"I fought back, you bet I did, but their dad is a lawyer, and my most useful skill at the time was hiding how broken I was inside. Since then, I went back to school and am now an addiction counselor. My kids are grown. They've heard this over and over. They appreciate what I went through for them. Sure, they grew up with their dad and Mindy for the most part, I had visitation and most birthdays and holidays. They saw me get stronger, and have stood by me, encouraged me, and sometimes helped me with my homework. They are my kids. They are here with me tonight," she said as tears filled her eyes while she looked at two young men in the front row. "This is the first time I have told my story in public, and they came to support me." The audience clapped, and two tall men stood and hugged Robin. "And on a really high personal note, Mindy gained one hundred pounds and my ex is now cheating on her. Karma is a sweet bitch sometimes," Robin said, pumping her fist.

As she made her way to her seat Ty couldn't suppress his admiration for this woman and stood and clapped his hands as hard as he ever had for anyone. She didn't credit anything with her sobriety except the desire to recover her life. Her strength was infectious as it beamed from her story.

Ty thought of Lilly in Robin's situation. If she had gone through anything like that, she knew the depths of the hell these people knew. Their stories were her story as well. He put his arm around her and pulled her into him. She had to be the strongest human being he had ever known.

"Why didn't you tell me?" he whispered into Lilly's ear after Robin had taken her seat. She stared up at him for several moments before answering.

"Would you have listened, Ty? Would you have understood?" Lilly asked, eyeing him wearily, her voice barely above a whisper. "You couldn't have any idea what life was like growing up in the shadow of the former Ms. Berger County and her perfectly perfect son. You haven't done anything wrong in your life, Tyler. You have no clue how I felt never being enough. I couldn't get a 'Good job, Lilly.' 'I'm proud of you Lilly.' Nothing. You've had her your whole life. What have I had? Huh? Hell, our dad even took off!" Ty's back stiffened, and his jaw clenched. Neither of them ever brought up their 'bio-dad.' He wasn't there, and that was all that had ever mattered. "I married a damned doctor, and that still wasn't good enough!"

"Lilly, it wasn't about not being good enough. She knows—"

"Yeah. I know." Lilly sized him up with her gaze and turned to look him squarely in the eye. "Have you ever woken up in the morning and your only thought is 'how can I hide it today? What will happen if I get caught? Will the whole world turn on me if they discover the truth about me?'"

Ty shook his head.

"Have you ever been unable to function, unable to know or feel that same shit you knew and felt a few years earlier, until you've had a drink?"

Ty continued to shake his head.

"To not be able to block out the monster that screams in your head until you've had enough to silence him? To know that you're locked inside? You're hiding behind the screaming beast, but still, you're in there?"

"Oh, God, Lil, I'm so sorry," Ty said, wrapping his arm around her shoulders and pulling her head to his chest.

Ty held her for as long as she let him while he mulled what she said. He wanted to say of course, he understood anything. He would have loved to say that he would have helped her, been there for her. But in truth, before that minute he had no idea how deep addiction was. In his profession, he saw the junkies, the drunks, and the crack heads come in for a night or two, clean up for just as long, and go right back to their juice when they left. He never gave much thought to the strength it took a person to walk away from it. Of course, he had seen people go through some horrendous detox, but he never gave much credence to the will it took to continue the sobering process.

He imagined himself going through the hallucinations, the seizures, want of the alcohol so strong that he would be willing to eat hand sanitizer or drink mouthwash just to still the thirst for it. He was not sure he could have gone through with it himself. But here he was, sitting next to the strongest person he had ever known. She beat that demon down, and she did it without him even knowing, much less supporting her. Ty's chest began to swell with admiration for his sister.

After the last speaker finished and the meeting was over, Ty, Ben, and Lilly walked out to the parking lot and stood face to face for a long while before anyone spoke.

"Love the hair," Ben said, leaning against the Crown Vic. Lilly reached up and ran her hand through her short hair, then ruffled the front. Her cheeks reddened when she looked at Ben and she had an odd, flirty smile. Anger rose from the pit of Ty's stomach as he fought to contain it. Something about Lilly and Ben together made him furious, but he would keep to himself, for now. *It may just be in my head*, he thought.

"You look so different like that. Why?" Ty asked her.

"Tired of looking like some damsel in distress," Lilly answered.

"You didn't look like that," Ty shot back. "So, you're an alcoholic?"

Lilly nodded.

"Is that how you met Drew?"

"I don't know exactly how I met him. It was a bad time, and I was drunk for a whole chunk of it, don't remember much," Lilly answered.

"Did you go into the clinic?" Ben asked.

Lilly shook her head. "No, when I started dating Drew, I think, I just stopped drinking. I don't remember having hallucinations or anything like some of them did," she said, tilting her head toward a small group from the meeting gathered by another cluster of cars. "I don't remember even wanting to drink. Until now," she said, her eyes dropping to the ground. "Did Ben tell you about today?"

"Yeah, he did," Ty answered. He knew Lilly had to be dying inside right now. In the past, he would have teased her about getting drunk and attacking his friend like any good brother should, but after what he just heard, and learned about her, it was inappropriate.

Ty leaned against the car considering how little he actually knew about what Lilly went through in the time she was gone. He knew about Drew and his mistreatment, about a possible child, which could have been a hallucination from the alcohol at this point, and her alcoholism. None of it explained how distant she had been that day at lunch. In fact, the more he learned of her life, the more questions he had. Ben gave Lilly his phone, and Ty saw the headlines of the article. It was the same one he'd read earlier about the charges Drew filed.

"Police brutality? Has he lost his mind?" Lilly stormed. "What the…." Her voice trailed off as she looked at a picture of Drew with a swollen eye and lip, then one of her and her mother in the park on the bench.

"He didn't look like that in the driveway," she said weakly, turning to Ty.

Ty shook his head. There was nothing he could say, Lilly was right. Drew hadn't looked like that when he left the jail either, but who was listening? When she finished reading she handed the phone back to Ben and wedged herself between the two men.

"I'm so sorry," she said.

"For?" Ty replied.

"All of this. Your badge, possibly your career, everything. I don't know." Lilly laced her fingers around the back of her head and looked up at the night sky.

"You didn't do it. He did hit you. He did attack you. Those are facts, and the facts are what got him arrested."

"It doesn't look like it in the picture they have of me," she said pointing to the picture of her and her mother.

Ty shrugged. Words weren't going to change anything right now. The only words he would have said would have been coated in the fury burning inside of his chest, and Lilly had seen enough of that kind of acrimony to last her for a good while.

Chapter Twenty

Ty couldn't possibly know how much his being there meant to Lilly. He would never grasp the weight she was finally relieved of since he knew about her alcoholism. It was embarrassing, to be sure. How stupid would she have to be to let herself become dependent on it? How could she let herself become dependent on anything or anyone?

Since Ben's question about her meeting Drew, she could think of little else. For years Drew would say things like, *"You remember that restaurant we went to on College?"* And of course she didn't, but she never let him know that. That time in her life was bleak. Brad had overdosed, and his family, the part of his life that she couldn't touch, cremated his remains. She had gotten a portion of his ashes to fulfill his wish and scatter them over Vegas. She kept the tiny amount she now wore around her neck, keeping him close to her heart always. The pain of losing him was more than she could bear. She did do coke from time to time, but her problem was with a demon that coke couldn't compete with.

Lilly knew the same truth that everyone at these meetings knew. Once the beast has control of your life, it is a living hell to get it back. Even though she did not remember having seizures and hallucinations as some of the others, she was wrapped up in a battle that, to her, seemed far greater.

Lilly's head had been pounding since she left the doctor's office that afternoon. Her throat was aching like she had sprinted through the desert, and her eyes were sore. More than anything she wanted to find the bottom of a bottle of anything. If the poison could take away the most painful year of her life, what chance did this horrendous day stand? Normally, going to the meetings made her stronger. Tonight, she feared, she needed more.

The voices were becoming quiet around her, and for the first time she was fighting not to see it. It was all lies anyway; nothing more than heart wrenching deceit. She did not want to hear them this time. She had no desire to see more, and certainly not to feel it.

She stared at Ty, who was watching Ben type on his cell phone. She could see his lips move and watch his animation of what was being said, but his voice had grown hush.

***

Lilly was in the white room, watching the light play shadow games with the spot on the wall. She had no idea how long she had been lying there, or how long she had been unable to move. The only certainty was she was cognate, not that anyone would know. No one was coming to check on her. No one seemed to care. She waited for the dark to take over and drown the shadows.

The door to the room opened, and a faceless person came in and stood by the bed, out of her line of vision. She could hear clicking, what sounded like water rushing, and felt ice running in her vein from her elbow to her shoulder.

The person stood there for several moments, blocking the shadow dances on the wall. Lilly's spot was darkened by a large outline of a person standing just behind her. Fear gripped her, making her heart pound so loud and hard she could feel it pulsating in her eyes. Her body tingled. It was the first sensation she could remember since she began staring at the spot.

First she moved her toe, hoping Faceless wouldn't notice. The shadow didn't move. Then she moved her fingers. Still, the figure remained motionless. She blinked and took a deep breath. The tingling grew more intense and her leg jerked. *"Dammit!"* she thought. The shadow walked to her feet and began pinching her toes.

"Ouch!" she yelped.

The faceless person walked toward her head. She looked up into his eyes and screamed. The haze in her mind blurred his face. His eyes, though, they were dark and expressionless, almost hollow.

***

"Lilly!" Ty shouted with a hand on each of her shoulders, shaking her.

Lilly opened her eyes. She could feel her body trembling between Ty's hands. The fear she felt in her memory hadn't dissipated as it usually did. She was panicking, staring into Ty's eyes. She put her hands on his arms to help steady herself.

"Where did you go?" Ben asked. Lilly noticed his hand was stroking her back.

"The same place as always," she answered, hearing the fear in her own voice. Lilly recounted what she had just seen. They could believe her or not. It did not matter. She knew it was real. She could still see the hollow emotionless eyes that were gazing into her soul. This had happened.

"I'll drive you home," Ty declared. Lilly shook her head and gazed in the direction she needed to drive. She wanted nothing more than to be alone, to process everything that she saw.

"I'm fine, Ty. I've been dealing with this for a while. I'm only going home and you two will be right behind me."

Ty crinkled his forehead and cocked his eyebrow. He squeezed her shoulders gently.

"You know I'm right here, I'm not going to let anything or anyone hurt you. I'll drive you if you want," Ty whispered as he held her in the embrace.

"I'm ok, Ty. Really," she said as she climbed into her car. She would not tell him that pins stabbed into her stomach every time she closed her eyes. The hollowness she had seen in the man's eyes haunted her. Whatever he meant to her, whatever he'd done to her, scared her to death.

Chapter Twenty-One

"She was drugged," Ben said flatly once they were in the car. Ty already knew that. "Whatever was being put in her system has messed with her."

"But where was she?" Ty said mostly to himself. He was watching his sister speed off into the dark in front of him. He and Ben rode in silence as the wheels in both of their minds were racing. It certainly made for a good theory. She had to have been drugged. But with what? What drug would make her lose her memory? Who did it? Drew? He was maniacal. But was that motive enough to give a patient, or, worse yet, his wife, something experimental at best?

"Are we certain that she was never a patient in the clinic?" Ben asked. Ty let the question sit in the air. The only thing he was certain about was that Lilly had lived through something horrific. It would make sense if she had been a patient there. Drew had used an unknown drug on the patients. That much was documented in the files.

"In her notebook did you read about anything that she saw around her? Anything that might give us a clue where she was?" Ty asked Ben.

"She was in a hospital somewhere. Knowing she was an alcoholic, I'm betting money that she was in the clinic."

Ty would put money on it too, regardless of Lilly's denials. "The records. The banker boxes," he said, thinking out loud. From the corner of his eye he could make out Ben's head nodding in agreement.

He stared straight ahead, trying to find his sister in the darkness. The moon was the only illumination on the narrow winding roads, and it wasn't providing anything further than their headlights could find. What waited around each curve was a mystery until they had come full circle around each one.

"Holy shit! That's what we were missing!" Ty shouted.

"What are you talking about?" Ben asked.

"The files in the banker boxes. The one labeled Patient 1. She was the only one that was never addicted to drugs. Every other patient was addicted to something, except her," he said smiling his broad, satisfied smile. The car could not move fast enough to get him back to the files. He knew they were about to get somewhere in the case now.

The headlights didn't seem to reflect from the silver metal guardrails, they just appeared in the center of the curve. The car was on their side of the road and not slowing down. Ben swerved to miss it, and Ty heard the metal scraping. The guardrail was made of thick aluminum, and it supported them from careening down the embankment.

The car, a dark colored Honda, pressed against the back driver's side, pushing them deeper into the railing. Ben opened his mouth as if he were shouting, but the sound didn't make it to Ty's ears over the loud metal clashing. Ty was certain the rail was giving way under the weight. He had worked more fatal accidents in this area than he cared to think about, but he could think of little else at that moment. He recalled the mangled automobiles carrying drivers who had planned to make it home each night. He could see the drivers and passengers as their lifeless forms lay strewn down the hill.

The metal cracked, and the car teetered at the edge. The hill was a 32% incline, there were signs stating as much all along the road. The Honda bore against them, tires spinning, engine revving harder, making sounds like evilness erupting from the depths of hell. Ty rolled his window down and unbuckled his seat belt. Ben did the same.

As the two men climbed out the window, the rail cracked and gave way. The Crown Vic rolled down the hill as they hung from the windows. Ty grabbed the metal railing and hoisted himself out of the car. He heard Ben shouting, and pulled himself toward Ben's voice.

Ben was lying on the pavement when Ty got to him. The Honda had sped away when the Crown Vic went over. Ben wasn't moving. Ty ran to his side and saw that he was breathing. He turned Ben over to face him and saw his eyes open. Ben breathed heavily now, and showed Ty his phone.

"Took 'em as he was driving off," Ben said.

The pictures weren't clear, there was no way they would hold up in court, but they would help the investigation. The driver was a male with dark features, as much as they could tell, probably in his late 20s or early 30s, but the pictures were too blurry to be able to make any sort of ID. He wore a light blue hooded sweatshirt, the hood pulled down over his eyes and covering most of his face. The license plate number was clear as day. It was an Idaho plate. They needed to run the tags, but Ty was certain it was a rental. Ty tried to call Lilly's cell number, but he had no reception.

"Dammit!" he fumed.

"Don't worry about it, I sent it in. We should have some answers shortly," Ben said, noticing Ty's frustration.

"Great. Really great. But what good is that gonna do us sitting here in the middle of nowhere with no transportation?"

"Seriously, Ty? A car is being sent to your house. We're, what, like two or three miles out? We can hike that."

"Let's go then. Try to keep up," Ty said, baiting him as he extended his hand to help him off of the asphalt. In the academy, Ben had set the bar for marksmanship. He could hit any target that popped up for him. Ty had been the runner, as much as his ankle would allow.

Ben laughed and jumped to his feet. They started walking using their cell phones as flashlights.

Chapter Twenty-Two

Sara tried to forget. She tried to put the past where it belonged, and leave it there. She had moved on. She had done a damn fine job of it, too. Until tonight.

What could they possibly want now? Why were they calling her out of the blue? They never left messages. No, that would be too easy. She had held up her end of the bargain. Fulfilled her good sister duties. She had taken her settlement and disappeared just like she was supposed to. Hell, she'd moved to Wyoming to be away from them. Why could they never hold up their end of the deal? All they had to do was leave her alone now.

She plucked the picture of her and Serena from the fireplace mantle that was taken when they were small children, long before the madness came, and held it as she talked to her.

"Damn you, Rena!" she said. She never denied what a beauty her sister had been.

Rena had lost something when they left Oklahoma. She'd lost the innocence that should have kept her sane. She started seeing older men. She loved to toy with them. Sara thought maybe, in the back of her mind, she blamed all men for what father had taken from her.

A long trail of destroyed marriages accompanied Rena wherever she went. Men volleyed for her attentions and she was only too eager to give it to them for a while. Kurt was no exception, until Rena got pregnant.

The phone bellowed, and a chill of dread knotted her stomach. She was about to learn what they wanted, and after nearly nine years of silence, it wasn't likely to be good.

Caller ID told her it was the same number that had called earlier. It was them. She picked up the receiver, hoping she was wrong.

"Hello, Sara," said the hoarse whisper on the other end. They always tried to conceal voices, but it was obvious who they were. She only knew one reason someone with an Ohio area code would be calling.

"What do you want?" Sara said, doing her best impression of someone who wasn't scared out of their mind.

"Just to make sure that you remember our deal."

"Of course I remember the deal. I think the forgetfulness is coming from your end. I leave you alone, you leave me alone. I disappear, you don't come looking. Sound familiar?" Sara said, feigning indignation.

"You take our past to the grave with you. You left that part out. Did you think we wouldn't know you have been blabbing? Did you think your little friend could keep his big mouth closed?" The person on the other end was growing irate.

Fear speared her chest. She had gotten close to only one person since Rena died. They spent one drunken night in front of her fireplace. He swore he would never mention a single syllable to another human being. He was the one she trusted to carry out one final deed after she died. The one thing that would set these spoiled, power tripping sons of bitches on their heels, and there wouldn't be a damned thing they could do about it.

"Your secrets are safe. I haven't told anyone here," she lied, hoping the trembling in her voice wasn't as evident as she knew it to be.

"Don't try to play me!" the voice growled. "Haven't you seen the news? Dear Serena's only son is in a ton of trouble. Don't pretend you haven't been keeping up with him. The FBI has shut down his clinic. Wonder where they got information. What do they know, Sara?"

"What? I don't... I haven't seen anything... I...." Sara stammered.

"Yes, that's what I thought." Click. The line went dead. Sara ran to the bedroom to gather what she could. The call had kept her on the line for four minutes. They could have been baiting her, expecting her to run. There were probably a dozen or so outside waiting to take her out. Inside was no safer. No, she had to take her chances. She had to get away.

She couldn't get the thoughts of Rena's son out of her mind. Sara had a picture of him tucked in the corner of another picture of Rena. He had been a perfect child, beautiful in every way. Perfectly rounded head, large dark eyes just like his mother's. It broke Sara's heart to leave him there.

He had a clinic now? That's what the person said. He must be a doctor. Rena's perfect little boy had, hopefully, escaped the madness that consumed his mother. Why was he in trouble? What had he done?

Sara was never allowed to know any details of his life. That was also part of the deal. Kurt, the rich bastard, ordered it that way. Why would they tell her now? Was it a mistake? Had they slipped? No, the answer was obvious. Her usefulness had vanished, and her knowledge was a liability. She might really never see tomorrow.

"God, please let Chris remember what he's supposed to do."

Sara heard a loud explosion as she saw the flash of light cross in front of her eyes. Drywall and plaster were showering her living room. She screamed, but the sounds of the house caving in drowned out her voice. She could almost hear Rena's voice cackling in the sounds of the wood cracking around her. Fire sprayed from the roof, and the walls buckled under the weight.

Sara ran for the door grabbing the knob, but it was useless. Fire lapped at the front windows all around the porch. The center of the house was barely above her head as she dashed through the kitchen to the back door. There was nowhere inside that wasn't alight. The explosion had blown the back door open and she was breaking for it. The ceiling was in flames, but she thought she had a few seconds to get there.

The closer she got to the door, the further away it seemed to become. It was just a few feet away. She was going to make it, she thought. The weight of the ceiling knocked her to the floor. Her back was in flames under the drywall. Pain ripped through her body faster than the fire had engulfed the house. She tried pushing it off of her. She knew she was trapped. They were getting what they wanted. She wasn't going to make it out. Darkness was growing larger, tempting her to let go and fall into it, like poor Rena had after he forced her to give her baby to the nuns. Sara fought it off for as long as she could. She heard the faint cry of sirens, but they were too far away. She could already feel the fire raging up her neck.

"Rena!" Sara cried out for the last time.

Chapter Twenty-Three

Momma was on the porch swing drinking her coffee when Lilly got back. There was a large rectangular box on the swing next to her addressed to Lilly.

"Did you take care of whatever was bothering you?" Momma asked. Lilly looked into her eyes and saw the concern of a mother. She had never seen it from her before. If it had been there, she'd paid no attention to it.

"Honey, I'm not so old that I can't see when something is wrong with my girl. Talk to me," Momma said in a voice that Lilly had only ever heard her use with Ty.

Lilly took a deep breath. "Momma, I don't even know where to start," she said, trying to dismiss her and walk into the house.

"I find the beginning to be the best place," the woman said, meeting Lilly with the same stubbornness she was famous for. "Tyler told me some things; some things that *you* should have told me. He's putting himself on the line for you, the least you can do is be honest. I can see your battle scars, they're all over your face, but I want to know, right here, right now, what is going on? What made you finally wake up and leave him?"

Lilly felt as though she had been punched in the gut. How could she look her mother or brother in the eye now that they knew everything? How could she expect to get any closer to her child if she did not?

"Okay." Lilly breathed deep, gathering courage as she eased herself next to her mother on the swing. Her fingers, accustomed to the long hair, ran easily through the short hair that covered her head now. She touched the spot on the back of her head where the blood came from in the memories. She had never had an urge to find it before now. Her fingers brushed across a slight bulge of skin that was once broken. There was a scar. She could feel it. Her heart lifted. She knew there had to be a scar. There was proof she wasn't crazy.

"What is the necklace you wear? I see you play with it, it has to be important," Momma said.

Lilly held the vial of Brad's ashes and closed her eyes. She wasn't sure she was ready to tell the world about him, but Momma wasn't the world.

"This is Brad," she said, holding the small red vial out for her mother to see. Momma raised her eyebrows and stared at the vial. "I met him at Bea's place a long time ago. We started talking and hanging out. When I left for college we moved in together." Lilly paused to gauge her mother's reaction. She didn't continue until she saw her mother didn't appear disappointed. "We traveled all over, Momma. He took me to Vegas, we went to the beach; he showed me things that I had only read about." Lilly could feel her lips curving up, and was powerless to stop it.

"Momma, you would've loved him. He was so good to me, good *for* me. He was wild. He was crazy. He was…." Her face was burning and her smile widening as she spoke. She knew her mother could see how much Brad had meant to her, she was smiling back at Lilly. "We were drunk a lot together. Momma, I am an alcoholic. I've been sober since I met Drew, but I drank a lot for many years." Lilly waited before she spoke again to let her mother absorb what she had heard.

"I didn't leave school when I married Drew, Momma, I'd flunked out in my second year." The embarrassment of having lied to her family about college rushed over her, and she shut down. She had never tried to tell anyone the full story of her past, and had no idea how insane it sounded until the words were swimming in the humidity around her and she could do nothing to pull them back.

"Anyway, Brad died on our last trip to Vegas. He overdosed on drugs. I woke up, and he was dead." The pain of that day beat down on her, overwhelming her emotions. She held the tears in check and plunged forward. "His family was… different. They wanted him to be something that he hated. They collected his body and cremated him. I was far from sobriety then, but a friend got some of his ashes and we took them to Vegas and spread them over the strip," she said, holding the vial out so her mother could see again. Momma nodded as she stroked the back of Lilly's head. Lilly's fingers rubbed the newly found scar.

"What are you playing with?" Momma asked as she placed her hand over Lilly's. Lilly moved her hand and let her mother feel the raised skin. "What is that from?"

"I'm not sure," Lilly answered. The memories, while she knew they were real, were presumably debunked by the doctor. Lilly told her mother what she remembered and what the doctor told her just today.

"So, there's still a chance that you were pregnant?" Momma asked raising her eyebrows. Lilly had seen that look in her mother's eyes before, though admittedly only with Ty. Angelica York made up her mind about Lilly's child, and no amount of doctors would be able to change it.

"Only a small chance, Momma. One in a thousand."

"That's still a chance," Momma said, wrapping her arms around Lilly's shoulders. "Don't discount your odds, honey. You know what you have seen in the memories. You know what you have felt." She pulled Lilly to arms-length and stared directly into her eyes. "Just because the odds are against it, doesn't make it any less real."

Lilly wished desperately for the blind faith that her mother possessed. To be able to hold her belief in the face of the nastiest of adversity was a skill that Lilly had never acquired.

"So, why did you cut your hair?" Momma asked. Lilly shrugged.

"Oh, I think you do know," Momma said, putting a hand on each of Lilly's shoulders. "My sweet, beautiful, brave girl." She wiped a stray tear from Lilly's cheek. Momma was beaming at Lilly. Warmth spread through Lilly's chest as a knot built in her throat. "Give yourself credit for leaving him and going after your baby. That took more than a little nerve, honey." Momma pulled Lilly's face to her chest. "It's not easy. It's never gonna be easy, I promise you that, but here you are, and here is exactly where you belong."

They sat in silence for a long while listening to the sounds of a southern Kentucky June night. Lilly was seated next to her mother, holding the box in her lap. Momma had her arm on the back of the swing, and her head on Lilly's shoulder.

"So, what are you going to do?" Momma asked.

"Momma, I've got a million reasons to stop looking. Everything in sight tells me that my memories are not real," Lilly answered.

"That's not an answer."

"I know. If I had just one reason, just one tiny little thing that said, 'keep looking Lilly,' I would keep going, but I'm so tired Momma."

"You don't need a sign from above, now, do ya? As I just said, you know what you feel when you look at the memories."

"I know, Momma."

"Let's see what's in there," Momma whispered as though someone was going to hear, and pointed to the box. They took the box into the kitchen where they had light. Momma already had a knife to cut the tape on it. Lilly recognized the box instantly. It was one of the banker boxes from Drew's office at their house.

Lilly was shocked it was still sealed when she got there. Momma was never one to put her curiosity on hold. The chemo treatments must have taken more than strength, Lilly thought.

On the inside of the box was a letter. The handwriting was unmistakable. It was Gretta's script and broken dialogue.

Ms. Lilly,

This was in Mr. Wilt's room. He call and say get the boxes out. I take this one. I want to give to you. Please, find what you need. I pray for you. Thank you for treat me good.

Gretta

The contents of the box were an odd assortment of things. Expanding file folders, pictures, and reports in plastic covers were all shoved inside. The reports were of no interest to her, they were on topics that Drew studied in med school. Inside the expanding file folders she found pictures of her and Drew from some of the fundraiser galas they attended shortly after they were married. How the years changed them. In this set, Drew was standing next to her with his hand on the small of her back. They were both smiling. They looked happy. Lilly barely remembered a time they were happy.

The next pocket contained pictures of Lilly and Anne. In most they were surrounded by people Lilly didn't recognize, which wasn't odd at all. Lilly didn't recognize most of the people at these soirees. They were power lusting snobs, and Lilly could care less about them. She and Anne were laughing and smiling in all of the photos. They managed to make a boring contest of who had the most into their own playground. The people around them never knew they were the butt of the jokes that kept both of them nearly in tears.

In the last pocket was a stack of pictures of Lilly and Brad. They all looked like photos from a security camera. There were scores of Vegas pictures from their first trip to the city. Lilly knew they were the first trip because they had only been there twice while he was alive, and the second time was when he died. They went to no casinos and only one restaurant. The rest of their brief time was spent with Brad snorting, both of them drinking, and having sex in the hotel room on the strip. Anger burned white hot in her chest at the thought of Drew having pictures of her and Brad. He had no right to that part of her.

Beneath the pictures were several green accordion files at least five inches thick each. Inside were pages upon pages of research. The authors of the papers were names she had never heard before. Each was written about a different subject. In the last file slot, paper clipped together, were black and white photos of a beautiful dark haired woman. Her lips were full as if in a constant pout, her cheekbones high and prominent. Her hair was cut in a silky short bob. As soon as Lilly pulled the stack of photos out, she knew who it was. She closed her eyes and turned away from the picture.

"Oh, my God. Tracey," Lilly breathed.

"Who is Tracey?" Momma asked. Lilly barely heard her voice, though she was only a few feet away. She saw Tracey as she was the last time they had spoken. Lilly's heart raced and pounded in her head. She stared at the picture in her hand and felt a knot tighten in her throat.

Lilly squeezed the pictures until she heard them begin to snap in her fingers. Her eyes were shut tight and she felt her mother's trembling hands cup her own. She was fighting this memory with everything she had, turning her head to each side and trying to think of anything else. Beads of sweat rolled across her forehead as hot tears puddled in her eyes. She did not want to see what was coming. She didn't know why, and she certainly didn't know what she was about to see; she just knew she wasn't ready for it.

***

"Penny for your thoughts," Tracey said, opening a bottle of water as she seated herself across the table from Lilly. Her silky black hair whisked into place.

"Penny first," Lilly heard her own voice chortle.

They sat at the table for the full 30 minutes they were allowed talking strategy to get out of this place. Guards loomed over them, their huge size casting shadows across the room. Making a run was impossible. Lilly wasn't even sure that she could get anywhere as big as she had gotten.

"You have to stop rubbing it. Once the baby gets here you're gonna want to get rid of the stretch marks," Tracey said, smacking Lilly's hand away from her large stomach.

"I just wish he'd get here already!" Lilly chimed.

A guard with 'Adam' embroidered on his shirt walked to Lilly's side and took her arm. She glanced up at him and rolled her eyes to Tracey. Another guard with 'Eric' on his shirt approached Tracey.

"You've got an appointment and today you will keep it," Eric told her.

Tracey's face was stricken. Her eyes darted around the room. Everyone in the place understood that having an 'appointment' meant you had to see Drew, and for Tracey, that was hell. She jumped to her feet and backed away from him.

"No! I'm not going to see him. I don't want to see him. You tell Drew that I'm not his property, I'm never going to want him that way," she said as she backed away from the guard.

Another guard larger than Eric grabbed Tracey under her arms and Eric lifted her legs. Tracey let out a howl that brought every motion in the room to a halt.

"Run, Lilly!" she screamed as she kicked at Eric and flailed her arms toward the other guard.

"Stop! Put her down! Tracey—"Lilly yelled with everything she could muster. Adam tightened his grip on her arm and yanked her in the opposite direction. Lilly pulled against him, watching the door Tracey had been forced through slowly ease shut and the other patients resume activity.

Adam loosened his grip on Lilly once the door had finally stopped moving and she tore her arm free. The door was on the other side of the room and she hobbled to it as fast as her body would allow.

It wasn't one of the many locking doors and opened with just a shove. Lilly felt Adam closing on her fast and forced her body through. The cold concrete on her bare feet was like shockwaves through her toes. Hairs on her arms and the back of her neck began to rise as she made her way through dark corridors. She could see Tracey's dark hallway ahead of her with a thin sliver of light illuminating an otherwise unlit area.

Lilly hobbled toward the hall, hearing Adam's shoes hitting the concrete behind her and Tracey shouting incoherently ahead. A familiar voice seemed to coo in between Tracey's protests. Lilly's heart sank as Tracey's voice became muffled and still seemed so far away. She held the wall to steady herself as she tried to catch her breath.

"You don't want to go down there. There's nothing for you there," she heard Adam say behind her. Everything in Lilly's being told her that he was right, but Tracey was the only person in the place that even cared about her. Lilly had to help her.

As she plunged forward, Lilly heard the cooing turn to what she could only describe as whining. He was saying things that didn't make sense in Lilly's mind. Tracey was perfect; she wasn't a 'whack job' as his words indicated. She hadn't attacked anyone.

"Why couldn't you just *love* me," she heard him sob.

The door to Tracey's room was only slightly opened. Lilly could see several nurses gathered close. She pushed it gently and her heart dropped. She heard her own scream reverberate from the bare walls and felt the cold concrete on her knees.

Tracey's dark eyes stared at Lilly in cold silence. They were double their normal size. There were no playful secrets swirling in them. There was no coy grin to bait Lilly into some crazy shenanigan. The terror that was on Tracey's face as she was hauled from the dining area still shone in her now hollow expression and bloodshot eyes.

"Say something!" Lilly screamed to her friend. "Please! Say anything." Lilly's chest heaved as she fought for air and her heart raced.

The door flew open and Lilly could see red markings on Tracey's neck, her arms strapped in place with the straight jacket. Her lips were pale and pasty. The faceless man walked toward her and grabbed her free arm and Adam pulled her other arm from the door.

"Get her to her room. She has no business in this hall," she heard Drew's voice say, no longer whining or cooing. The sharp tone and bitter anger Lilly knew well.

Lilly felt her own body go limp, her head bobbling as she was being dragged through the halls. Silent tears streamed her face, gathering at her chin, threatening to drop off. Silently, step after step, door after door, she was remembering this place. She was remembering her prison. Nothing was moving, nothing was speaking; it seemed as if time had stopped. Life was turning black and white as the color faded.

As they approached her room, the faceless man turned the knob, and Lilly glanced up into his hollow eyes. Ian's face stared back at her.

***

"Oh my God! They killed her! Momma they killed her!" Lilly shouted as she paced from corner to corner in the kitchen. "I saw it! They killed Tracey!"

Ty and Ben bounded through the door as Lilly paced the kitchen floor, her heart pounding. Momma rushed to Ty, dabbing at a cut above his eye just as his cell began ringing.

"What happened? We heard someone screaming," Ben said as he struggled to catch his breath.

"I remembered something more−" Lilly told him as she listened to Ty talking on his phone.

"Hey Kari, what's up?" Ty said, while Momma worked on his wound, a look of worry on her face. "When?" There was a pause. "I'm here now. I don't see anything." He was walking out the door as the words came out. The pins nabbing in the pit of Lilly's stomach were sinking lower. Lilly ran to catch him.

"Ty!" she shouted. Ty kept walking and looking in the darkness. "Tyler! What's wrong?"

"I don't know, have you seen Papa?" Ty asked.

"What? What's wrong with Papa?" Lilly asked, frozen in her spot on the porch.

"I don't know. Kari said that medics are on their way to him. Go find him."

Lilly ran to Papa's room and stopped cold at the door. She heard a shrill screech surrounding her, and took several moments to realize it was coming from her. She backed away, trying to keep the pain inside the room, away from her. "No!" she screamed, willing her eyes to be fooling her. Ty and Ben ran in past her, flipping on light switches.

Papa's head was on his pillow and his feet were on the floor. His eyes, fixed on the spot where Lilly was standing, were glazed. There was a tiny trail of blood from his ear to his pillow. Ty put his finger on Papa's neck to check for a pulse, then lowered his head. Lilly was screaming in her head, but could make no audible sound. Her knees buckled, and she fell to the floor. Tears streamed her cheeks, she could feel their wetness.

This powerhouse, this giant was crumpled in his bed. Ben put his arms around Lilly's shoulders, picking her up and wrapping her in himself, pushing her back into the study. She wanted to close her eyes. She wanted all of this to go away. Papa was fine. He was always fine. Nothing could hurt him. He was Alvin Jefferson Clay York for God's sake. Of course he'd be okay.

The medics came in with the gurney already raised. Ty came out of the room wiping his eyes with the back of his hand. He took Lilly out of Ben's arms and wrapped his arms around her. His body was shaking, and her emotional overload was freed. She fell into her brother. Her strength vanished.

"He's gone," Ty whispered. Lilly hadn't needed the confirmation.

There was a tap on Ty's shoulder, and Lilly heard a female voice telling him Papa pushed the medical emergency button on his wristband. His finger was still on the button.

The medics wheeled Papa out to the ambulance covered with a sheet, and left the driveway. Lilly watched their lights fade through the window in the study. She sat across from Papa's chair and stared at it as though he would appear there at any moment wondering what all the fuss was. People were moving about the house, questioning everyone, looking at everything, and taking Papa's medication bottles. It seemed as if time stopped for Lilly as they went on with their jobs.

She heard the questions Kari Spear was asking her. She couldn't vocalize any answers, and just nodded or shook her head in response. She couldn't take her eyes from Papa's spot. That was where he was supposed to be. He belonged there. He wasn't supposed to go yet.

Momma's voice was somewhere in the background. "He had a headache today," Lilly heard her say. "The nurse gave him–" Momma's voice trailed off as she left the study with the officer.

***

Lilly's mind played the images of the day Papa took her out to walk the grounds. She was a small child, maybe seven or eight.

"Papa, will you live forever?" she heard her own impish voice ask. Papa stopped walking, and leaned on a tree stump.

"Lilla girl," he said, putting her on his knee, his voice full and booming as it always was, not the frail sounding echo that it had become. "God wouldn't put that on anybody. I don't want to live forever. That would be the worst thing. Once I have been here long enough to learn everything I'm supposed to know, I'll be called home. Just like all the others before me were. As long as somebody who loves me stays here, then I'll still be alive. Right here," he said, putting his finger in the middle of her chest.

"But, what would happen to me if you weren't here, Papa?" Lilly asked.

"Oh, my girl, I think you'll be just fine. You've got a good heart in your chest and a good head on your shoulders. You will do fine."

***

Slow hot tears traced the framework of her face. It couldn't be his time. It just couldn't. She glanced to the long cherub bench and thought of the first time her heart was broken. The day Ricky Drake had shown his loyalty. She cried on the bench by the door for hours until her insides were raw.

***

"Why would such a pretty girl waste her time and tears on a no account punk like that Drake boy?" Papa asked, standing over Lilly. She looked up into the old playful eyes and wanted to smile with him, laugh with him, but her heart was bursting.

"Papa, he was supposed to be meeting me there. We were gonna... well, it was our night," she said.

"Oh, my Lilla girl. You are too precious to be putting thought into that kid. He's just like his old man. He'll be here in Rock Holler until he keels over. Same as the rest of them. Come on in here, let's look at the pictures."

She had gone into the study with him and sat in the very same chair that night. Papa pulled out the pictures and they looked at the York family through the years.

Her heart was pounding; there was no doubt everyone around her could see her body shake with each assault in her chest, just as it had the morning Brad left her.

***

"Tell me what you're mad about," she could hear Brad's voice rumble in her mind. The object was for her to answer with *I'm mad about you*, to which he would proudly display his blank-eyed, full grin expression until they fell into each other. He perfected the art that was winning Lilly's heart. He, and he alone, could take her to the brink of the universe then slowly, as if it were nothing, draw her back to his—their—reality. Thoughts of him reminded her she had once known happiness, she had touched it. It was real.

"Desolo unum," she whispered to his vial. It meant *abandoned one* in Latin, their commonality.

Lilly twirled him around her finger. The song they danced to all over the Vegas strip on their first trip was playing in her head. Every club they walked past would boom the song until her body pulsated with the beat. Brad loved to make her laugh. He would do his impression of modern dancing, which was jumping straight up in place, until she was doubled over. Then he would take her into his arms and twirl her around like she was Ginger Rogers and he Fred Astaire. She could see those big eyes full of wonder as he looked into hers.

***

The house was stale and stiff. Lilly was suffocating under the weight of the pain this day had brought. She had to get out of the house. She needed to be away from these people. All of them.

She walked out the front door and waited on the porch. The swing swayed gently back and forth with the slow breeze that was building. The staunchness followed her. She still couldn't breathe. Her car could easily back around all of the vehicles parked in the long driveway. Taking a last look at the scene inside, she started the car and drove aimlessly. She had no destination in mind, but anywhere would be better than at that house at that minute.

Chapter Twenty-Four

"Dammit! Dammit, dammit, dammit!" Drew was pacing in his home office. He hadn't heard from the kid for hours. Today was supposed to be the day. The kid was supposed to call him as soon as it happened. He could not fail now. Drew was already barred from the clinic. That damn FBI guy made sure of that. He would get his. Sissy would see to that.

Sissy was pissed, just as he knew she would be. Gretta was collateral that he couldn't afford right now. Sissy just couldn't understand that yet.

She walked in with her lips pulled tight so they formed a straight line, and started barking orders. Four guys that Drew didn't know jumped at every command. After the body was taken out of the house she turned on her heel and glared at him, fire roiling in her eyes.

"What kind of idiot are you?" she said. "How in God's name did you manage to even make it through med school, much less first in your class? You better pray to whatever you believe in that nothing happens to precious little Lilly now after all the stink she has caused, because you my dear baby brother, will be the first person that goes down, and I'll be damned if you take me with you!"

"I'm not going down and I'm not taking anybody with me!" he protested. She always knew exactly how to push every button to piss him off. "Did I not keep her in check for over nine years? Did I not keep her from asking questions for that long? Could I have done that if I were some kind of idiot?"

"You didn't do any of that without my help, or do you not remember that part?" she said. "And you started to come unhinged when the FBI was questioning you. You have to get control of yourself."

True enough, Sissy helped. Not as much as she credited herself with, but she had helped. As far as coming unhinged, she had no idea. He was going nuts staying in this damn house, the unintended gift from their father. Drew could see all of his sins scrawled across the walls here. His mother's voice clucked them in his head. She had been howling the night he'd struck Lilly.

"*Shut her down!*" she'd screamed over and over until he punched her. He was truly sorry for having done that. He would have apologized for having gotten physical if she had not run away. She was easily swayed when he needed her to be.

"*Just like you controlled the other one?*" his mother's voice chortled.

"Shut up!" he shouted in his mind. His anxieties were growing every second he didn't hear from the kid.

"*Or you'll kill someone else?*" his mother's voice shrieked. Drew clutched each side of his head to steady the room as her words bounced from the walls. "*It's three now, isn't it? Tracey, your half-brother, and now the housekeeper. You should have silenced your little woman when you still could,*" she hissed as though the words themselves would save Drew from whatever fate lay before him.

Sissy rolled her eyes at him and left, slamming the front door. He watched the glow of tail lights until they were gone.

"Where the hell is that kid?" Drew shouted, silencing his mother's taunts. It was past ten o'clock already; if that damn kid had gotten himself caught, Sissy would have both of their heads. He walked to his desk where he left his phone just as it started to buzz. It was the kid.

"Finally!" Drew boomed into the phone.

"It's done. He's gone," the kid answered. "The police have been at the house for hours. I need to get out of here. Now."

"Are you crazy? You can't disappear now. How do you think that would look? Old man dies and you can't be found? Damn suspicious! That's how it would look!"

"Strokes aren't suspicious, especially for the aged. And they aren't murder. That's why you sent me." The kid was so calm. The time he had spent with Haim had emboldened him to a fault. It was good; he needed to be toughened up.

"No, just wait a few more days. After everything settles down there, then you can vanish again."

"Does mother know I'm here yet?"

"No. I don't plan to tell her. She's pissed at me right now," Drew admitted.

"What did you do now?"

"Never mind, it's no matter. You just sit tight, report in just like you should. You can get a feel for how everything is going. Find out what they know," Drew instructed.

"He's gonna make a mess of everything. You have to take care of this yourself. Stop depending on your father's family," his mother hissed.

"They have two boxes of your files," the kid said.

"Only two? Where's the third?" Drew asked. He was stunned. What could have happened to the other one? Maybe he had less to be concerned about than he thought.

"I don't know, but there are only two at the house. I saw the cowboy trying to figure them out. They have no idea what to think of them. The FBI guy hasn't even made a connection. Yet."

"If they don't have the third they can't. It's perfect." Drew couldn't help the grin. His confidence was rising, his mother was silencing. "Just sit tight, Ian, we can get you out in a few days."

"I'm going by Phillip, uncle."

"Yes. Yes of course you are." Drew thought of the day he named the kid. Sissy had quietly given birth to him in Canada—father couldn't have the family reputation marred with a grandchild out of wedlock. The sisters were hushed over him. Drew had known then this child was going to be the end of his imprisonment. He would get to be a part of the family he so desired. Father would finally, without hesitation, openly admit that Drew was his son. Not just his son, his favorite son.

The nuns, with all of their rules and commandments, and punishments for wicked children could be damned! Never would father look at him in disgust as he had the day Drew tried to make Cheesely, the ferret that Father Downey kept in his office, love him as he did the others who would play with him as long as they wanted. He squeezed the little ball of fluff in his arms. Drew did not mean to hurt him; he only wanted the nutmeg colored prankster to accept him as Cheesely did the other children.

He'd heard father telling the nuns that Drew's mother was crazy and that Drew was likely going to end up just like her. In the end, father sided with the nuns and Drew was stripped naked and given forty stripes, locked away, allowed out of his room only to attend class in a specially assigned seat next to Sister Blanche, the meanest of them all. He did not see dear old Dad for weeks. After that instance, Father's visits began to get fewer and further between. Then Drew set his mind on proving himself to his father. He would earn his father's respect and be as powerful as the old man.

Sissy had given birth to what would eventually be the vehicle that would catapult him to his success. He named him Phillip Ian because in the Bible, Phillippians had been the end of imprisonment for the apostles. The nuns drilled that lesson, among many others, so deep into his skull, a neurosurgeon would never be able to reach it. Phillip Ian would bring about the end of the days of shame, the end of Drew's imprisonment.

They broke the connection, and Drew poured himself two fingers of bourbon. Celebration was near, he could feel it, taste it. He would soon be back at the clinic, just like always. He would deal with Lilly when everything settled down. He just had to be patient. She would give up this ridiculous search now, he was certain of it. He had outwitted the cowboy and the FBI and, with Sissy's help, he would move on.

He never tried to figure out why Sissy forced him into this situation. He knew the story all too well, but only Drew knew what had happened with his half-brother. Drew had never told Sissy, nor would he. She went goo goo eyed over 'The Chosen One' just as father did.

He owed her for sure. After the mess with Tracey, he owed her big. But, if Sissy hadn't denied him, they would not be in this mess. If she had just let him get rid of Lilly to begin with, none of this would matter.

"No, the child could need something only his mother could give him. He's born to an addict. Surely I don't need to tell you, doctor, what that could mean. She stays alive," Sissy had insisted. Now she stayed alive because it would raise so many suspicions if something happened to her. Drew grimaced. Lilly would get hers. In due time, he would see to it.

Chapter Twenty-Five

Ty always hated this part of the job. It was worse now that it wasn't his job, but it was his family. Cold, sanitary hospitals gave him chills. Morgues gave him goose pimples on his arms.

Kari had gone with him so he could have information as soon as she got it. She was a good cop, would make a good sheriff if he wasn't cleared in the trumped up brutality charges. She was ambitious, but he didn't think she had played a role in the charges even though she'd confided in Ty she wanted to be the first female cop in Berger County. She'd succeeded.

Dr. Maggie Lindell was the examiner on staff. She came to The Hollow on the night of the murders of the two boys with the coroner. She liked to get a feel for what a person last saw. It was only practical in the case of a murder or a car accident. Maggie had worked in Chicago for years before coming back to Rock Hollow to practice near her roots.

"He had a stroke," she said flatly, taking a seat next to Ty. "From what I can tell so far it was a natural death, but I can order an autopsy if that's what you want."

Ty shook his head. "There's no point. Papa was old and old people die. An autopsy won't change that."

"How long had he been taking blood thinners?" Maggie asked.

"I didn't know he was on them. Why would he have been on blood thinners? I don't know exactly what he was on, but I don't remember a blood thinner."

"Well, there are many reasons that a doctor would prescribe them. Most commonly they are used to treat certain cardiac conditions. Sometimes they are used to treat deep vein thrombosis or blood clots."

"He doesn't have a heart condition or blood clots," Ty answered. This was not sitting right with him. "Are there any other reasons he would have been on them?"

"There could be. Just from a preliminary exam he seemed healthy. For his age, I'd say he was extremely healthy. I can't speak for his heart condition, but in his records I have there isn't anything noted. The listing of medication I have doesn't include warfarin, the blood thinner. That's why I asked. Do you have any idea who prescribed it?" Maggie asked as she was thumbing through all of the files the hospital kept on Papa.

"He would only see Dr. Farmer," Ty said, recalling the disagreement Papa was having with the home health guy. Papa was adamant he was being given a pill he wasn't supposed to take.

"Dammit!" He did not mean for it to be audible. Both Kari and Maggie were glaring at him with wide, expectant eyes. "Nothing, just an argument he had with his home health worker."

"About?" Kari asked.

"His medication. He was convinced he was being given the wrong thing," Ty answered. A pain Ty could not stand settled into the pit of his stomach. His cheeks flashed red hot. Ty had told Papa his medication was right. He encouraged him to take what that person was giving him. He thought that his grandfather was just being stubborn.

Lilly's face flashed through his mind as she sat helplessly staring at the chair Papa resided in for as long as either of them could remember. She looked lost in her own life. Papa had been her hero since they were children. The two had been together every day until she left.

Ty paced as Maggie gave Kari the rest of the details.

"Kari, call LifeLine Partners and get every bit of information they have about their employee Phillip. He's the one that's been coming to the house for a little bit. I want to know where this guy went to high school, where he has worked before, if he has family and who they are. I want to know the last time he took a dump."

"You got it, boss," Kari said, turning back to Maggie. "Give me just a few to get the prelim from here, and I'm on it."

"Better yet, I'll go with you," he said. "Then I can find out everything I want to know."

"Good that you trust me," Kari whined.

"It's not about trust. This is my family."

Chapter Twenty-Six

The car rolled to a stop at the remnants of The Sunken Ship, the bar Bea Drake once owned. The only thing left was a pile of lumber, blackened by smoke from the fire that had brought the place down years ago. If rumors were true, Bea set the fire herself so the insurance money could pay off what she owed. Lilly had known Bea well enough to figure the gossip was probably true. No one could ever know for certain, since Bea had been killed in a car wreck four years ago. Lilly had fought the urge to come home back then.

"You damn huckleberries, I don't get it. Somebody dies and you have to go flying down there. What can you do? She's dead, you can't help her. Can't you cry here?" Drew had laughed.

The walkway that had once led to the door of the old burned out building was still visible even in the darkness. Lilly stared at the place where she first laid eyes on Brad's bike. She could still see the chrome gleaming in the moonlight. Maybe Brad had been her undoing. Maybe her life would be calm and sensible had she never met him. Maybe. For sure her heart wouldn't break at the thought of his large playful eyes or that blank expression. The rumble of a motorcycle probably wouldn't drive her to tears. She also may not have ever known what incandescent happiness looked like. She certainly wouldn't have ever known what being wanted by the person she would eagerly die for meant. No way would she have known the peace that came as she lay in his arms, listening to his heart beat in the rhythm of her own.

Pain, rage, and guilt stabbed at her chest, and she dropped to her knees. With her arms circling in front of her body, she let out a howling sob. Her heart had ripped open when she'd seen Papa lying in his bed, and now it was going to gush. She was bleeding emotions as her forehead found the gravel.

"Why?" Lilly screamed. The sound reverberated up the hill behind the lumber pile, seeming to bounce from the trees to the red dirt where it would land. She lay in the gravel, giving in to the desire to drown herself in the flood of pain that spilled out. "Why?" she cried softer, pulling herself up, the gravel tearing into her palms.

Her tears blazed a trail between the rocks. Lilly's heart was beating in her wrists. This place was sacred to her. The hallowed ground where her tears were landing had become a makeshift altar to the life she once knew.

A breeze caught her tear soaked cheek, and she looked up. She wasn't sure if she expected to see Papa standing there, or a translucent Brad walking toward her, but what she saw was a full moon beaming onto the now wet ground.

She sat back and leaned against her car door. She could still hear the song coming from the building that once stood here; Stevie Knick's voice singing about a strong woman giving her heart over to the love of a man. She could see Brad leaning in to kiss her just as she was laughing at his craziness for the first time. Her guard had been down. She was recovering from a stupid high school fling that had left her hollow. Brad had no competition. He was classy. He had been through things that made him carry a certain wisdom that Lilly could not resist. Once his eyes were locked on hers, her heart caved in.

Her stupid, crazy, lying heart. Never once had it told her the truth. Maybe she only thought she loved Brad so wildly. Maybe she was hollow. Maybe she was just nuts. Drew said that for so long. He was the expert. He was top in his field.

"I'm broken, Lilly. Irreparably broken," she heard Brad's voice in her mind say as he had so many times.

"Maybe you were the broken one back then. So why am I the one needing to be saved now?" she whispered into the breeze that was continually whisking past her and winding its way up the hillside.

She had not heard any cars since arriving here. Out in the middle of nowhere she could feel, she could think, she could breathe. Her stomach was raw and she was quivering. Nothing made sense to her. She hated everything and everyone, and that was okay. Who the hell was going to tell her it was wrong? Who had that right? Papa would have told her that good energy cost too much to be wasting it on hate. He was probably right, but he wasn't here.

"Consider the dandelion, Lilla girl," Papa had said once when they were walking the grounds. "It's just a common little weed. It blooms into a pretty flower, or you make a wish and blow the cotton tops off of it. But it's just a weed. We pull them up or cut them down and they grow right back. They don't sit back and crook their nose and whine about how hard it is to be a weed. I read an article the other morning that said now that little weed can help heal people. But it's just a little weed." He twirled the yellow flower he just plucked from the grass.

Lilly's tears were flowing all over again. She pulled a dandelion that was growing in the gravel, twirling it in front of her own eyes. The little weed, as Papa had put it. She hugged the flower as if it were Papa himself.

"Why do you keep going away?" Ben's voice startled her, making her jump as he spoke. Embarrassed at her reaction, she rolled her eyes and sighed.

"Why do you keep coming to find me?"

"Maybe I think it's worth the effort," he said as he slid down the side of the car and sat next to her in the gravel.

"Maybe you're just nuts," she spat. He shrugged. "Why are you here?"

"Why are you?" he retorted.

She stared at him wondering what his story was. Why did he always show up when she needed someone? She had not seen him before the night Drew would have most likely killed her. She certainly never called and asked for his help.

"I couldn't breathe at the house. Too much has happened there," she said finally, leaning her head back against the car.

Ben nodded. She doubted he had any idea what she was going through or how many emotions were coursing through her every moment with every breath. He seemed so young, so green.

"So, can you breathe out here?" he asked.

"So far so good," she said.

They sat in silence for a long time as memories of Brad and Papa swirled through her head. They were nearly colliding at times. Given the fractured state of her memory she feared they would become intertwined and cross with one another. She was not willing to part with anything she remembered from either of them.

"The night my wife died I left the house because I couldn't breathe there," Ben said, his voice hushed, his gaze down on the gravel. He seemed lost in memory. "Everything reminded me of all the dreams she would never get to see to fruition, all the Christmases she wouldn't be able to over-decorate, and play her corny tunes at full blast. I couldn't understand why someone so young, so vibrant was taken just like that," he said snapping his fingers.

"I'm so sorry, I didn't know. What happened?" Lilly asked the question feeling worse than she had before. Now she had thrown herself at a man who was grieving the loss of his wife.

"She had taken one of her sisters to pick up her fiancée. They were expecting a child together, she and Viv were due about the same time; the whole family was at the house waiting. Everyone was afraid they were going to elope. They'd threatened to a half dozen times. Viv was taking her sister to meet her boyfriend." Ben stared at the stars in silence for a long time before Lilly touched his hand. He reciprocated by lacing his fingers through hers.

"She never even had a chance," he whispered. "The car rounded the curve on her side of the road. The officer that worked the scene said that he was going over one twenty. He was drunk. She was killed instantly. Her neck broke, her rib cage was shattered."

"Oh God, Ben. I'm...I'm sorry. I didn't—"

"I know. You didn't know. You had no reason to know. I couldn't even open her casket at the funeral. I held onto anger for a long time. Her sister and the fiancée got married, and the baby was born just fine, no issues. My wife and child were still gone, though."

They sat in silence as Ben gazed at the stars for a while. Lilly stared at the gravel unsure what to say to him.

"That was six years ago. I hadn't known Ty very long when it happened. Then he and my sister broke up and the rest, as they say, is history."

"I didn't know Tara was your sister."

"You'll laugh at me, but when Ty and Tara first moved here and I came to visit, I saw your pictures everywhere in the house and couldn't help having a crush on you. I figured you were way out of my league, married to a rich doctor and all, but Ty had told me stories about you and, well, I was smitten."

"Out of your league?" she laughed. "I think that's the first time I've ever been accused of that."

"Tell me what you're thinking about," Ben said after long moments of silence. *Why is it so damn easy to just be when he's around?* Lilly thought. She turned to see he was staring at her.

"I was thinking about Papa."

"What about him? Tell me."

"I was…. well…" she stammered. "I was remembering the first time Papa took Ty and me to the lake. We were so young and Ty got sick. The whole time we were on the boat, Ty had his head hanging over the side throwing up." Lilly laughed.

"He was a great man," Ben said. Lilly nodded her agreement. Papa was more than a great man, he was and would always be the rock in Lilly's otherwise muddy, sinking life. "The day I met him his first words were, 'Now boy, if I tell you to do something, you do it. Right?' I said, 'Yes, sir.' He said, 'Ok then. I'm telling you to straighten out this mess of a cup of coffee Angelica offered up to me. It tastes like hot water. Looks about like it, too.'"

Lilly couldn't help smile at Ben's story. She could see her mother and grandfather arguing over the smallest of things that turned to bigger things and eventually an all-out war.

The sky was alight with its brightest shades of magenta and tangerine while lavender swirled its way through the brighter colors. Lilly watched as darkness rolled past and the beauty of sunrise overtook the hills. Papa loved to watch the sun come up. He would sit on the back porch in his rocker drinking coffee and reading the newspaper every morning for as long as she could recall.

Lilly put her head on Ben's chest and listened to his heart beating as he rested his chin on the top of her head. She could feel his warm breath in her hair. It made her feel at home. The rhythm of his heart lulled the turmoil in her world. As the storm around her settled, Ben's hand cupped her chin and she stared into his glassy eyes. He brushed a kiss across her lips. Her heart pounded its response as she lifted herself up to meet his lips. She let herself be consumed in the peace of his embrace.

She listened to his heart thumping a rhythm, cooing her into tranquility. His chest felt unnatural, surreal. Crickets and frogs sang a chorus as the sun blazed higher in the morning sky. Lilly closed her eyes to its brilliant rays.

"So, you had a crush, huh?" Lilly asked, fighting with her face not to betray her.

"Yeah," Ben laughed. "A crush."

Ben's phone chirped, breaking the serenity settling around them. He lazily pulled it from his pocket and sighed.

"Ty needs us at the house," he said.

"I figured," she answered. "Peace can only last so long."

Ben climbed to his feet and extended his hand. It looked so far away from the place her body had carved in the gravel. She thought she must have gained twenty pounds sitting in the spot as she struggled to reach his fingers.

"We will make it through this. I promise," Ben said as she steadied herself on her wobbly legs.

"Promises don't work out for me," she replied, unable to meet his gaze.

"Trust me," he answered.

"If only," Lilly managed as he held her hand and walked her to her car.

She did not think to argue as he slid into the driver's seat and started the massive machine, pulling onto the highway. Lilly watched the early morning fog hanging low throughout fenced farmland as they passed. Trees at the edge of hills barely poked through. Papa would have said it was a sign of a sticky day on tap. As she thought of his words, a warm trickle inched its way down the side of her cheek. She was not interested in masking her pain; she had the right to grieve.

Chapter Twenty-Seven

"Phillip Ian Shelburne. Twenty-four years old. Graduated high school at sixteen, started college in Cincinnati but the records are a little weird after that. He worked for a lot of big pharma companies, some hospitals, some medical clinics, but I don't see what year or where exactly he graduated from," Kari said as she looked over the forms the home health agency faxed. Ty took them and began scrutinizing every letter.

"Bachelors of Nursing from Columbia," he said, pointing to the line displaying the information. "Run him. See if he's got any priors."

"His background is with all of that. LifeLine checks them out pretty good," she said. He glared at her until she turned on the computer and began clicking at the keys.

Something was missing from all of this. Phillip Shelburne. From where? There was no high school listed on the forms. Either he was home schooled or went to a private school, and those would not have to be listed. Most of the time people were proud to have been able to afford them. It would be part of their dossier. No parents or family of any kind came up in his background. There was no emergency contact. This guy just appeared from nowhere.

The knot forming in Ty's throat was closing. There was no such thing as a mystery person. He came from somewhere. Ty punched in the cell number listed on the forms and got an electronic voice telling him that the voicemail box had not been set up.

"Ty," Kari said from her computer. Ty walked to the desk and looked over her shoulder. On the screen were several Phillip Shelburnes and not one of them was this guy. There was nothing to go on. Kari held up a finger then typed in the social security number listed. The records for

Phillip I. Shelburne displayed on the screen. He was born in nineteen thirty, married in nineteen fifty-two, was the father of Julian Shelburne and Jackson Shelburne, and passed away in nineteen ninety-six.

"Print that," Ty told Kari. He retrieved the paper from the printer and started toward the door. "I'll be at the house. If you get anything, call me." She nodded as he walked out the door.

Ben and Lilly were at the house when Ty walked in. Lilly looked like hell. Her eyes were swollen and pink, her hair disheveled on top of her head, and her clothes looked like she had been crawling in mud all night. The way she looked at Ben made him uneasy. He shook off the urge to scream that this was not the time to both of them.

He slapped the papers down in front of Ben who was stirring a cup of coffee. He started thumbing through them as Ty went for his own dose of caffeine.

"Hey! I may have found something," Ben said, shuffling the pages. "Our Phillip worked at Glick Pharmaceuticals until…." He paused looking for the end date, "well, I guess he still works there. The termination date is blank."

Ty, on full alert now, grabbed the page from Ben and stared. How had he missed that? He could feel his eyes crossing as he scanned the tiny words again. His lack of sleep was catching up with him.

"He had a stroke because of warfarin?" Ben asked looking at the hospital report Maggie had given him. Ty nodded taking a seat across from him. Lilly stared blankly into the cup of coffee she was cradling with both hands. She didn't seem to hear anything they were saying.

"Ian," Lilly said without looking up from her cup. Ty and Ben turned to look at her. "The nurse that was coming here, I thought I had seen him before. He wore a badge that said Phillip, but his name was Ian."

"Yeah, Phillip Ian Shelburne according to the background LifeLine Partners gave Kari. Problem is, the social he's using belongs to a man who died in nineteen ninety six."

"So who knows who this guy really is?" Ben said.

"I'm telling you, his name is Ian. Before you got here last night I remembered something more. Ian was at the place that I had the baby. They murdered Tracey," Lilly insisted.

"They who?" Ben asked.

"Drew and Ian. Well, they were in the room when she was killed, I can't be certain that they did it."

"How do you know she was killed?" Ty asked.

"I saw it in the memory. When I saw the picture of Tracey last night, it triggered something. I saw her; she was sitting with me at a table, just talking. Then the guards came and drug her away. I tried to help her, I chased after them but she was dead before I got there. I saw her body. That's what I was seeing just before....everything last night."

"How do you know they killed her? How can you be sure that she didn't die of something else?" Ty asked.

"Because I had just been talking to her. At the table. We had just been sitting across from each other."

"But, something with a medicine or something like that can happen pretty quickly. Why are you positive that she was murdered?"

"She was in a straight jacket on the bed. Her eyes were cold and glassy. She had red marks on her neck. I do not think it was medicine."

"What is that?" Ty asked, pitching his chin in the direction of the box from Drew's office which had arrived the day before.

"It's the third box that Drew had at the house. That's what I was doing last night, going through it. There are pictures in there of Tracey, the girl I'm telling you they murdered," Lilly said, her voice sounding urgent. Ben ripped the lid from the box and he and Ty each grabbed stacks of papers and pictures.

Ty grabbed pictures of Lilly with a man he had never seen. They were from what looked like a casino. Ben was going through photos from restaurants and convenience stores. Lilly and the man were in each photo. The last picture made Ty's heart ache for his sister. In it, Lilly's head was on the chest of the man and she was beaming directly into the camera. It looked like it had been cut from a strip taken in a photo booth. She was happy. She was in love. But the man wasn't Drew.

"Who is he?" he asked Lilly, still holding the picture.

"Brad," she said, her voice hoarse, as if the word was rusty on her vocal cords.

"Brad," Ty repeated. He hadn't heard the name before. "Who exactly is Brad?"

Lilly cleared her voice. "Someone I knew before Drew."

"Seriously? After everything, there is still more that I don't know? Dammit Lilly! What else is there?" Ty demanded. Lilly glanced up, tears filling the bottom lids of her eyes, and dropped her head just as they began to fall.

Guilt pierced his chest at his own anger. "You have to tell me everything. Even something that seems like nothing to you could be huge." He put his hand on her shoulder. "Where were these pictures taken? Why would Drew be keeping pictures of you and this guy? Doesn't that seem odd to you all?" He glanced from Lilly to Ben.

"No, it seems odd that he would even know about Brad," Lilly said, knitting her eyebrows. She seemed to struggle to focus. "I have no idea. I don't know how anyone would even get these pictures."

"It's easy enough to get them. You would normally need a reason to want them, though. Where were they taken?" Ben asked.

"Most of them in Vegas, on our first trip there."

"First? How many times did you go?" Ty asked. Sleep deprivation made his voice rougher than he intended, and anger made him rub his stubble with his palm to keep himself in check.

"We were together for four years. We went to Vegas twice. The second time we were there is when he died. He overdosed. Brad is the father of my baby."

"What was Brad's last name?" he asked.

"It was Davis."

Ben typed Bradley Davis into his laptop he had just turned on as Ty looked over his shoulder. There were plenty of hits, but none of the shots in the system were the man in the pictures. Ty took the computer and did a database search for Lilly and Brad's names together.

The first hit was from Vegas. According to the wedding certificate from August eighteen, ten years earlier, Lilly R. York and Bradley Davis Hodge were united in matrimony in a ceremony in the Viva Las Vegas Wedding Chapel. Ty showed the record to Lilly and Ben.

"No. We had a pretend wedding. We never got married. That's why he used the fake last name. We were drunk and just messing around, saw the wedding chapel and said what the hell, why not? So we had a certificate and all, but it wasn't real."

"Oh, it was very real," Ben told her. "This is an official record." He continued pecking on the keys as Lilly tried to absorb the latest bomb. Ty watched her play with her wedding ring from Drew, and stare blankly at the wall.

"But, he used a fake name," Lilly said weakly.

"I don't think so. Look at this," Ben said pulling up an arrest record with a mug shot from the early nineties. Ty read over her shoulder, Brad had been arrested for possession of an illegal substance and drug paraphernalia.

"He told me about that. He didn't want to go to law school, his family thought he had to, so he started doing everything that they hated. They had money, but he could only touch that wealth once he graduated. He never graduated, never got the money," Lilly said, looking desperately from Ben to Ty like she was seeking confirmation.

Ty poured himself the last cup of coffee and started a new brew. Ty typed Brad's full name into the search bar and nearly dropped his cup when the results appeared on the screen.

Chapter Twenty-Eight

"What was the senator's name? The lady you know?" Ty asked, his eyes remaining focused on the computer screen.

"Anne," Lilly answered.

"Her last name smart ass."

"Hodge. Anne Hodge. Why? Oh my god, no!" she answered, realizing what he was implying. He turned the screen and on display was the entire Hodge family, Brad included. Her heart climbed to her throat, determined to gag her. She kept swallowing. The vial on her chest seemed to be rattling him back to life. "Oh," she gasped. "Oh my God."

"What?" Ben asked.

"This whole situation," she said, fanning her arms across the table where the entire contents of the third box were splayed. "Apparently he and I were really married, for a minute at least. I know Anne, and if the rest of the family is anything like her they would never have approved of us, hell they never approved of him. Brad, obviously, would never have cared about that."

She tried being upset about his not telling her his last name but, try as she may, she couldn't. She stared at the photo on the monitor. Brad on the left of their parents with his hand on his mother's shoulder, and Anne on the right, hands folded in front of her, their father's arm around her waist.

He told her more than one story about his sister, though he never mentioned she was the current U.S. Senator. Brad could not have been more than 16 or 17 in the picture. His hair was long and honey colored, braces shown prominently from his naïve smile. Lilly chuckled, staring at the picture, and took her hand to her mouth. She would've never thought Brad the braces kind of nerd.

Anne looked awkward, like she was far out of her realm. She was obviously much older than Brad. He'd told her his sister was twelve years older. Her hair hung in long spirals, the fashionable style of the day. She was tough looking even then, which made her resemble a sour headmaster with a blond girl wig. Given the things Brad had told her about his sister, she had really never been the girl next door.

The picture was from a Cincinnati newspaper. The caption below it read *"Kurtis Hodge and Family, from left, B. Davis Hodge, Mr. Hodge, Karen Hodge, and Anne Hodge."* Brad was supposed to become a lawyer who answered to B. Davis Hodge. Lilly thought of how the name would have looked scripted on a nameplate, had Brad decided to embrace his father's vision for his life. It was a true life comedy and tragedy. His family had never known who he was. What they did know of him they rejected.

If they had known anything about him, or even tried to, they would have known he would never have answered to "B. Davis." They would have known he was a beautiful man with a soul that couldn't possibly die. He was easy to love. He was full of child-like wonder. He loved nothing more than living, seeing, and doing things. He wanted the full experience of life. He used to say, *"If I make it to a grave, I'm already gonna look like hell so I'll fit right in. I'll probably die from over using my body anyway."*

"Brad was an amazing man." Lilly said more to herself than to Ty and Ben, though they both stopped what they were doing and turned to look at her. "He was so cultured; he had been everywhere, done everything. Even the way he walked told you he was somebody. He didn't flaunt that, though. He had a little sparkle that lit his eyes when he was about to do something crazy, and you just had to see how his shenanigans worked out."

The hot tear shocked Lilly. She hadn't given Brad the credit he deserved in her life. She hadn't realized how deeply she loved him. She had realized that she would never stop.

She looked up into Ben's eyes and saw that her words had cut into him. Her heart ached and she turned away. She would never do anything to hurt him, but she could not deny how deeply she had loved Brad.

Ben and Ty were disseminating the family bonds of the Hodges. Ty's cell phone rang and she watched him leave the room. Ben stayed at the table on his computer.

"Thank you for being here for all of this," she said, watching him work on the laptop.

"There's nowhere I'd rather be."

"Don't lie. Most of us would rather be just about anywhere else."

"Nah. I'd like the circumstances to be different, but I'd still want to be right here."

"You're too sweet."

Ben snapped his head from the computer and stared into Lilly's eyes. "I'm not being sweet. I'm not just saying words that I hope you like. I want to be here. I want to know you, I want to keep you safe. I told you before, no one is going to hurt you again."

Lilly put her hand on Ben's and smiled. She wanted him right where he was as well. Ben squeezed her hand and returned to his clicking keys. She stared at his eyes as he worked. The smoke grey glinted the images on his computer screen. She watched him grimace when his resources didn't turn up what he wanted and his eyes light up when they did. She felt safe, at home just being in the room with him; a stark change from being the leech to Drew.

Chapter Twenty-Nine

"You're not going to like this boss," Kari said.

"I'm listening," Ty told her.

"Phillip Shelburne doesn't exist. LifeLine sent me a packet of information they collected and nothing in it makes any sense."

"What's in it?"

"Basic stuff, demographic information, drug screening results, the usual pre-employment stuff. The really strange things are copies of his driver's license and passport. I've never seen anything like it," Kari explained.

"I'll be there shortly. Did you run his background?"

"Yeah. The original Phillip Shelburne had some traffic stuff, nothing big. This guy has nothing. And, Maggie called. She was right, it was a stroke. His blood was too thin. Warfarin was in his system. His medical records have nothing about that drug in them."

Ty hung up the phone and stared out at the vast land. He'd thought there was something off about this guy from the day he met him. His gut picked up on it. He knew he should always trust his gut. He never really liked Papa's home health workers. He heard the door rattle behind him, and turned to see Ben walking onto the porch. He hoped his own face didn't show the same exhaustion as Ben's. He didn't have time for a nap, and he had no idea when he would have it.

"What's the plan?" Ben asked.

"Station. Kari has some more stuff on Shelburne or whoever he is."

"So, Brad, Lilly's dead husband and the senator are siblings," Ben said after they were on the highway.

"Seems that way. I'm trying to figure out how Drew plays into it, though. Why does he have all of that stuff in the box?" Ty answered, rubbing his temples. "And we have a guy with the home health that, I would bet, gave my grandfather the wrong medication on purpose. Once is an accident, but he had to have given him the blood thinner repeatedly for it to have made him stroke."

His mind seemed to be forming a numbing zone. All of his thoughts were crowding each other, and nothing made sense.

"Has anybody been dispatched to the address listed on his employment files?" Ben asked, reading Ty's thoughts. Ty lifted his shoulder. Kari hadn't given him that information.

Ty had been on suspension for too long. Pulling into the parking lot, a simple action he'd been doing daily for the past four years, seemed foreign to him. The building itself wasn't welcoming like it once was. No longer was it the home it had once been.

Kari met him at the door, files in hand, shoving the small stack of papers into his gut. Ty looked through them, handing them to Ben after he finished.

"This is crazy. Here's the passport," Kari told him, showing him the copied version of the identification. The passport was stamped by several different countries, and by some countries several times. The picture of Phillip Ian Shelburne was nearly unrecognizable. In it he had longer hair, and his features seemed altered. Ty had only seen him once that he remembered, but he thought he looked different. When he compared the picture to the driver's license there was no doubt, something was off.

"The nose is different," Ben said after looking at them for several minutes. "Different nose, cheeks are fuller, lips are thinner. That's a different person." Ty held them closer and examined two pictures.

"You're right. Totally different," Ty said. Kari left the two of them in Ty's office with her latest information.

He caught her attention and motioned her into the room. "Has anybody been out to the address he listed?"

"I sent Reid and Longacre. They couldn't get an answer at the place. Reid said the apartment looked empty."

"Come on, Ben. Let's check out this empty apartment."

"Hold on a minute, boss," Kari called. Ty stopped and turned toward her. "I just want you to know that I had nothing to do with your suspension. I wasn't even here. Reid told me that Jay and the DOJ guy were pointing the finger at me, but I didn't do anything."

"Thanks, Spear. I needed to hear that."

"Now go, solve cases, save the world, be Sheriff Ty York, before this gets weird," she smiled and rolled her eyes at him.

"Told you before, we are the same kind of weird." Ty winked at her and walked out the glass door.

***

Ty was back to life. The adrenaline high made him antsy. The apartments Phillip had listed on his employment forms were in an area Ty was all too familiar with. He had been there making arrests at least a hundred times. Usually it was drugs, but sometimes he got a domestic disturbance. Those could usually be attributed to drugs too, though.

The dilapidated building sat just off of the highway about three miles east of town. The siding hanging loose on two of the four sides of the building had been needing repair for at least the past couple of years. The owner of the apartments lived somewhere in northern Kentucky. Ty doubted they even knew the condition of the building. The people that rented here weren't living a lush life; they were getting pretty much what they paid for.

A sign was sticking out of the grass separating the run down place from the highway advertising a two bedroom for $300 a month. With a view from the outside Ty was sure that was still asking too much.

"Apartment B201," Ben read from the stack of pages between them. The two men climbed the concrete stairs amidst stares from children dressed in oversized t-shirts with their hair mussed and dirt on their cheeks. Several adults were outside when they parked, but had scurried in as soon as they saw Ty. He knew they hated him here. He could feel the hate oozing from the concrete under the blazing noon sun.

"Mr. Sheriff?" Ty heard an impish voice behind him say. He turned to see a small young girl with a messy pony tail wearing a red pajama bottom with an oversized blue top. "Are you gonna take my daddy again?" she drawled.

"I hadn't planned on it. Do I need to take your daddy somewhere?" he asked her, bending down so their eyes met.

"No!" she said shaking her head violently. "He just don't like cops cause you always put him in jail whenever you come here. And his friend is gonna be leavin' soon to get some ham and I don't want daddy to go." As she spoke Ty saw that she was missing several of her teeth, which coupled with her drawl, made understanding her difficult. She pronounced 'ham' as haim, with a long a sound. He thought of how Lilly would love to tuck her child into bed, their recently lost tooth under the pillow, and watch them fall asleep. His heart was heavy, but his adrenaline high. He patted the girl on the head, did his best at a reassuring smile, and climbed higher up the stairs.

Apartment B201 was the very end unit on the second floor. The door was closed and the blinds drawn, the norm for this area. Nobody wanted to know anybody else's business. Ben banged on the door loudly enough to cause the neighbors in the unit two doors down to investigate.

"Ain't nobody lived there for over a month," a portly man in a white undershirt holding a bottle of beer said through a thick black mustache. Ty recognized him as a man that he'd picked up on a few occasions for driving drunk.

"Did you see the person who lived here then?" Ben asked.

"Well yeah. When a girl's got four screamin' young'uns you can't help but see 'em," he answered.

Ty dug through the papers and found the license. "It wasn't this guy?" he asked, handing him the picture. The neighbor shook his head. "You haven't seen that man then?"

"That girl had every kind of man comin' and goin' in there, but I don't think I saw that one," he grunted.

"Thanks."

"Dammit. I guess I didn't really expect to find him here, but I damned well hoped," Ty said to Ben as they were getting back into the car.

"Yup. But it does beg the question, who and where is he?" Ben said.

"Wait a minute!" Ty shouted. "That little girl said her daddy's friend was leaving to get some ham."

"Yeah," Ben answered.

"Where is she? Did you see which one she went into?"

Ben pointed to the unit on the bottom floor at the end of the building. Ty saw her standing in the crack of the door watching them. He and Ben approached the apartment with their hand on their guns as the little girl slammed the door. Ty banged with his fist balled and waited until a woman with scars, some fresh, covering her face answered.

"I didn't do nothing," she slurred.

"Is your husband or his friend here?"

"Husband? If you mean Zach, then no, he ain't. As for his friend, I don't know where that boy runs off to."

"What's the friend's name?" Ben asked.

"I think its Alex, or Aaron. Something like that." She inched the wooden plank door closer to shutting.

"How long has he been here?" Ty put his foot across the threshold to keep the door opened.

"Did he do something?" she asked.

"Please just answer the question," Ben demanded.

"I don't know. He came here right after, no it was before, right before school was out. About a month I guess."

"Thanks!" Ty turned and headed to the car.

"Wanna tell me what that was?" Ben asked as he hurried from the parking lot.

"The little girl said the friend was going to get ham soon. I thought it was her missing teeth, but he's not going to get ham, he's going to see Haim. Remember, Glick?"

"And how did you make that connection?" Ben asked, giving Ty a side-eye.

"His passport. It was stamped by Switzerland many times and according to the dates of the stamps, he stayed for long stretches at a time. Then, there's the little girl. I could still be wrong, but it does seem to fit."

"So, are you thinking that the good doctor had his friend, Haim, send the Phillip guy over here?"

"I'm not sure about that part yet. Lilly remembers him from when she had the baby, so he's been here for a long time; maybe helping Drew? I don't know yet."

"Damn, York. You are a genius. Who are you calling?"

"Kari. I want Reid and Longacre out here. When this *Phillip* comes back, I want them to be here. They can bring him in."

The sun was high in the late afternoon sky as they drove back to the house with their new information. Ty was anxious to get back to the computer to try and find a trace of this guy. He thought of the conviction in Lilly's voice telling him and Ben about Tracey's murder. He had tried to convince himself that Tracey could have had a reaction to medication or something less sinister than what Lilly described. He did not want to admit that what he feared she saw was a hallucination from the alcohol withdrawals. He didn't think that he or his sister could tackle that demon right now.

Chapter Thirty

Lilly's head barely hit the couch cushion when she began to see images of the Vegas strip. The signs announcing the latest starlet who had taken up residency, the impersonators of every variety, including children's television favorites, and tourists dressed in every way imaginable faded in and out of her view.

The sidewalk was crawling with people. People who had no idea they may be wearing a small piece of the greatest love she had ever known. Randy, Brad's best friend and most often accomplice, was walking beside her. Neither speaking, just walking. The sounds that filled the sidewalk were painful. She wanted to run, to scream, to lash out at everyone and everything that was happy and laughing, enjoying their lives. The people were spinning around her, their laughs taunting her. She had awakened beside death in this city only three weeks earlier, they had no idea what pain was. They were just vacationers hoping for a quick cash load up.

Her stomach was lurching and roiling, made worse by the lights and people swirling around her. The mouths of every one she saw were amplifying in her face. One after the other the faces made their way onto the carousel in front of her. She wanted to vomit. She wanted to find Brad and hold him. She wanted her life back, their lives back.

Randy put his arm around her waist and led her into a lobby decked out with flashing lights, pictures of the monthly casino specials, marbled counters and floors, and a fountain with a continuous flow of water going through a cherub's vessel. He got them checked in and helped her to the room. She sprang through the door and ran to the bathroom, throwing up until there was nothing left but heaving. She had not been sober in over a month. If her eyes were opened she had a drink in hand. Randy rubbed her back and held her hair trying to comfort her. He was hurting for Brad, too.

When she could stay on her knees no longer she lay across the bed and sobbed. Randy had brought whiskey to the room, and she drank it from the bottle. He watched her from the other bed as he flipped through the television channels.

"I miss the crazy dude, too," he said finally.

"My feet are killing me," she said, rubbing her toes as her tongue stumbled around her mouth.

"Did you do the test yet?" he asked.

Lilly had forgotten she had the test. She held to the walls to get to the bathroom and found it on the sink. Randy had not been merely trying to comfort her, he was waiting for the results. She had not thought about having missed her period since they arrived. Pouring her boyfriend from the Eiffel Tower in Vegas made everything else in her world a distant afterthought.

She pulled the wrapping away from the stick and did her best to get enough urine on the felt part to test. She recapped it and waited, praying for the results to bring her closer to Brad. Randy appeared in the door holding the now nearly empty bottle. Lilly had her back to the stick and was afraid to turn around.

"What if I am pregnant, Randy? What will I do? Oh God, what if I'm not?" The thought of having a small part of Brad inside her had been keeping her going since he'd died.

A tiny smile began inching across Randy's lips between his sandy mustache and goatee as he opened his arms wide to her. Her heart raced and pins stabbed at her stomach. Everything inside urged her to look at the stick laying on the counter, but she couldn't. No matter what the results, she didn't feel strong enough to handle it.

"Congrats, mommy," he said as she fell into his arms.

Sobbing tore at her chest, and she cried, clawing to Randy's chest. She was going to have Brad's child. Their child. She would do everything in her power to make sure this baby knew what kind of man his or her dad was. What an amazing man. And as soon as she got back to Kentucky, she was going to get sober. For the baby. For Brad's baby.

***

Lilly woke up on the sofa in the study. The first thing she saw when she opened her eyes was Papa's empty chair. Her heart ached for him, for Brad, for her child she was losing hope of ever finding. Her emotions, like her body, were tired and worn. She wanted a break from pain.

Something gnawed at her about the dream. Something wasn't right. Had someone else been in the room? Was it even real? Drew's voice howled in her head, *"Stupid hick! How many times do you have to hear the words before you accept it? There is no kid!"*

Lilly put her hands on both temples and inhaled as deeply as she could. She had to drown out Drew's taunts.

She and Brad had lived by the motto, "No regrets," but she had regrets; so many that her stomach stayed tied in a tight knot. If she could have been sober enough to remember clearly, she wouldn't doubt everything. She would know, without question, she had been pregnant and given birth. She did not even remember with any clarity having scattered Brad's ashes. She was only certain that it had happened by the vial she kept of them.

As she walked into the kitchen her eyes fixed on a large brown envelope lying on the table. It was addressed simply to 'The York Family' and was unopened. A knot tightened in Lilly's throat as she picked it up. The knot grew as she slid her finger under the fold and opened it. She wasn't sure what she expected. She believed it was something concerning Papa's death, but thought it was too soon for something to have been mailed.

She pulled the contents of the envelope out and began reading the letter that was addressed the same as the envelope.

York Family,

If you have received this envelope then something has happened to me. My name is Sara Wilt, I am the sister of Serena Wilt.

Lilly nearly dropped the pages onto the table. Why would Serena Wilt's sister be writing a letter to her family? Since when did Serena even have a sister? Serena, Drew's mother, had been dead since he was in high school. That's what Drew told her. What could possibly be accomplished with words at this date?

I am not proud of the things I was forced to do. I do not want you to think I liked doing what I am about to tell you, but there was no other way to protect my sister, or her child.

Rena was a free spirit since we were children. She loved life, but apparently life didn't love her back. When we moved to Ohio from Oklahoma our father joined the law firm of Kurtis Hodge. Rena later went to work as an assistant there, after our father passed away. She was a beauty and most men found her impossible to resist. Especially Kurt. Rena was pregnant within a year, and determined she was in love with him. He tried to push her away, tried to pay her to just leave, but she wanted the three of them to be a family. He told her that wasn't going to happen, and she started making threats. She was going to kill herself and his child if she couldn't have him. She threatened to expose their affair which would have ended his marriage and caused him to lose standing in the community and a lot of money in a divorce.

Instead of playing Rena's game, Kurt found an old friend of his to take the baby and put him in a foster care facility where he grew up. She lost her grip on reality from that point and did try to kill herself. The first time, I found her passed out on the floor, among spilled pills, bottle lying by her head. The second time she was hanging from a bed sheet tied to a hook in the ceiling, her naked legs kicking the air beneath her. I nearly lost her then.

Rena snuck into Kurt's house a few nights later. He woke up to her standing over his sleeping wife holding a knife from the kitchen. If Kurt hadn't woke up, who knows what she may have done.

Kurt paid for everything for the child, but no one ever knew the truth of his paternity. Rena was cared for in a clinic until she passed away five years ago. Kurt paid for that as well.

Kurt played on my love for my sister. I had to be the one that took the child to the foster care building. I had to be the sister that visited Rena every week to keep her doing well, keep her from asking the wrong things. Kurt did save her life, he did provide for her. I will give him that. But the deal was struck, he took care of the finances, I got paid a nice stipend for my trouble, I disappear. No questions. I have no idea what became of Rena and Kurt's child, I can only hope that he is happy.

How your family became involved is a little less clear. About nine or so years ago I got a phone call from Anne, Kurt's daughter, threatening to cut off Rena's care and send her to prison if I didn't do one last little favor for the family. Not wishing Rena to be turned out into the streets, or worse, I reluctantly agreed. My job was to once again take a baby to the foster care building and leave it. I had no idea to whom the child belonged until I got him there. Sister Agnes Marie took him into her care. I gave her the envelope, just as I had with Rena's baby, with the child's birth certificate inside. Sister Agnes Marie had no idea who I was so I had to prove that I was not Lilly York. That's how I knew who you were.

I realize that this will be coming as a shock to you. I have enclosed the address of the facility and the copy of the birth certificate the sister gave to me. The only reason I have kept it is for the purpose of sending it to you. I am likely dead now, they can't hurt me any longer. Poor sweet Rena has been gone for years, they can't hurt her either.

I truly hope that you already have Lilly's child back in your care. I have no idea if she survived the childbirth or whatever her problems were, I hope so.

Good luck,

Sara Wilt

A pang of joy struck Lilly through the chest, crackling and etching its way to her tingling spine. It had been so long since joy had shown itself in her life she nearly didn't recognize it. Finally, she was going to make progress on finding her child. Finally, she could teach him—the letter said him—about his father. Tears threatened at her eyes, and she blinked furiously to keep them in check. She had shed so many of them in the past few days she was tired of them.

She heard Ben's car in the driveway and ran to meet him and Ty. She waved the letter and the rest of the pages from the porch as they were opening the dusty doors. She must have been beaming because both men looked like they had seen a ghost.

"I found him! My baby! He's real! I found him!" Lilly shouted.

For a moment her brother looked at Lilly like she was mad. For another moment, he measured her up and down like he was considering restraining her. But when she just stopped and opened her arms wide, he ran to her side and yanked the pages from her hands. He read through the letter quickly, probably focusing only on the essential. Ben put his arm around her waist, resting his hand in the small of her back and was reading over Ty's shoulder.

"Drew? This is Drew's aunt?" Ty asked.

"I guess. That's what she said," Lilly shrugged.

"I want to analyze it. I don't want to trust this just yet," Ben interjected.

"What? Just go to the address that she gave us and let's get my son!" Lilly was growing furious. To hell with caution, she wanted her child.

"Look at what's going on with Ty, Lilly. Drew arranged that. I can't prove it, but I know it and so do you. Do you really want to just go flying up to Ohio only to be crushed again or worse?"

Lilly couldn't stop fuming. She knew that Ben was right; she knew she shouldn't have gotten so worked up, so hopeful.

"Can you just look it up? See if the place actually exists?" she asked.

"Of course. But even if it does, that's no guarantee that it isn't some sort of trap. Stuff like this just doesn't appear."

"See if you can find anything on Sara Wilt. If the woman is dead like she believed she would be, then there should be some sort of obituary somewhere," Ty said, turning the envelope over in his hands. "Check Wyoming. That's where this stuff was mailed from."

Ben began clicking on the keys of his laptop and soon had the newspaper article from Gillette, Wyoming chronicling the explosion and fire that took the life of Sara Wilt.

"That says she died two days ago," Ty said, reading the screen over Ben's right shoulder while Lilly peered over the left.

"Yeah, but keep reading. There was a gas leak at the side of the house that caused the explosion and the rest of the house was completely engulfed within minutes," Ben pointed out.

"Couldn't she have gotten out?" Lilly questioned.

"Not necessarily. If an accelerant was used, fire may have overwhelmed her. If natural gas caused an explosion and the fire department was on scene within five minutes, there more than likely was," Ben said reaching for his phone.

"Who are you calling?" Ty asked.

"Cam. I think we need to look into this as well. We may have enough right here to tie this to the case with Drew. I'll also start the filings to get Anne Hodge brought up on charges."

Betrayal as Lilly had never known before was setting itself up in her chest. Anne befriended her as soon as she and Drew had gotten married. She used to stick up for Lilly. She taught her how to socialize with the privileged few. All the while knowing where her child was. Where Anne's own nephew was. She had to have known about the baby's paternity. Had she known she was her sister in law, twice? She must. In the most twisted way, it made perfect sense.

"So it looks like Drew is your ex brother in law turned husband. Keep it in the family, I always say," Ty said. He had a sick sense of humor with things like that. Lilly's eyes narrowed as she seethed at him. She knew it was his way of helping her cope.

"Weirdo," she said.

Chapter Thirty-One

"Cam's going to call me back. I need to get copies of this to him to get the charges going," Ben announced as he hung up the phone.

"What about the fire?" Ty asked.

"He pulled the same article that I did. He's called the sheriff in Gillette to get the facts that they have collected. We have an office not too far from there that can handle the investigation."

"Use the scanner in Papa's office," Ty said. Lilly winced. The study had been his office since they could remember. He could run the mill from there, and did a lot of the time, especially since Lilly had left. It broke his heart. Momma said that he stayed at the house in case Lilly came back or called.

Ben went to the study and scanned the pages. When he came back he had a picture in his hands. He was staring at the smiling face of a young boy with perfectly round, translucent blue eyes and large honey blonde curls falling onto his little head. He had three freckles on his left cheek and a small dimple on his right.

"Who is this?" Ben asked.

"Looks like me," Ty answered.

"It does look like you, but your eyes aren't that light," Lilly said. "Where was it?"

"It was on the glass of the scanner."

Lilly stared into the eyes and her heart began to ache. She knew those eyes. They had haunted her dreams. Urgency rushed over her chest.

"Those are Brad's eyes," she said, choking on her trepidation. "If this isn't him, then it's my son."

Ty snatched the picture out of her hands and put it with the letter and addresses Sara had sent them.

"How did the picture get there, Ty?" Lilly asked, hoping her voice was not quivering.

"I don't know. Papa was in there most of the time and so were his home health aides." Ty answered, still shuffling the pages into the large envelope.

Ben's phone chirped, and the tension in the room grew. Lilly wanted to be excited, she wanted to celebrate. She was on the cusp of finding her child. Until the child was safely in her arms and there were no further threats from Drew and his family, there would be no party.

A pleasant ding came from the laptop and Ty turned it toward him. He clicked the mouse buttons and tapped the keys.

"Do you know a Randy Walls?"

Lilly's heart jumped into her throat. She had not mentioned Randy to either Ty or Ben.

"Randy was Brad's friend, he's not involved in whatever Anne and Drew have going on."

"But you know the guy?"

Lilly nodded.

"How close was he to you and Brad?"

"He was always around. He rode with us when we took the motorcycle out. He drank with us a lot. He may have been with me when I scattered Brad's ashes, but I'm not sure."

"May have been?" Ty cocked one eyebrow and Lilly gazed into his eyes.

"Alcoholic? Remember? You don't get that way by being sober little brother."

Ty nodded and looked back at the computer. Awkward tension filled the room. Lilly watched Ben pace as he listened to whoever was on the other end. He glanced at her and winked, setting flutters loose in her stomach. She felt heat rising to her cheeks as she remembered his large arms wrapped around her, the taste of his lips on hers, and how her heart pounded when she inhaled his essence.

"So, what's going on with Randy? Why did you ask about him?" she inquired, tearing her eyes from Ben and breaking through the tension.

"Oh, he was picked up with Brad a couple of times when they were kids, we figured they were buddies. Ben found his contact info and I wanted to talk to him. See what he knows about the family, about Brad, that sort of stuff. How much do you trust him?"

"Fully. I would put my life in his hands. You've got his phone number? I haven't heard from him in years." Lilly allowed her mind to wander back to the dream she'd had.

Ty typed the number into his phone and pushed the button for speaker.

"Let me talk. He knew me back then, he doesn't know you at all," she said as Ty laid the phone on the table.

Voicemail answered the call. Lilly tried to think of what she could say to a computer that would make Randy call back.

"Hey Randy, it's Lilly. Brad's Lilly? Listen, give me a call, I really want to talk to you," she said. She looked at Ty with her eyes wide. He shrugged and touched the button to disconnect the call.

Ty turned his attention back to the computer. As he tapped on the keys, Lilly watched Ben. He seemed so comfortable piecing the shards of her life together. He handled every new bit of information that came to light as if no matter how the story unfolded, he was going to be fine with it. She had heard him on the phone with whomever he talked to at the office; she knew he was tough and demanding. He was a cop, he had to be. When he touched her, her heart raced and her head was dizzy. She saw the gentleness in his eyes when he looked at her. She felt the vulnerability of his heart when they kissed.

Ty's phone sprang to life with a high-pitched ring startling Lilly. She felt her cheeks redden as Ty glanced from her to Ben. Ty nodded and slid the phone to her. She pushed the button to answer and hesitated before she spoke.

"Hey Randy, how are you," Lilly said as she answered.

"Aww, sweetheart, you know me. How's my god child?" Randy asked. "And how is little Ms. Lilly?"

"I'm… um… I'm okay, Randy. But my brother has some questions he wants to ask."

"Your brother? What is he a cop or something?" Randy gave a throaty laugh.

"Yeah. He's a cop."

Randy choked on his own laughter and swallowed hard. "Sure. Shoot."

"I'm gonna put you on speaker phone if that's okay," Lilly said as Randy tried his best to laugh again.

"Hi Randy, I'm Ty York, Lilly's brother. I wanted to ask you a few questions if you have a few minutes."

"Sure, ask me anything," Randy slurred. "Well, almost anything." Lilly smiled to herself. She had been almost certain that he would have been drinking. That was his way. She had never known him to be as bad as Brad or even herself, but he had always loved his whiskey. "Is Lilly okay?" Randy asked, sounding much like the man she knew him to be.

"Physically, she's fine. Listen, we have some arrest records for you and Brad, we know the two of you had a long history, do you or did you ever know Anne, Brad's sister?"

"Nah. Brad didn't want anything to do with his family. Didn't go around them. I only met her at the wake for a few minutes. Fancy bunch of people. She wasn't really thrilled to give me some of his ashes for Vegas, but she said she knew her brother, knew he probably did want that. Poor old guy. I imagine he did hate growing up with those people with sticks up their asses."

"Did you know who his family was? I mean, how did you recognize them? Had you seen them before, or−?" Ty asked.

"No. I never met his sister before that day. Crachety woman. She told me to meet her at Jarvis' Funeral home, but not to come in. She came out to the parking lot and gave me some of Brad's ashes. Guess I was too low brow to be seen inside." Randy almost laughed. Lilly could hear guzzling as he took a pull from a bottle. She had seen him do it so many times; she could almost see the bottle emptying in her mind.

"So you never actually saw that there was a wake going on inside? You don't know for certain that the ashes she gave you were Brad's?"

"I didn't run tests on them or anything, no. I assumed they were exactly what the old bat said they were, Brad's ashes."

"That's what I needed to hear. Thanks for your help." Ty started to end the conversation when Randy mumbled something. "I'm sorry, what was that?" Ty asked.

"I just wanted to tell Lilly that if she needs anything, anything at all, please let me know. Brad was nuts about her, I don't want to let me buddy down, ya know?" Randy slurred.

Heat rose to Lilly's cheeks as she recalled so many times being on the back of Brad's bike and turning around to make sure that Randy was still behind them. He had their back. Always.

Chapter Thirty-Two

Ben ended his conversation and rubbed the bridge of his nose. He was exhausted, they all were, but they needed to keep going. They were just so close, Ty could feel it. He suspected Ben could as well.

"Cam has the charges. I'm going to have to go question Drew and the senator. What did Brad's buddy say?" Ben asked.

"Okay," Ty said. "Aside from this letter and everything else, Brad's buddy says he had never met the sister before that day. Also, the buddy can't confirm that the ashes Lilly has are actually Brad's. His sister met him in the parking lot of a funeral home."

"I know, heard that part. Let's go with the theory that everything Lilly sees in her memories is an actual account of the events. That's going to mean she really could have had a brain injury," Ben said.

"I don't think so. I think it's something else," he said, rifling through the research files again. He found a paper written by Drew in college about the effects of scopolamine and handed it to Ben.

"So...?" Ben questioned after he skimmed the article.

"So, this was what he was studying. It's in with a bunch of other articles about mixing it with morphine." Ty took the paper from Ben and searched for the paragraph he had seen earlier. "Here, it says it can cause anterograde amnesia, the inability to form new memories while the drug is in a person's system."

"Okay," Ben said, staring blankly at Ty. "That would explain a sliver of her memory being gone, but she doesn't remember a large chunk of her life before that."

"Yes, I know. As she has reminded me a few times, she's an alcoholic. She didn't get there through sobriety."

Ben's face looked as though he was holding the kite with a key when the lightning bolt struck. "Okay, that's why she doesn't remember."

"Eureka, Sherlock!" Ty hooted with a broad grin. "Now, we have to prove that theory. Can you call Cam and…."

Ben held up a finger as he put his phone to his ear. Cam would be pissed at the rapid fire calls, but having even more to run with would make it worth everyone's effort and lack of sleep.

"Why is there a question about the ashes? Of course they are Brad's," Lilly said, glaring at Ty.

"Maybe. If they are Brad's, then so be it. It's a lead we are checking out, that's all. Trust me, sis. As soon as I know more, you'll know more."

Lilly left the kitchen and headed up the stairs. Ty took the last stack of pictures out of the accordion file. They were of an attractive woman with silky dark hair. In each picture she was heading away from the photographer, making Ty think she wasn't aware her photo was being taken. Except one. In it she was seated across the table from the admirer, and appeared to be enjoying their company. She had a playful smile on her lips, her head tilted allowing her dark locks to fall over one of her eyes. Around her neck was an unusual coin charm on a dark colored chain. This had to be the Tracey that Lilly had seen.

"Cam is heading over to the clinic now. He said they didn't go into the pharmacy when they were there. Told him to grab everything and start tox on it," Ben said, picking up the stack of black and whites. "Who's she?"

"Just a guess, I'd say Tracey," Ty answered as he was dialing Kari's phone. She picked up on the third ring, her exhaustion and annoyance apparent in her voice. He explained what he needed, and she agreed to meet him at the station.

Chapter Thirty-Three

"They have the third box. I saw it there yesterday," Phillip told him.

"You didn't try to get it?" Drew asked, hatred bubbling into his throat.

"I couldn't. They were in and out of the house. The old man was complaining, and I had to keep up the caregiver bit. Get my mother involved. I need out of here."

"Not yet. How is the family dealing with the death?" Drew smirked.

"No idea. I haven't been back since yesterday. I can't go in there right now. I know they are on to me, my friend at LifeLine called and said they had gotten my records from them. I need out, uncle."

"Look kid, we are too close to start getting the jitters now," Drew spat, reminding himself why he never wanted children. He took a long sip of his scotch, his constant companion recently, and a deep breath. "Once your mother gets the approval from her buddies, I'll be back at the clinic and you and Haim will be there researching with me. It's just a matter of time now. Sit tight for another day or two. The senate hearing on the price gouging is next week. After that, it's smooth sailing."

"You don't know, Drew. They are getting too close. They are going through the papers in the box. I'm certain they will figure it all out. They aren't as stupid as you think. I thought the cowboy was, but he's not. I need out. Now! If you can't do it, then I'll call mother."

"Dammit! What did I just say? She still doesn't know about the old man! She doesn't need to know. It will get Lilly and her bunch of idiots off our asses so we can get back to what's important. I know Lilly. I know how she thinks, what makes her tick. She's done. She's probably cried her poor little eyes out, but she's done. I just need you to wait it out."

Phillip hung up. *Damn kid, if he ruins everything when we are this close!* Drew thought. He shouldn't have trusted him to get this done. He should have hired the people Sissy used. She had a list of them. Father handed it down to her when she took her office. How much better it would be if he were still around.

He thought of the day father had shown up with his mother. Drew was only seven years old at the time, and had never met her. Father came by weekly to visit. He said he wanted to see to it that his boy was getting the proper training. Drew knew what he meant, he understood the unspoken innuendos.

His mother—Rena father had called her—had been a beautiful woman. She had long hair as dark as midnight. Her large eyes rivaled the deep chocolate that the sisters withheld from him unless he finished his weekly chores and school work. Her cheeks bones jutted out just below her eyes giving her an angelic look. At his tender age he thought she was his dark angel. He never cared much for the teaching of the Sisters or the Father, less so once they locked him away in his room, away from the other kids. Having a 'fallen one' in his corner was perfect.

"Oh, my little man! Come, give your mother a hug!" Rena cooed. He fell under the trance of her voice. He wanted to live in her light and let her sultry tone envelope him. She put her arms around his shoulders and pulled him into her ample bosom.

Father left the two of them alone and he and his mother spent the afternoon playing on the playground, talking about his school work, and sitting on a bench. Drew devoured every second of it.

"We'll get out of this, sweetie," his mother said. "One of these days, we'll catch the old goat off guard and you and I will disappear. No one will know where we are. No one will come looking for us. It will just be us."

It was music to Drew's ears. He wanted to disappear with her. He wanted father to come, too. He couldn't wait to talk to father about the idea. They could be like a real family then.

I was a fool. I trusted a kid. And look at you, about to get your ass handed to you by one, his mother's voice echoed in his head.

"Leave me alone, Mother!" Drew shouted. He argued with her over and over since Gretta's death. Having nothing but time and nowhere he needed to be he rambled around the house, plotting.

If Sissy would just listen, he had every detail worked out. It would work, it was already starting to. Lilly wouldn't be a problem anymore. He could sense it.

Three loud bangs at the front door jarred him from his thoughts. He peeked out the window to see four dark SUVs parked in his driveway. *What the hell?* He thought.

He yanked the door open expecting some of Sissy's henchmen bearing good news. What he saw were several men and a few women wearing black jackets with FBI written in large white block letters across their backs.

"Andrew Wilt?" the youngest of the men asked. Drew nodded. "I'm agent Cameron McDonald, I need you to come with us. We have some questions for you."

"Have you spoken with my lawyer?" Drew smirked.

"He's already at the office waiting. Come with me please."

Drew placed the last scotch glass he had not smashed against the fireplace hearth on the half-moon dark cherry table, Lilly's only contribution to the furnishings in the house, and closed the door. He didn't even bother locking it. He'd be back before morning.

Chapter Thirty-Four

Ty jumped out of the car as soon as it was parked heading into the sheriff's office. Kari was standing on the walkway in jogging pants and sneakers waiting for him. He shoved the pictures of the attractive woman, Tracey he assumed, into her hands and breezed past her. Ty was barking orders to Kari who was flipping through the pictures and laying the best of the bunch onto the scanner, as he was clicking away at the computer.

With a quick flash of light from under the lid the pictures were uploaded and scanning numerous data bases for a match. One after the other the computer displayed close matches. Dread and despair sank into Ty's chest as image after image displayed and disappeared with a rating of eighty percent or less.

There was a long beep, and the scanning stopped. The screen displayed the face, name, address and biographic information of the woman in the pictures. Her name was Tracey Elizabeth Penney, and she had been missing since August, ten years ago. She was from East Greenwich, Rhode Island and had graduated from the University of Cincinnati three years prior, returning for her last year at Baylor. She was last seen leaving her parents' home at 11:00 a.m. on the morning of August twelve on her way back to school.

In the picture from the database the charm on the necklace she wore showed clearly. It was a penny, which, according to Lilly's account, was exactly like the one in Drew's watch that he loved dearly.

"There's our good old penny," Ty said, pointing to the charm.

"All pennies are identical. We talked about that before. We can't tie him to her with that," Ben said.

"Maybe not, but it's the same girl. Look at the similarities," Ty said holding the original picture next to the digital one on the screen. "In fact, I think it's the same picture."

"It is," Kari chimed in. "Look, same clothing, same tilt of the head."

"Ok, so, our picture is the same picture of this girl that's missing. What else do we know about her or, more specifically, what do we know about her connection to Drew? You know it has to be concrete," Ben said.

"We know that she went missing right around the same time that Drew was getting all sorts of grant money and interning at the clinic," Ty said.

"Yes, but she went missing from Rhode Island. That's a long way from the clinic."

"We also know she went to the University of Cincinnati, the same as Drew. She would have graduated in the same time frame."

Ben studied the pictures and case file on the screen. "Her pictures were found in a box that had been in his possession for who knows how long," he said, mostly to himself. "Okay, suppose we charge him on her disappearance, then she shows up."

"I hope she does," Ty said, "but I think you and I both know that she won't. Lilly's memories have all panned out so far. Look at her, Ben, she's gorgeous. He was obviously fixated on her. Look at all of the pictures the poor girl surely didn't even know he was taking."

"I know, I'm with you. Drew does have good taste, I mean your sister is kind of gorgeous, too, in case you haven't noticed. But why the obsession with this girl?"

"Thanks for noticing my sister," Ty spat. "Look, it's not our job to figure out why he's a sick bastard, just to prove he is. We have the burden of proof, and I'm thinking a box full of pictures of a girl that's been missing for over ten years is kind of telling. Circumstantial? Maybe. Could they have been friends in college? Sure. Why would he keep this stuff though? Especially after he married my, as you say, *gorgeous* sister," Ty asked, brows crunching until they formed a line.

Ben pretended not to catch the question in his friend's scowl, and printed the file from the computer and paper clipped it with all of the photos from the box. He pulled his phone out just as it started to ring, so he walked into the interrogation room to answer the call. Kari was seated at the desk shuffling through papers, looking like she was trying to stay distracted from what they were doing.

"I appreciate it, Spear," Ty said as he bundled all of the papers into a manila envelope.

"Just get your lazy ass back in here York, I don't like your job," she said with seriousness. Kari was ambitious. That was one of the things Ty admired about her. She had to have ambition to be a cop and a woman in Rock Hollow, much less the acting sheriff of Berger County.

Ben was bouncing as he walked out of the interrogation room. He grabbed the envelope from Ty and went out the door.

"Well?" Ty asked as soon as they were in the car.

"Well, we got the scopolamine and morphine. It was clearly labeled on the shelf in the pharmacy at the clinic. Big surprise here, Glick Pharmaceuticals was the distributor, and, drumroll, Lüx Pharmaceuticals was their distributor. Remember? Lüx has more?" Ben waited for an acknowledgement before continuing. "Cam said there was some mixed in syringes in bins with patient numbers on them. He's sending it up to tox to see exactly what is mixed in, because it's not just the scopolamine and morphine. Wilt was dabbling with it alright because nobody that was in the clinic a week ago was there for pain. Cam's picking him up for questioning in a little bit and I'll be heading up there."

"And the girl?" Ty asked impatiently.

"One thing at a time my brother," Ben said, equally impatient. "Charges have been filed against Anne Hodge, too. She will be there."

"I'm going with you to question them. I just want to see his face," Ty said.

"You're there as an assistant to me. No questions, no involvement. Understood? Your presence could jeopardize the whole damned thing."

"Got it. I just have to be there." Ty was too anxious to sit still. Drew was about to get his just rewards, and Ty was reveling in it. He only wished he could film the whole thing for Lilly to watch later.

"There's more," Ben said grimly. Ty bore a hole into the side of his face with his eyes anticipating the boom to be dropped here. Expecting that Anne Hodge found a way to wiggle her senate loving ass out of it. "Cam found the foster care home. He's got two of the guys stationed outside of it so no funny business can go down there with the kid. It doesn't mean Lilly's child is there, but no one wants to run a risk."

Chapter Thirty-Five

The drive from Rock Hollow to the FBI office in Louisville was only a few hours, but to Ty, this trip was taking eons. He wanted to see Drew squirm. He wanted to make him answer his questions. He also knew he had to stay in the background. With the brutality case sitting around, he couldn't be kicking in the door, guns blazing, and demand answers. Though in truth, that was exactly what he wanted.

Putting a serious scare into the asshole and making him sing made Ty's toes curl. He loved getting to the truth and, if in the course of an investigation he made a little bag like Drew Wilt cry, well, even better. Avenging Lilly was a thought, of course, but not the only one. He had a strong feeling that Lilly was right and Tracey Penney was not alive, and Drew knew why.

He also had a strong hunch the senator and Drew knew what had happened to Lilly's child. He had no idea what he would say to her if it was bad news about the baby. She had already been through so much he didn't want to give her any further hurt.

Cam was a tall, broad man with long curls all over his head. He looked more like an NFL linebacker than an FBI agent. He wore a dress shirt and tie, no jacket. Ty thought the jacket would have made him appear even larger.

"The senator's pissed. Says she doesn't have time to sit around an FBI office for some fluke questions." Cam laughed, inviting them to sit down. "I told her to sit tight, you'd be here and explain everything shortly."

"Bet that made her day, huh?" Ben teased.

Cam shook his head. "Not much is gonna make her happy right now, and you know it."

They walked into the office where Senator Hodge was seated, tapping furiously on her phone. She was dressed modestly in a pin striped pantsuit and flat shoes. She glanced up as Ben and Ty entered, then resumed her tapping.

"Senator," Ben greeted her as he sat on the other side of the desk. She looked at him emotionlessly scanning him up and down like a robot.

"What do you want with me, Agent... um... what's your name?" she asked pointedly.

"Hale. Benjamin Hale, ma'am," he answered, extending his hand. She briefly touched the tips of his fingers, just enough to have considered it a handshake.

"Well, Mr. Hale, I am certain you realize we have constant threats to our security, partisanship prevailing so nothing gets done for anyone, and lobbyists beating our doors down all day. I would hope, with that in mind, you have brought me in here for something substantial and will keep it brief."

"Of course. I have some questions about your brother, ma'am. Bradley Hodge?" Ben said.

Anne's eyes narrowed. Her focus shifted from whatever she was tapping on her phone to the present. "What about him?" she said much softer.

"Well, we know that he passed away some years ago," Ben said.

Anne nodded. "Ten years ago. I miss him every day." She looked at the floor as if recalling memories of him.

"Yes, I'm sure you do. Our questions are more geared toward his relationship with Lilly Wilt. What did you know of the two?" Ben asked. A muscle moved on her face when Ben mentioned Lilly.

"I didn't know they had any relationship," Anne said, looking flabbergasted. "Lilly is married to Dr. Wilt. We've been together at several functions. She's never mentioned knowing my brother. What exactly was their relationship?"

"They were married," Ben answered, the words falling like an anvil in an old cartoon. Anne stiffened in her seat. Her once stone visage seemed to melt, and the person seated across from Ben now could have been anyone.

"Brad was never married. I'm afraid–"

"Yes, Ms. Hodge, he was. I have the certificate if you'd like to have a look at it," Ben said, patting the manila envelope. "He and Lilly were married the night before his death."

Anne shook her head. Ty thought he saw a brief moment of emotion, but before he could be certain it was gone.

"Is this what *she* is claiming?" Anne asked, venom oozing from her words.

"No. She didn't remember it. Seems poor Lilly has some problems with her memory. You wouldn't know anything about that would you?" Ben tempted her.

"How would I know what problems she has?" she snapped. The ice queen returned.

Ben shrugged. Ty would have to admit, watching the senator squirm was as much fun as he'd hoped it would be. He remembered her commercials when she ran for office. *Tough, because America needs her to be.* That was understated, Ty thought. Dragon because America needs her to be sounded closer.

"What is your relationship with Lilly?" Ty asked, avoiding eye contact with Ben. He could feel the weight of Ben's glare.

"We are acquaintances," Anne said. "And you are?"

"Tyler York."

"York? Related?"

"If you're only acquaintances, how would you have affiliated her with the last name York?" Ty asked. When his eyes met hers there was a moment he saw a flicker of the hatred he'd experienced with Drew in her. She glared at him with the toughness that her campaign ads promised. She should have been a poker player, Ty thought. There was more to this woman than anyone he had ever experienced.

"So, the family of some whiny little tramp can sit in on questioning now?" Anne said.

"I'm a sheriff, not just some Joe Schmoe, senator," Ty said.

"And my partner in this case," Ben added.

She pursed her lips into a straight line and stared directly at Ty. Tension thick as butter filled the room.

"Senator, can we cut the crap here?" Ben began. Her mouth fell open. It was obvious no one spoke to her this way. Anger radiated from her entire body. "Look, we know you and Drew are siblings. I can order a DNA test if you'd like. Of course that would make this much more public, but we can go that route. It's up to you. Does the name Sara Wilt mean anything to you?"

The senator's eyes grew as her mouth dropped. She was being backed into a corner. A tremor of fear rumbled through him at the thought of what she may do in retaliation. Not to him, but he worried about Lilly and the child.

"I don't know the name," she stammered.

"That's odd. A packet was received at the York home this morning. In it there is a letter written by Sara Wilt. She's your half-brother's aunt? Of course you know that. She referenced you having called her, threatening to cut off her sister Serena's care and send her to prison if she didn't take care of a last problem for you. Any of this ringing a bell?" Ben slapped the copy of the letter and the story from the newspaper describing the fire and Sara's death onto the desk in front of her.

Anne looked at the pages briefly and turned her face away from them. "You have no idea," she mustered.

"Then enlighten me," Ben replied.

"Rena was a nightmare. She tried to ruin my father, tried to kill my mother, damn near destroyed her own son, and would have killed him. My father provided her treatment, I mean she was nuts, and paid for everything for Drew. He was raised in a good environment with the Sisters. He has never wanted for anything. Neither did Rena."

"And Sara?" Ty asked.

"I have no idea what became of Sara. She left town several years ago. After she buried Rena." Anne stared at a spot on the long white table and refused to make eye contact with either of them.

"She's dead," Ben told her flatly. "She was killed in the explosion and fire that destroyed her home. Oddly, even though the newspaper called it a gas leak, she had arranged with someone to deliver these documents to the York family in the case of her death. If you'll look at the letter written by Sara, she explains—"

"I don't need to see it. Both of the Wilt sisters were trouble. They always were. Sara wasn't crazy like Rena, just a clueless bitch," Anne spat.

"And Lilly and Brad's child? Where is he?" Ty asked.

"It would seem, *sheriff*, that you already have that answer. You do appear to have more knowledge than I at this point," Anne said, a cruel divisive grin etching its way across her lips.

"I want you to say it," Ty baited. Anne smiled further, her lips refusing to part, defiance pooling in her eyes. "Fine. Don't tell me, it's your call. As you say, I do know where he is, or have an idea. He will be reunited with his mother soon enough. Tell me why, though. Why would you put Lilly, a person you don't even know, through all of this hell? And don't give me the 'I didn't know she had a relationship with Brad' crap either. We all know that's bull."

"She's a gold digger. She was with Brad, who as I'm sure you can figure out, would have been practicing law in the firm our father built, had it not been for that little hick, and he would have been immensely wealthy. But you are sadly mistaken if you think I had anything to do with whatever may have happened with her. I met her after she and Drew married."

"You took—" Ty started, rage bubbling from his voice.

"Thank you Senator. We will be back in shortly," Ben cut him off.

Both Ty and Ben stood to leave the room. Anne was staring at the letter Ben had placed in front of her. *Read it, bitch*, Ty thought.

"Oh." Ben opened the envelope. He pulled out a copy of the picture that Ty saw earlier showing how happy Lilly and Brad were. They looked like two people who belonged together. They belonged to each other. Ben handed it to Anne. She stared down at the picture with disgust and flung it across the desk.

Ben put his hand up in surrender and left the room. Both of them watched her through the closed circuit cameras.

"She's lying. She knows exactly what happened to Sara Wilt, and she is up to her elbows in what happened with Lilly's baby," Ty said.

"Obviously."

"Did you see her face when she looked at the picture?" he asked.

"Did you see her face when I told her I was interested in both Brad and Lilly, not just Brad?" Ben chuckled.

"Yeah, it's about to get real," Ty said, watching Drew through the shades in the office across the hall. "You didn't mention Tracey Penney."

"In time, man, in time," Ben said, watching Drew as well. "I'm talking to him. You'll snap if you're with him in the same room. You almost did with Senator Hodge, too. I told you no questioning and what do you do?"

Ty shrugged. He had tried to stay quiet, leave the questions to Ben. Try as he might, he could feel they were on the cusp of breaking through the walls that had been built to protect Anne and Drew, and he wanted to be there to help tear them down.

Chapter Thirty-Six

The sun had just started to sink behind the trees when Lilly walked into the house. She was completely spent. Her emotions had been on a roller coaster for so long she wasn't sure what to process or how to attack it. Lilly wanted to rest. Just for a while. Just until Ty and Ben were back and she could squeeze whatever information out of them they were able to pry out of Drew. She could imagine Drew, blue crack in his forehead flashing like the neon lights on the strip, crazed with anger and no outlet for it. She would not be there. He could scream in her head, but she didn't have to listen. He could pounce on all of her insecurities, but she did not have to feign confidence to compensate.

She laid her head on her pillow and thought about Brad. What he would do if he were alive. What he would say if he knew about the baby. He never wanted a child, he'd told her that. He never even said I love you. Neither of them did. Lilly hadn't believed it to be an emotion. Brad just didn't see the point.

"You say all these words to somebody but they don't mean anything. Not really. It's just words. I don't do that," he had said one morning after they'd made love. He would stare into her eyes and fill her with his life. He never needed to say the words, she knew.

Her eyelids were getting heavier and her mind fuzzier. She held the vial of Brad and closed her eyes. She was more than a bit timid what she was going to see.

Pictures of Papa, how he was when Lilly was a child, how he had walked, how he had talked, began to flood into her mind. She saw him as he made his trips around the rim of the property, his straight back and hefty legs making it look easy. There was a serene look on his face as he plunged through the tall grass, snapping tiny branches that had fallen from a tree. He turned his head and winked, as he would always do when Lilly was with him, and marched forward.

Lilly could hear Papa's footsteps snapping twigs and rustling tall grass long after he'd disappeared over the hill. His steps began to sound like heavy thumps on wooden stairs. She looked around at the peaceful field and saw nothing.

She awoke, bolting straight up in her bed. Footsteps were clattering up the stairs. She looked out the window, hoping Ben's Crown Vic was back. No such luck. A dark green car Lilly didn't recognize was in the driveway.

She opened the bedroom door and her face was inches away from his. Her chest pounded until she was dizzy. She knew he was capable of anything. She had seen the terror scripted all over Tracey's face. Ian's eyes and snarl were boring into her. She backed into the bedroom and tried slamming the door. She heard his fingers crack against the doorjamb as he threw it open.

"You bitch!" he yowled.

He burst into the room and pushed her onto the bed. Her heart raced as the needles ground in her stomach. She flailed on the bed, kicking at him with both feet, narrowly missing his groin. He grabbed her arms, wrapping them around her abdomen, and stood her up. Her body was trembling wildly.

"Aunt Lilly, you haven't changed at all. I really thought you would have learned by now," he said. "I guess it's up to me to toughen you up."

"What do you want?" she screamed. He shook his head and tied her hands behind her. As he tucked her under his arm she heard a car pull into the driveway.

Please let that be Ben and Ty, she prayed. *Dear God, just let it be anybody besides Momma.*

Chapter Thirty-Seven

It was nearly dark, and the house was silent when Ty and Ben walked in. Momma usually went to volunteer at the hospital during the morning, but Lilly's car was there, meaning Momma was home. Lilly was likely in her room, sleeping. Ty could not wait to tell her about the debacle with Anne and Drew, who had fumed through the entire interview. Ty watched the interview on the monitor, and Ben did a skillful job of tearing him apart. He was close to cracking when Ben slapped the letter from Sara Wilt on the table in front of him. Ty thought he saw a tear balling in the corner of Drew's eye when Ben pulled out a picture of Tracey Penney. Then his lawyer walked in and Drew pulled himself together.

Ty ran up the steps two at a time leaving Ben at the bottom. Lilly's door was open, which was odd; she always closed it whether she was in there or not. He signaled for Ben to come up and the two of them approached the room as if there were a suspect lurking behind the wall.

Her bed had not been made, and her purse and cell phone were on it. She had been under the blankets at some time, he could see that. Ben checked the rest of the rooms on the floor and reported there was no one there.

Ty ran down the stairs, dialing Kari's phone on the way. Ben was right on his heels. He told Kari both women were missing and to send uniforms out, though he was going to keep looking. They could look around and collect evidence without Ty this time. He grabbed Lilly's keys from Momma's purse. Her car was faster. Ben had been on the phone with someone but hung up and followed.

Ty had no idea why Momma had parked so far down the driveway. She was so into taking as many steps as possible every day. Each step he took sent another wave of panic through him. He wanted to be in the car searching already.

He saw on the senator's face she would exact revenge on Lilly. He thought she was plotting it during the first round of questions. He should have been more prepared for this. He should have had Kari park somebody outside the house until he and Ben returned.

"Kicking yourself isn't doing your sister any good," Ben said. Ty knew Ben's story and knew if anyone understood how helpless he felt right then, it was him.

They scrambled into the car and took off before either had even thought of a seatbelt. Ty peeled out of the driveway sending gravel spraying all over.

"What the hell?" Ben said as the tires were touching the pavement. "Hold on!"

Ty followed his gaze and saw a small light flickering on the third floor. The Amanda floor. It was brighter than a candle, but not bright enough to be a light bulb.

"Somebody was just standing in the window," Ben said. "They watched us pull out. Can you drive around back or something?"

Ty thought for a brief second then floored the gas. He passed the second entrance to the house and drove to the paper mill a mile behind it. He knew the paths between the mill and the house better than anybody except Lilly herself. He knew he could get to the house through the paths in the woods without being seen.

There was a pile of blankets in Papa's office at the mill, and protein bar wrappers all over the floor. Papa had not been to the office in over a year, and the supervisors at the factory didn't have a key.

As he approached the house a tall figure came out the back door and went to a dark colored car. Ben and Ty dove behind the car to avoid being seen. Ty recognized the figure as the one they chased into the woods several nights ago. He motioned to Ben to go to the other side of the car in case he tried to run again. The man retrieved a large file folder from the car and bounded back up the steps, stopping at the top and casting a long gaze at the place Ben had just been crouching. Ty wanted to see where Ben went but he could not rip his eyes from the tall man. There was no doubt about his identity. Phillip charged into the house, locking the door behind him.

"Shit," Ty whispered. "Where'd you go?"

He saw Ben's hand wave just behind the lattice of the porch. Ty pointed to himself and then up toward the roof. Ben crawled out and looked up.

"How do you think you can pull that off?" Ben asked.

The lattice was old and made noise as Ty touched it. Trying to climb it would alert the man inside. Ty reached into his pockets but knew he left his keys inside.

Ben held up a finger and charged off. Ty crept along the side of the house, looking through windows into dark undisturbed rooms. The only light was in the Amanda room. Ty could see a shadow moving across the floor in front of the window. The shadow paced left then right again, over and over.

The back door crept open slowly, and Ben's face leaned out the side. He waved Ty over and they entered through the back laundry.

"Window in the study," Ben whispered. Ty nodded. He noticed it had been unlocked the night Papa died.

Ty patted the wall as lightly as he could, looking for the door that led to the back staircase. He had not used it since he was a child but was certain it was still in working order. Papa had been a stickler for upkeep on his home.

He found the door and tugged on the small knob. It was an antique brass knurl that never turned. He pulled with one hand, holding the other behind the door to keep its opening quiet. Ben had his weapon drawn in case Phillip was on the other side of the door anticipating their arrival.

He tugged again. The door was stuck. It had been so humid all summer that every door in the house at some point stuck. The paint on it was even sticky. Ben grabbed a towel and crammed it in the tiny crack that Ty's tugging had made and gave the door a hard yank. It opened freely, releasing the smell of matches being struck.

The two of them climbed the stairs, avoiding the ones that Ty remembered were squeakers. They could hear Phillip's voice in a low growl, and Lilly sniffling. The words were indistinct, but judging from Lilly's reactions, he was not offering to help her.

As Ty approached the top of the stairs he could see the shadow of Phillip. It looked as though his back was to the open door that led down. Ty leaned out slowly to make certain that Phillip did have his back toward him. The first image he saw was his mother sitting on an old red velvet chair, her eyes wide and mouth agape. She was terrified. Lilly was seated next to her on a wooden high back bar stool. Her face was pasty, her eyes were swollen, and her nose red as if she'd been crying hard. She was shaking her head ferociously.

Momma was staring at an old wood stove and slowly began to shake her head. Ty inched along the wall, toward the cupola until he could see what they saw. The tall man was standing over the small antique wood burning black stove striking match after match and throwing them in. Ty crouched behind an old secretary's desk and peered out between the letter shelves until he saw a stack of green accordion files, the ones from the third box, Phillip had placed on some logs.

Ty watched him through the shelves, anticipation sending pins through his chest and sweat beads down his back. His neck pulsated with each passing second. He looked at Lilly, who was watching Phillip try unsuccessfully to light the fire. Momma looked helpless sitting beside her.

Being less than twenty feet from Lilly and Momma and unable to do anything made Ty's stomach knot up. If he made too much noise Phillip may shoot one of them. He couldn't see Ben, he had not noticed where he went when he left the stairs. What he could see was the handle of the revolver that Phillip had sticking out of his pants. Ty's weapon, usually in his shoulder holster, was on the front seat of Ben's Crown Vic currently in the driveway three floors below him. He had taken it out on the ride back from Louisville.

He was unfamiliar with this part of the house. He and Lilly used to sneak up the back steps and peek through the keyhole to try and see the forbidden room, but their adventures had never offered them any insight into what was on the other side of the door.

Ty looked around the room as much as he could without being heard to find something, anything, he could strike with. There was an old shotgun on the wall opposite him. To get to it he'd have to get in the open and grab it before Phillip could do anything to either of the women. Then he would have to hope it had rounds inside of it for it to be useful.

There was furniture pushed together in the corner. What appeared to be two cribs with blankets and pillows still inside, made and ready for a baby to sleep. It was the creepiest part of the house Ty had seen. *This is the twins' bedroom*, Ty thought. They were babies when they died, there likely wouldn't be anything in here to deliver the type of blow he wanted to plant into Phillips head.

The smell of the cast iron stove heating was filling the room. The smoke made it difficult to see. The accordion files would soon catch fire and the evidence they offered would be gone.

In his peripheral he saw a moving shadow at the other entrance across the room. Phillip did not seem to have noticed, he was busy swearing at the matches that, from the appearance of the box, were last used when Amanda and the children were alive.

Ty heard glass break and saw Phillip throwing a lamp onto the top of the stove. Tiny glass rocking horses and farm animals were sent careening onto the floor. *Is he really having a tantrum?* Ty thought. Everything that would break was sailing into every corner of the room. An oil lamp with a depiction of Noah's Ark was in pieces at Momma's feet as she stared at it in disbelief.

Ben lifted his head from against the wall to watch the scene. The flashing lights of the cruisers were getting close, and Ty bit at his lip trying to force himself to come up with a plan to get the women out of the house. He hoped he could neutralize Phillip without killing him, or Ben killing him given Ty's absent weapon, but if circumstances favored taking a shot, then so be it.

Lilly's shrill scream pierced the stuffy attic and was only increased when Momma joined in the shrieking. Ty and Ben pounced at the same time, converging on Phillip from both sides of the room. A rack obstructed Ty's view momentarily, but he heard a scuffle followed by the sound of something dropping to the floor.

The light from the stove illuminated Lilly's face as she lay motionless at Momma's feet. Momma was bent over, reaching for her. The man had the butt of his revolver ready to smash into Momma's head.

"Put it down!" Ty yelled, raising a coat rack, the only object that was within his reach, over his head. Phillip raised the gun higher, pointing it directly at Ty. Ty saw the flash, heard the boom, and heard his mother scream.

When he opened his eyes, Phillip was laying on top of Momma with a bullet hole in his shoulder and blood covering the back of his shirt. Momma pushed him off of her and fell to the floor, cradling Lilly's head, crying and screaming. Ty joined her at Lilly's side, brushing the hair off her face.

"My sweet, brave, beautiful girl. Please, be strong," Momma said as tears fell from her eyes and onto Lilly's forehead.

Ben got the revolver out of the man's hand and kicked it out of his reach. Ty saw a thin red trickle coming from the corner of Lilly's eye. He put his fingers on her wrist and waited until he was certain there was a steady pulse. His mind raced as he took off his shirt and put it over her. He took her head out of Momma's arms. She watched him as she backed herself out of the floor.

Ty heard Kari and Simms banging on the front door and motioned for Ben to go let them in. Ty shouted at Kari to get the medics but doubted she would hear him from the third floor. Simms came lumbering up the main staircase, stopping to watch Ty as he tried to make his sister comfortable. He had been with Ty for two years, learning everything he could shove into his head. He would be a good cop.

Ty stayed on the floor with Lilly until the medics arrived. Several ambulances were in the driveway when they got down to the porch. Momma was in the back of one of them telling the medics she was fine. Phillip was being loaded into the other along with two uniforms and three more following.

Ben gave Ty the accordion files, along with a manila envelope, that Phillip had been trying to light on fire. The edges were charred, but they were otherwise intact. Ty opened the manila envelope and saw the letterhead of The Sisters of Nazareth Foster Home. They had made a transaction with someone 9 years ago, according to the letter. He tucked them under his arm and he and Ben left for the hospital. The scene was in good hands, Kari was handling it. Ty could go with his family.

Chapter Thirty-Eight

As soon as the blow landed on Lilly's skull all of the noise around her stopped. She was once again in the hallway with bare feet, her contractions nearly constant, her back feeling as though it would snap if relief did not find its way to her. She held one hand to the wall to steady herself, the other tried to massage the worst areas in her abdomen.

The bed looked so inviting, so warm, but she wasn't able to get there. Even after she stumbled into the room, it kept withdrawing itself further from her. She begged her voice to scream out, to cry, do anything to ease this, but nothing happened.

The door slammed behind her, startling her. She tried to see who entered, she could feel a presence, smell cologne, hear breathing, but couldn't force her head to turn. She could sense the tension had amplified since the door closed. This was it. Her baby was coming now.

Her legs were as useful as jelly. She tried to steady herself with the railing of the bed, but could only force her elbow to it. Her legs were giving way and she braced for the fall.

The deafening blow of the spackled concrete sent a cracking through her body. She heard the voices of the women ordering each other into action. She looked around the room for any comfort as her body froze and began to seize. Her head was slamming into the floor again and again. Her contractions gave her no alternatives, she began to push with everything she could muster. She looked toward the tiny window in the door and saw a fleeting woman with dark hair and large eyes looking frightened. She really wanted Tracey here. She pushed again and again, her head smacked into the concrete floor. She could feel warm sticky blood from her head pooling under her, and had no control.

She looked toward the window again as the voice on the other side of the door shrieked, pleading for help. She looked into her eyes and gave the hardest push she could. Her head made one last lunge at the floor and the window and the door and the room faded into darkness.

She heard the baby cry in the darkness. She could hear the suction tubes; she could feel hands stitching her as the baby lay on the outside of her abdomen. She could feel him.

"He's gonna be a strong one, look at him holding on!" the raspy voice said.

"Get him out of here! She's not going to know anything about him, take him downstairs. Someone's waiting for him," Drew's voice commanded. "And for God's sake get my mother back to her own room." He was angry already. Lilly tried to force her eyes to open. They refused to cooperate. She tried to make her leg or arm or even finger move as she had in the first room here. Nothing would work.

The icy surge erupted in her arm, just as it always did when the darkness was about to take over and she would have no knowledge of what happened to her time. She fought with all she had to stop it. She had to know where he was sending her baby. Her son. Brad's son.

When the blackness cleared, she felt light. Like she had lost a hundred pounds. The morning was bright, the curtains were open, and she was ready to go. She was going to go start her life with her new husband, Dr. Andrew J. Wilt, and nothing from her past would ever bother her again. He told her everything was going to be okay, and he would take care of her forever. Waking up for the rest of her life in this castle where she was the queen would take some time to get used to.

Chapter Thirty-Nine

The Sisters of Nazareth of Columbus, Ohio had entered into an agreement with Sara R. Wilt nine years ago. She was surrendering a child, born out of wedlock, to her brother and his girlfriend, now deceased, according to the file the Sisters had sent to Ben. Both had overdosed on illegal drugs. The baby was eleven days old when he arrived and, as far as the sisters could tell, may still be recovering from his own addictions. The Sisters were cautious when taking in any children, especially if they presented possible health risks. They were afraid the boy had been born with fetal alcohol syndrome. The cost associated with his health care could be enormous, and they struggled financially at times.

Sara had no money and no way to raise the child on her own. She was a single woman living with friends of her parents while she worked as a secretary at the law office of Hodge and Hodge. Though the firm was affluent, they did not pay their secretaries very well. The sisters called the firm; Sara was indeed the secretary of Anne Hodge, the managing partner who offered to help offset some of the cost for the child. She was apparently fond of this secretary. She expressed she may want to promote her to legal assistant Sister Agnes Marie had noted.

Sara had one request of the sisters. She wanted to be able to visit the child at will. The agreement was signed and the child was a permanent resident of the home. The sisters gave him the name Elijah Andrew. They reserved giving him a surname in case his aunt was eventually able to take him with her.

There was one single picture of the child in the file. He was a tiny, red, bald boy. Ty stared at the single dimensional view of what had to be his nephew until his eyes were crossing. The baby had Lilly's nose. He could see the tiny peach fuzz on his head. It looked like what Momma called angel's breath. He was a handsome little guy, the York genes landed right on top of his bald little head. He held the baby's picture next to the picture of a slightly older boy and the resemblance was undeniable. The older child was Lilly's son. Ty could see so much of himself in his face.

The desire to go straight to Columbus and bring him back here to meet his mom when she woke up was overwhelming. Ben was working on the formalities to reunite baby and mother, Ty had to be patient. Lilly, on the other hand, would move heaven and earth once she was coherent again. He could not wait to show her the picture. The doctors had already taken samples to do a DNA test at Ben's urging. He knew it would be a requirement.

They were waiting to be able to interview Phillip in depth. The doctors were not letting them in the room until he was recovered from the surgery to remove the bullet. Ty knew Phillip held the answers he and Ben needed to nail Anne and Drew for everything. Human experimentation without their consent had been a huge federal thing years ago and was very illegal, and Ty was certain that was exactly what they were doing.

He watched Lilly as she lay in the hospital bed. Her eyes were darting around behind the lids. He wanted to see what she saw. He wanted to undo the hell she had been through. He wanted to. He had, for years, sensed that something was not right with her. He always had to trust his gut. He knew that she'd see Drew for the low life piece of shit he was, he had just hoped Drew would not turn out as bad as he'd feared. No such luck.

Ben opened the door and stared at Lilly. Ty could sense the tension between them. He could see his friend was developing feelings for his sister, and it infuriated him. She had been through enough.

He held her hand and wished he could take it all away and give her room for the happiness she was so deserving of. Ben, Ty knew, would be good to her, good for her, but he had his own baggage with the death of his wife only a few years before. Still, he was one of the good guys. And Lilly would need a man in her life at a certain point. If it wasn't Ben, it was bound to be someone someday, so maybe....

Ben cleared his throat and Ty turned to see him waving him outside of the room. The two of them walked to the waiting room and sat before either spoke.

"Cam found Serena's grave. The date of death on the tombstone says nine years ago, but Rena only died five years ago. I'm thinking that Tracey Penney's body may be in there," Ben said finally.

"Then where is Serena?" Ty asked.

Ben shrugged. Ty watched him typing away at his keyboard, which kept him busy through most of the night. Being an FBI agent gave Ben access to an ocean of resources Ty couldn't even fathom in his small county sheriff office. He could not tap into many of the things Ben had opened and running at that moment, much less the information available on a simple request.

"The Penney family has been notified and Cam is overseeing the digging. The grave will be dug up in half an hour. Drew is denying everything. His lawyer is threatening a counter suit. He's afraid Hodge may get out on bail if enough judges owe her favors."

"The letter from Sara Wilt should be evidence to at least keep her in until we can find more," Ty said.

"Hopefully. I just wanted you to know about the graves. I have to go, this is my case."

Ty saw the look on Ben's face. He knew this was his job, his case. He also knew Ben wanted to be there when Lilly woke up.

"Look, I know there's something between you and my sister. I get that. But you gotta know, she's been through hell, man. She's not ready for anything–"

"Ty, one thing at a time here. I have to get through this case. Yeah, Lilly and I have gotten close, but getting the people that put her through that hell is my first priority."

Ty slapped his friend on the back. He could see this whole thing was taking a toll on him as well.

"If our boy's name is in fact Phillip, I know why he's in town," Ben stated looking through glassy, sleep deprived eyes at his computer. Ty gazed blankly at him. "Seems that Anne Hodge had a son some twenty-six years ago, when she was only sixteen; not many people knew about him. Kurtis Hodge, daddy dearest, took him to the Sisters of Charity of Nazareth, ringing any bells?" Ty nodded, still amazed. "They named him Phillip Ian. He has spent his life in their care, left when he turned 18, went to college, failed out of med school, now he's a nurse. Spent some time in Germany, studying." Ben used his fingers to make air quotations as he said the word studying. "Came home from the land of milk and honey over there and started working in Memphis. At Glick Pharmaceuticals. Seems to be a lab guy."

"Damn, you can find out more about a person in a few minutes than I could in a week," Ty said. "Any word from the doctors about when we can talk to him?"

Ben shrugged. "As you know, Glick was in bed with Lüx. I've looked at the connection, and one foundation keeps popping up. They give grant money for different things, research being one of them."

Ty took the laptop and started pecking at the keys. He may not have all of the fancy databases of information available to Ben, but he knew how to dig without them. He'd been doing it for years. He googled the name of the foundation, Foster's for Healing. The foundation's website was at the top of the list. It was a dot-org which, in Ty's experience, is usually pretty legit.

On the website, the president of the foundation was listed as a William Henry Foster, great grandson of the founder, James Foster. The picture of William was especially unflattering with a toothy grin underneath a dark thick mustache, one hand on a hearth, and a rounded stomach pooching out past his trousers. Ty was certain he'd seen the man before. He studied the face and squinted eyes and tried to remember where he'd seen him.

"The pictures from the third box," he said aloud. Ben looked at him confused. "That's where I've seen his face before. He's in some of the pictures from that box. He's in the one of Lilly and the senator."

Ben stared at the floor and slowly began to nod.

"Gentlemen, he's awake if you'd like to speak with him," a young doctor wearing light blue scrubs said.

**

Phillip was in bed with one arm covered by a large gauze. He didn't acknowledge they had entered the room, or when they sat on either side of him.

"We need to talk," Ty said, watching Phillip's face for the slightest reaction. There was none. "I need to know everything."

"Why? You already know everything I do. That's what the reporters say," Phillip answered.

Ty cleared his throat.

"Did you think your self-righteous bullshit would mean anything?" Phillip chuckled. "My mother will squash you, you have to know that. Money is power, and the person with power wins. Always."

"We get that. Money is a motivator. By your mother I'm assuming that we are talking about Anne Hodge?" Ben asked. Phillip let out a large sigh. "Ok, tell us what is going on here. Start at the beginning."

"You already know. Backwoods cowboy wins this one," Phillip said, making a circle in the air with his forefinger.

"You killed my grandfather," Ty grunted under his breath. Ben stalked to the door, locked it and stared through the window, making sure they weren't disturbed.

"Humor us," Ty said, not hiding the impatience coursing through his veins.

"Why would I give you anything? After what your sister has done, why would you think I owe you one bit of information?" Phillip asked.

"What my sister has done?" Ty asked, suffocating with indignation. "What did she do, pray tell? Besides bear the child of your uncle, lose any memory of it thanks to your other psycho uncle, and have no knowledge of the baby's whereabouts thanks to your mother? Besides that, what the hell did she do that made you uneasy?"

"I told you, you know as much as I," Phillip answered.

"Enough!" Ben roared. Rarely raising his voice, when he did it was an event, and Ty took a step backward, clearing Ben's path. "I've listened to your poor little rich boy bullshit all I intend to. You are accused of murder in the death of Alvin Jefferson Clay York. If you want to help yourself, I need to have a compelling reason to even listen to another word that falls from your lips. I know you wormed your way into LifeLine Partners, I know you switched Mr. York's medications."

"Ah, you know this, but can you prove it?" Phillip smirked.

Ben, red in the face and eyes wide, reached for the gauze and pressed his thumb into it. Phillip yelped and sank into the mattress. "I have security cam footage of you in the pharmacy department at the Fentonville location, which also happens to be where Mr. York's medication was dispensed from. I have the false documents that you submitted to LifeLine to ensure employment. I have enough to get a warrant and keep you under twenty four hour watch," Ben hissed. "Do not try to toy with us. I'm fed up with you already!" he scolded as Ty lifted Ben's shoulders, pulling Phillip from his grasp.

Ben and Phillip stared at one another for several moments. Phillip winced as he repositioned himself on the pile of sheets, now disheveled.

"My mother had a brother, you know that, Brad," Phillip said, holding the wound and breathing heavily. "He had a large, and I mean very large, inheritance he would have got his hands on when he graduated from law school. He never went to law school. A clause of the inheritance stated that if he didn't go to law school, or if he passed away and my mother was the only living heir, she would get the money ten years after his death, as long as Brad was buried in the plot next to my grandfather."

"So Anne wanted the money," Ty said.

"Yes, and no. She wants power. As a senator she has power, but she craves more. My grandfather was a powerful man. When he spoke, people trembled. That's what she idolizes. Then Brad finds himself in love with Lilly, and marries her. They have a child. Lilly and the child are entitled to Brad's share of my grandfather's estate, not my mother. She wanted Lilly out of the way, the money, and to keep the child hidden with the sisters until he is old enough to do the things his father refused. She was recreating Brad with his child while amassing an empire. If the boy would join her in the fight to gain power, she could be more powerful than Kurt Hodge even dreamed."

"And feeding your other uncle's sick desires at the clinic," Ben inserted.

"No. Not really. Drew is testing various therapies. Some of it works, some of it doesn't. It's a process. His research will be groundbreaking. He is a healer. He will always be a healer. Don't doubt that," Phillip implored.

"How did Brad die?" Ty asked, chancing that maybe Phillips loosened tongue would lead to information.

"Drug overdose," Phillip winced.

"I know the official cause. I want to know the full truth."

Phillip stared coldly at Ty. "Brad denounced everything that he had been given in his life. He was born to a privilege that most people are not and he chose to cast it aside and place his lot with your sister. What happened to him was his own doing."

"Answer the question you were asked," Ben threatened, stepping closer to Phillip's wound.

"No, it was not just cocaine."

"And let me guess, psycho healer uncle was responsible?" Ty asked.

Phillip rolled his eyes, shook his head, and looked away. Ty didn't need him to answer, it was obvious.

"Totally dipped and dyed in the Drew Wilt BS isn't he?" Ty said once he and Ben were in the hall. Ben nodded and they set off to find the evidence in the stack Ben retrieved from the stove. "And then there's Tracey."

"There's more than Tracey," Ben said looking at a text that had just came to his phone. "Looks like a missing person was filed for a Margarite Chavez, aka Gretta. Her last known employer? Andrew J. Wilt."

"You have got to be kidding me," Ty said. He was astounded by the brazen arrogance Drew would constantly display. "When was the report?"

"Two days ago. She never made it home from work," Ben answered, shaking his head.

Chapter Forty

The morning sun was just beginning to peek into her room as Lilly opened her eyes. She could feel the weight of a hand on hers and the presence of someone in the room. Her head was throbbing like all of the rush hour traffic was detouring through her skull. Even her eyes burned with pain in their sockets. To turn her head and see who was with her would surely bring more pain so she lay still.

She heard the door squeak open and heard someone moving. The nurse came to her side and she looked directly at her. The nurse was startled, probably to see Lilly's eyes open, but smiled warmly.

"Do you need something for pain?" she asked. Lilly tried to nod, and pain etched through like a Taser. "Okay, I'll get you fixed up."

Lilly heard the door open and close again, then she heard her mother humming. Momma's face appeared in Lilly's sight, staring down at her with moist eyes. Momma was at peace, she was happy. Lilly saw the reflection of a new person, a better person beaming back at her in her mother's eyes. Once Lilly could think clearly, she'd pound the idea out.

Momma lightly stroked Lilly's face. She'd never tell her, but every touch was like knives jabbing into her skin. Instead, Lilly lay there and enjoyed the feeling of her mother doting on her.

The nurse returned with a syringe and a new person. "This is Dr. Bellow, he's been treating you since last night." She grinned.

"Good to see your eyes open, Mrs. Wilt," the doctor said. "With that nasty fracture I wasn't sure how long it would take you."

Lilly wanted to protest being referred to as Drew's wife, but couldn't find the strength. The familiar feeling of ice entering her vein made apprehension whisk through her. She knew this was not like before; she wouldn't lose time from this one, but the thought of not being in control of what happened to her chilled her spine. The thought of not having something for the pain in her head nauseated her. Maybe the nausea was from the bump on her head, she couldn't be sure.

"I apologize for this, I know it's going to hurt, I just need to see inside," the doctor said as he shined a blinding light in her eyes. The pain was like a bomb going off in her brain and was reverberating off of her bones. "I'm going to get another CAT scan and some more pictures. There was an old fracture that had healed in the same place as the new one from the other night, so I want to keep a close eye on the healing this time. Just make sure it goes the way it should. It doesn't look like there was a lot of treatment to the old one."

Lilly closed her eyes and whispered a prayer of thanks. The doctor patted her on the shoulder and left the room. The pain was beginning to ease and she could open her eyes fully. She tried turning her head toward her mother, and it wasn't as bad as she expected. The nurse watched her until Lilly was moving more freely.

The memory of Phillip and the papers outlining her baby's life came flooding back at once. Her heart ached, and she wanted to get out of bed. She wanted to find the papers. Pulling herself up in the bed was a massive struggle, but she forged ahead with it. Momma raced to her side and held her hand.

"Where's Phillip?" she asked.

"He's in a guarded room upstairs," Momma answered.

"Why is he in the hospital?"

"Because Ben or Ty or somebody shot him."

"Is he going to die?"

"I don't think so."

"Good. I need to try and find out about the baby. He burned those papers."

"No, he didn't. He never got the fire going. Tyler has them."

Lilly's heart lifted, and pain flooded in. She didn't care about the pain, she had to see what was on the papers.

"Where's Ty?" she asked her mother, bounding up from her pillow.

"He and Ben are gone to the FBI office. Drew has been arrested, the senator is being detained, which I can only figure is how you say that a government person has been arrested, the senator's husband has been brought in for questioning. It's a big thing, sweetie. It's been on TV since yesterday when they made all the arrests. My boy and Ben's faces are all over the place," Momma said, pride glowing from her face. "One reporter even called Tyler a special FBI person."

"Turn on the TV, Momma. I want to see what they are saying."

Momma clicked on the television, and before the picture came into view, Lilly could hear the news anchor beginning the story.

"Breaking at this hour, a doping scandal that has nothing to do with sports. Senator Anne Hodge of Ohio is being detained at this hour for her alleged involvement with what's being dubbed The Tuskegee-Gate Trials involving a clinic treating mental illness and addiction. Here with the details is our Andie Payne, Andie." The TV picture was displaying a young dark haired reporter standing in front of a large gray stone building. The caption below the reporters name said *"Congressional Doping Scandal."*

"That's right Jackie, I'm outside of the Federal Building today where Anne Hodge has been taken into FBI custody. According to the records released just a short time ago, Senator Hodge and her husband William Henry Foster have been funding the Sounds of Hope Clinic for the past thirteen years. The foundation, founded by Foster's great grandfather, was also giving large grants to several pharmaceutical companies supplying the clinic with the medications that were being used. According to Agent Benjamin Hale of the FBI, and special agent to Detective Hale, Tyler York, the clinic was using a combination of morphine and scopolamine, formerly used in a process known as twilight birth. The combination was discontinued due to the deaths of many of the women who could not control their bodies and thrashed violently after having been given the drug. All of this was done without the consent or knowledge of the patients. Dr. Andrew Wilt, who was the director of the clinic, was taken into custody several days ago, and just yesterday murder charges were filed against him. No further information has been released. No word on whether or not more charges will be issued against any of the people involved. Back to you."

"Do we have any word on how many victims of the clinic there were or how many murder charges will be filed?" the news anchor in the studio asked.

"There is no word on how many women were used in this trial yet, but we are being told that it will be a large number. So far we are told that there are at least three suspected murders including Senator Hodge's brother, Bradley Davis Hodge, nearly ten years ago. His body is to be exhumed this afternoon."

"What?" Lilly shouted at the television. "Brad's body?"

The reporters moved on to the next story and Lilly silenced the television. Brad was murdered? How could they exhume his body? He was cremated. Drew, or Anne, one of them was responsible for his death? Nothing made sense. A silent tear trickled down to her chin.

Momma filled Lilly in on Phillip and his connection to the whole thing.

"Anne had a child?" Lilly repeated. Momma nodded. "I wonder who his father was." Momma shrugged. "From what Brad told me it could have been almost anyone, including Brad. Not by Brad's choice. He said his sister never offered him a choice."

The telephone on the nightstand beside Lilly's bed rang and Momma answered, then handed Lilly the receiver. She heard Ty's voice before she spoke the first word.

"Ready for some good news?" he asked.

"What do you think?" she said.

"Well, while you were sleeping we had samples taken from you for DNA testing with the boy at the Sisters. Ben and the Federal Prosecutor got the results about five minutes ago. Congrats, Mommy, we have found your boy!"

Tears poured from Lilly's eyes. Words were in another realm. A place where clear and present thought melded. A place Lilly had left. Her baby had been found. She would get to hold him, touch him, and protect him from the things that his father's life couldn't be protected from. She dropped the phone and covered her face with her hands as she sobbed. Momma put her arms around her and the two women held each other, weeping.

Momma wiped her eyes and started straightening up the room. She was fussing over every little thing. Nothing would or could ever be clean enough for her. Lilly watched and wondered if she would become her once her son was with her. She hoped she could be half as amazing as this woman. She wondered if Momma had surrendered her whole heart to Lilly and Ty's father the way Lilly had to Brad. She had never asked, Momma never volunteered.

"Well, we have to get you well and get you home. We have to get his room ready, get him plenty of toys, and get him started in school. There's just so much to do!" she said looking around the room for something else to clean.

"I bet he'll love macaroni and cheese. I've never met a kid who doesn't."

"Momma," Lilly said, her emotions spilling all over her face. Momma stopped trying to clean and wrapped her arms around her again. She had no idea what this feeling was that had sprouted in her chest and caused her heart to race, but she wouldn't have wanted to feel it without her mother.

Chapter Forty-One

Sister Agnes Marie greeted Ty and Ben as they entered. She wore a pleasant smile and had a motherly demeanor. She was plump with deep gray hair. Ty expected to see the habit and black robes he had seen on television, but the woman here had on a modest skirt and blouse.

The building itself was built in 1921 as the sign etched into the brick proclaimed, but had been well cared for. It wasn't modernized, the floors were wooden, the walls, 30 feet high each, were stucco and beautiful. The stained glass windows had depictions of Jesus on the cross, Jesus with the halo of light around him, and the nativity scene. It smelled of old books throughout.

"Would you care for something to drink?" Sister Agnes Marie asked. Ty and Ben both shook their heads. "Very well," she said as she slid a file across her desk with "*Elijah Andrew*" scrolled across the front.

Ty opened it and started rifling through the photos and achievements of his nephew. His health records, his grades, his milestones, all were documented in the file.

"It's a copy, you can take it. I thought his birth mother would be with you," the sister said.

"She's in the hospital. As soon as she's able to stand on her own I'd bet the devil himself couldn't stop her from getting here," Ty said, then thought about his words. "I mean—"

"I know very well what you mean, Detective. Is she still using drugs? I would have reservations about letting Elijah be in her custody if that's the case," the Sister asked as her features sharpened.

"No, she's not using. She's in the hospital because she was attacked. It's been a bit of a wild ride," Ben answered.

"Yes, I follow the news, Detective. I have heard," the sister chimed. "The two of you are enjoying a bit of a celebrity status." She gave a knowing simper as she watched their reactions. "Would you like to meet Elijah for yourself? He's a wonderful boy."

"I think his mother should be the first to meet him, but I would like to see him," Ty answered.

Sister Agnes Marie nodded and rose from her desk. Ty followed her up the stairs and out a door leading to a narrow bridge. He looked down onto an indoor playground where several children of varying ages and skill sets were playing. Sister Agnes pointed to a boy who was playing alone with an old metal dump truck. The child had bright blond hair and square shoulders, just like his uncle Ty had as a boy. He looked content. Ty was anxious to get him home and introduce him to football.

He thanked the sister, grabbed the file from Ben and they left. He looked through the pictures of Elijah and thought he could have been looking through his own pictures from school. Lilly would jump out of bed, skull fracture be damned, when he gave her this file. That sideways grin was already apparent on this boy. His eyes were not the York eyes, though. The York's had dark blue, almost sapphire, eyes, except Lilly and Momma, of course. This child had eyes so light they were nearly translucent. It was like staring into the lightest part of the sky on a cloudless day. He must have gotten his dad's eyes, Ty thought. Seeing the way Lilly's face lit when she spoke of Brad, Ty wished he could have met the man.

Chapter Forty-Two

The digging was nearly finished when they arrived. FBI agents, the sheriff's department, and the local law, all of which wore the jackets announcing their department, circled the mound of dirt. Cam stood with a group of examiners waving Ty and Ben over.

Cam introduced everyone, including an investigator representing the Penney family. Her name was Erin Bent. Ty couldn't tear his eyes from her. She had tight auburn curls ringing their way out of a ponytail. Her eyes were two emerald circles that pierced him. He was stumbling for words, and frustrated with himself. He had never been stricken speechless at the sight of beauty. He had grown up with Lilly and Momma, for goodness sake.

"I brought Tracey's dental records for comparison," Erin said. Cam took the brown envelope from her and handed it to the examiner's assistant. "It's been a long ten years, I hope we have finally found her so her family can have closure. They didn't come, they've been let down so many times already."

"I understand," Ben said, looking past her at the machinery flopping its last shovel of dirt onto the already tall mound.

Ty heard the crane's jaws clasp around the metal box and the gentle hum of the machine lifting the coffin into the air.

"Hold it!" Cam shouted. Ben and Ty went to his side and gazed into the hole.

"No friggin way!" Ty said, accusing his eyes of lying to him. One coffin was dangling in the air above him and another was sitting inside the grave waiting to be discovered.

"I'm betting we find Tracey in that one. Serena probably really is up there," Ben said, pointing up to the dangling casket. Ty nodded his agreement, he could not utter words. He glanced in the direction of Kurt Hodge's monument, it was far too large and elaborate to be called a tombstone, and saw a smaller grave marker, as though for a child, with freshly dug mud. Ty's heart fluttered and his stomach ached. He was certain what would be inscribed on it, but he had to see it.

"B. Davis Hodge, our beloved boy, has joined us at last"

He found Lilly's Brad. What she wore on her necklace may have given her strength and helped her through a battle that Ty could never have imagined, but it wasn't Brad.

"Body was exhumed yesterday. We should have the results pretty soon." Cam said over Ty's shoulder.

They got in the car and sped over to the examiner's office to wait for the dental matching. Jon, the examiner, told them it could take hours or even days to get a positive match. Time wasn't the issue, but faster was better.

Within the hour Jon handed Ty and Ben the news they already expected. Tracey Penney was buried beneath Serena Wilt in the grave. Erin called Tracey's parents, who were relieved to have found her but devastated she was deceased. Ben and Cam ordered toxicology testing and an autopsy to determine the cause of death. Cam was going to put the evidence into the case for the prosecutor, Ben and Ty were going to Lilly.

"One more thing," Cam said, handing another page to Ben. "Prelim just came in on Bradley Hodge. It looks like he may have been poisoned. Cocaine, cut with a substance tox is working on identifying, were found lodged in his nasal passages."

"Keep in touch special assistant York," Erin said pushing her business card into Ty's hand. He nodded and climbed into the car with Ben and they left.

"What are you going to say to her?" Ty asked when they were nearly at the hospital. With both men exhausted beyond measure, the drive was mostly silent until then.

"Probably that I am in love with her. Maybe that I can't promise she will never think of the pain in her past again, but I would like to be a part of her present and future. Her and Elijah's future, that is."

Ty considered protesting. Lilly needed time without a man so she could heal. Time to discover her child and his likes, wants, and needs. Ben was right. She would think of the pain in her past, likely all of the time. Certainly every time she looked into her son's eyes and saw his father. But with someone like Ben in the picture, Ty could rest assured her future was a better place to live than the past she had known.

Lilly was sitting up in her hospital bed when they walked in. Ty laid the file Sister Agnes Marie gave him in front of her. She opened it to see a picture of Elijah smiling up at her. Tears trickled down her cheek as she drank in the image of her son. Ben sat on the bed next to her and put his arm around her. She laid her head on his shoulder and Ty and Momma left the room.

"She's about to find out what it feels like to be happy," Momma said.

"She's known it once before," Ty said. He still had reservations, but he would keep them to himself. Ben was going to be a stark change for her. A good change.

Chapter Forty-Three

Two weeks later

"Can't this car go any faster?" Lilly asked. "You're driving like a grandma."

"Really. *I'm* the Grandmother in this car," Momma said. "I swear Tyler James, sometimes you take this following the law thing to far!"

"Seriously, man! Either step on it or pull over and let me drive," Ben teased.

Ty shook his head and laughed. Lilly wanted to get to Ohio like nobody's business. It killed her to wait this long. She'd stared at pictures of her son, which Momma had framed and hung all over the house, every day since Ty and Ben brought the file to her hospital room. Sitting still was killing her. It seemed further away than it already was. The anticipation of putting her arms around her child was making her crazy. They were only two hours into the trip and it seemed like they had an entire day left to go.

Ben laced his fingers through hers, picked up her hand, and kissed it. She smiled at him as he did. Her heart was pounding. Her anxiety was rising, and she could feel heat rushing to her cheeks. Every glance at him made her feel it. He drew the letter I, then a heart, then the letter U on her leg. She blushed. He could be so corny.

Momma was in the front seat next to Ty trying to make conversation, but they always ended up reverting back to Elijah. She hadn't met him yet, but since she'd had the first memory her entire life had revolved around him. Maybe it had since that day in Vegas so many years ago when she and Randy had seen the results of the test.

When the wheels finally stopped rolling in front of the old rusty red brick building, Lilly's heart was racing. She stared at the building for several minutes before moving forward. How the tides had turned. Today, Brad would finally win. Today, they both would win. Elijah, not what she would have named him she didn't think, but at that moment, the only name in the world that meant anything, was coming home.

They all got out of the car and stood on the sidewalk staring up at the huge steeple with an enormous bell waving slightly in the breeze at the top. Ben stood at Lilly's side, Momma and Ty stood behind her. She took Ben's hand and headed toward the door.

Sister Agnes Marie was there to greet them. Lilly had spoken to her several times on the phone. She sounded wonderful, and she cared deeply for Elijah. She told Lilly she had been the sister to have taken him in at eleven days old. Lilly knew she herself was living a nightmare when Elijah was eleven days old.

Sister Agnes Marie told Elijah about his mother and about her coming to get him. According to the sister, Elijah's response was, "I knew she'd come." He was a smart boy, like his father. From the pictures he looked like his uncle with his dad's eyes. He was more beautiful than she could have imagined. Her arms ached to hold him. Her heart broke for the things she'd missed. Never again would she let him go.

Sister Agnes Marie smiled the warmest, deepest smile Lilly had ever seen and motioned her inside.

"He's waiting for you," she said.

Lilly could see a hundred yards away, on the front pew of the church, the tiny silhouette of a round head with blonde curls. He wasn't moving. He wasn't turning around. He sat there, with his little head tucked, looking at his fidgeting legs. A warm tear found her cheek and her feet began moving toward him. Ben let go of her hand and waited at the door.

This, at last, was their moment.

Elijah looked at her sideways as she rounded the pew he occupied. Brad's eyes stared through her as they had so many times. Tears streamed her cheeks forming tiny droplets on her chin.

"Hi," she whispered.

"Hi. You're my mom, aren't you?" Elijah answered. He stood and wrapped his arms around her waist.

Lilly drank every instant of her son's embrace, wrapping him in her arms and lifting him until his head rested on her chest. She had missed the chance to cradle him as a baby. She would never miss another chance to comfort away any fears, sickness, or heartbreak that may come his way. She would never let him go again.

About Shanna Nichols

Shanna Nichols has been writing since she figured out how to hold a pencil way back in the day; whether it be short stories, poetry, dramas, novels, or anything in between. When not writing you can find her with her nose stuck in a book, running, cooking, or just hanging out on the couch with her family and cats. As an avid lover of everything that makes her feel alive, she enjoys hiking, running marathons, biking, swimming, gambling, and laying on a beach with a cute little umbrella drink. Growing up between rural southern Kentucky and Louisville, she saw many different cultures and landscapes and fell in love with them all, weaving something that has touched her into each of her stories.

Acknowledgements

I have to mention my family, Mike, J, and MaRita, without whom I would have given up on this dream ages ago. You three have kept me going forward, encouraged me, and put me in my place when I needed it most. Thank you.
In college, which I loved by the way, I had many professors that inspired me to be more than I thought I was, dig deeper than I thought I could, and excel higher than I thought possible. I can't possibly mention all of them, but I would be remiss if I did not thank two of them. Dr. Lynn Pohl, the greatest history professor ever, thank you. I loved going to class and hearing the lectures, especially the history of medicine. Look for more of those lessons to be woven into future stories. Dr. Laura Detmering, thank you for believing in my writing and encouraging me to continue. I hope you enjoy reading!

www.ingramcontent.com/pod-product-compliance
Lightning Source LLC
Chambersburg PA
CBHW070912180626
46817CB00003B/1024